The Widow's Secret

French Legacy Book 2

Rose Pascoe

Published by Flax Bay Books, 2020.

Copyright

To my amazing son, for making the world a better place.

Contents

The Will

Inside the office, the only sounds were the ticking of the mantelpiece clock and the beating of three heavy hearts. The incessant clamour of London in the new era of Queen Victoria was muted to a soft hum by thick drapes of burgundy velvet.

Elisabeth Godwin sat straight-backed in an over-stuffed chair. Her hands remained still in her lap, resisting the urge to scratch her neck, which was prickling under the torments of the over-heated room and the tight black crepe of her mourning dress. Only her eyes moved as she scanned the room. Mr Price, their attorney, was checking his pocket watch and shuffling the papers on his desk again. Elisabeth's sister-in-law, Anne, had her eyes closed and her jaw clenched, and was crumpling a handkerchief between restless fingers.

Row upon row of legal tomes dominated one side of the room. Their gilt-inscribed leather bindings protected thousands of words on every aspect of the law, as defined by the rich and powerful, though little ink was wasted in pursuit of equality or compassion.

As the minute hand on the clock clicked around to the quarter-hour, the door opened, and her brother-in-law strode in. Frederick placed his tall silk hat, overcoat and silver-topped cane on the hat stand. He paused for a moment to adjust his collar and tie in the mirror. The collar was so starched that it pushed up a roll of fat on his neck, but he gave his reflection a satisfied nod nevertheless.

He moved the vacant chair forward, so that he was seated closest to the desk, in front of the two women. 'Sorry I'm late. Important business. Couldn't be put off. Now, let's get this over with, shall we?'

Elisabeth smelt onions on his breath and noted a fleck of pastry on his moustache. Important business indeed. Frederick was only twenty-eight, a year younger than Elisabeth, and had far less knowledge of the family business than she had. She took a deep breath, ready to have her say whether or not it was welcome.

'Mr Price, I feel it is too soon to read my husband's will.' She could hear the quaver in her voice, as raw emotion threatened to overwhelm her determination to remain rational. 'I realise that two months have passed since he was lost at sea, but–'

Frederick didn't bother to turn his head to face her before cutting her off. 'Really, Elisabeth. He has officially been declared dead. His fall was witnessed.'

She exhaled slowly, knowing it would serve no purpose to be dismissed as an over-emotional harpy. In a calm voice, she continued. 'The witness had been drinking and visibility was poor. Surely, it is still possible that a vessel from a distant port picked John up and he is lying injured somewhere.'

Frederick turned and glared. 'Elisabeth, you're being hysterical. For heaven's sake, John was wearing an overcoat and heavy boots and he never surfaced. Our vessel searched for hours and there were no other vessels in the vicinity.' He snapped his head back to the attorney. 'Mr Price, please proceed.'

The attorney raised not just one, but both of his hearth-brush eyebrows, which was equivalent to an indignant shout from anyone else. A sheen of sweat dappled his forehead. He was a gentle soul who had looked after the Godwin & Sons' business with exemplary efficiency, as his father had done before him, but he coped better with paperwork than with conflict.

Mr Price looked to Elisabeth, not proceeding until she signalled her reluctant agreement. Frederick was John Godwin's brother and heir, and she was merely his wife. Even with a woman on the throne these past four years, a woman's legal rights were virtually non-existent except as an extension of the man who commanded her. Father, husband, and now brother-in-law. She counted herself lucky to have had outstanding men filling the first two roles.

The attorney picked up a letter and adjusted his bifocals. 'Before I read the last Will and Testament of Mr John Percival Godwin, I have been instructed by him to read a letter. The letter is dated the thirtieth of May 1841, two weeks before his death.'

Frederick jerked upright. Red blotches bloomed on his neck and rose up his cheeks.

Mr Price read:

'My darling Elisabeth, you made the sun shine on the darkest of days. I loved you from the moment I met you and will carry on loving you for eternity. Dearest Anne, how proud I am of the extraordinary woman you have become. Frederick, I ask that you look after these two precious women. You will inherit Godwin & Sons' Shipping and the house, but I expect you to use both to benefit the whole family. I trust that your goodwill will be sufficient to respect my wishes. If not, Mr Price has the power to ensure that you meet your obligations. Your loving husband and brother, John Godwin.'

The attorney looked up to ensure there were no questions before the formal reading of the will. Frederick was on his feet and hovering over the desk, but he stifled whatever comment he was about to make. Instead, he prowled the room, his eyes narrowing as the attorney listed a series of sentimental bequests.

It was John's wish that Elisabeth should keep all the gifts he had given her over the past decade, including the sapphire and diamond necklace he had bought her as a wedding present, as well as keeping her own family jewellery. She was also bequeathed all of John's books, with the exception of his collection of bibles, which went to Anne. To his faithful employee, Mr Rivers, John left a model of the first Godwin ship, made by Mr Godwin senior. To the Palmers, their butler and housekeeper, he gave the silver box in which his father had kept his cigars.

Frederick's frown deepened, but he kept quiet, evidently willing to relinquish a few minor items rather than fight for his right to everything.

Mr Price continued, reading the clause that Frederick was waiting for – the bulk of John Godwin's estate went to his brother and heir, Frederick Godwin. At that, the prowl became a strut. Elisabeth watched his ill-concealed glee without a flinch, knowing Frederick had been worried that John would cut him out of his inheritance.

Mr Price called in his clerk as a witness and handed a document to each of them. 'By signing this, you attest that you accept the terms of the will as read.'

Frederick signed with only a moment's hesitation, Elisabeth with a combination of resignation and relief, and Anne only after receiving a discreet nod from her sister-in-law.

'There is one final item,' Mr Price continued. 'Shortly before his death, Mr Godwin entrusted me with a copy of certain documents. He asked that I unseal and read them only if I feel that his wishes in respect of Mrs Elisabeth Godwin and Miss Anne Godwin are not being adequately discharged.' He kept his gaze squarely on Frederick. 'I trust that no such action by me on Mr John's behalf will be required.'

Mr Price extracted the sealed documents from his pile of papers and transferred them to a filing drawer, before locking the drawer with a symbolic flourish.

'What documents? Where are the originals?' Frederick's nostrils pinched together over an out-thrust lower lip, a familiar sign of barely suppressed anger.

'I do not know the nature of the documents, nor who holds the originals. I am only repeating Mr Godwin's brief but explicit instructions to me.' Mr Price gathered his papers together. 'And may I once again express my sincere condolences on this terrible tragedy. Mr John Godwin was a great man.'

The attorney kissed Elisabeth and Anne on the cheek and shook Frederick's hand. 'The transfer of ownership will be ready in a few days, Mr Godwin, if you would care to make an appointment.'

Frederick disappeared immediately, leaving Elisabeth and Anne to thank Mr Price for his long service and soothe his ruffled feathers. He spoke again of his deep regret at John's tragic death and assured the women that he would do whatever he could to assist them.

They travelled home in silence, making one stop at the premises of Mr Arthur Postlethwaite, a dealer specialising in antiquarian books. When they arrived at the house, they were surprised to see Frederick's carriage in the courtyard, as they had expected him to return to work.

The butler rushed out to open the carriage door with unaccustomed haste, his face the colour of beetroot. 'Mrs Godwin, Mr Frederick is in the house, making a fearful mess. I tried to stop him, but he told me he owned the house now.' The beetroot darkened a shade as he added, 'He threatened to let me go if I tried to interfere.'

Elisabeth felt her own face flushing at his words. Their butler and his wife, the housekeeper, had been with the Godwin household since the days of Mr Godwin senior and were more like family than servants.

'I'm very sorry, Mr Palmer, but there is nothing we can do to stop him. Frederick owns the house now, or will soon, but he had no right to treat you with such disrespect.'

Elisabeth suggested Anne retreat to her room while she dealt with the situation. Her determination to remain calm vanished when she saw the state of the library. The room, which had been their private sanctuary, was no longer. Documents from the safe were scattered on the floor, along with the contents of her late husband's desk. She finally found Frederick in the master bedroom, searching through the bedside drawers.

Suppressing, with difficulty, the overwhelming urge to slap him, she strode forward and seized her jewellery box, ripping it from his hands. It was one of the few things she had to remind her of her mother and more precious than a mercenary like Frederick could ever comprehend. Legally, her husband owned everything she possessed, so it had been a relief when Frederick had agreed to her keeping her family jewellery. Not that she would have given it up even if he hadn't signed the agreement, but that was a battle best avoided.

Elisabeth stood her ground in front of her brother-in-law, barely reaching his chin and a fraction of his bulk, her face red-hot from the anger boiling within. 'You have no right to touch my possessions, Frederick.'

Rather than back off, Frederick leaned in and held her shoulders so hard she could feel his fingernails digging in. 'Where are the documents, Elisabeth?'

'I have absolutely no idea what you are talking about. John never said a word to me about any documents.' She could see by his expression that he was inclined to believe her – no doubt thinking that John would not have trusted her, being a mere woman and therefore of inferior mind. Still, he hesitated. 'Really, Frederick. I will swear to it if you wish. Now will you please leave my bedroom, so I can recover from a stressful morning.'

He released her and retreated to the door, but didn't leave. 'It's a beautiful jewellery box, but you don't seem to have a great deal in it. Did you not have a valuable pearl necklace?'

'I might ask what concern that is of yours, as you have signed a document acknowledging my rights to my own family jewellery.'

'And I might ask how a farm girl came to be in possession of valuable jewellery. Show me the necklace.'

Elisabeth ignored the intentional snub, as she had done for the past decade. 'John was desperate for money a few months ago, so I offered to sell the pearls.' Which was true, as far as it went. She had offered, but of course John had refused to sell the pearl necklace, knowing how much it meant to her. She held Frederick's accusing gaze until he blinked. 'I believe there was a problem with financing the business. Would you know anything about that?'

Her words had the desired effect. Frederick slammed the door behind him without replying. She locked the door and threw herself onto the bed, finally letting loose the surge of grief she'd been struggling to control all morning.

Choices

Elisabeth's eyes were dry again by the time she heard a tap on the door. Mrs Palmer entered with a pot of tea and a platter of her favourite food. Freshly baked bread rolls wafting a yeasty aroma, a crusty wedge of Stilton with slices of pear, and delicious little raspberry and chocolate tarts. Yet even these delights turned her stomach.

Without speaking, Mrs Palmer removed Elisabeth's widow's cap and the many pins needed to keep her waves of rebellious blonde hair tightly reined in. The constricting gown of black crepe and corset followed, allowing her to take a full breath for the first time that morning. She would definitely have to get another dress if she was to survive ten more months of mourning, if only she could find the spare time to attend a fitting. With a sigh, she slipped into a dressing-gown John had bought her, luxuriating in the soft caress of the loose satin on her skin.

Elisabeth sat at her dressing table, enjoying the rhythmic pull of the hairbrush through her loose hair. As Mrs Palmer worked the knots out, Elisabeth applied a soothing cream to the rash from the itchy collar, revealing the red arcs left by Frederick's finger-nails on her shoulders. The brushing stopped and Mrs Palmer's reflection in the mirror met her gaze with narrowed eyes and a tight mouth.

'If there is anything I can do for you, Mrs Godwin – anything at all – please don't hesitate to ask.' Mrs Palmer lowered her gaze and concentrated on tidying away the brushes.

'Thank you, Mrs Palmer. I couldn't have coped without you these last few weeks. But I have all I need right now.'

Mrs Palmer hesitated for a moment, then turned away to straighten the rumpled counterpane on the bed. 'Mr Frederick Godwin has informed me that he wants the house thoroughly cleaned before he and his wife move in tomorrow afternoon. Perhaps I misheard?'

Elisabeth was dumbfounded by Frederick's gall. Typical that he didn't have the decency to tell her himself. She had been mistress of this house for a decade, but it seemed he would not give her more than a day to come to terms with the new regime, even before the paperwork was signed. But she had known this day would come and had taken steps to prepare for it.

She realised belatedly that Mrs Palmer had spoken it as a question. 'Thank you, Mrs Palmer. I was not aware they would wish to move in so soon.' She took a deep breath and went on with as much dignity as she could muster. 'They will want the master suite of rooms for themselves, naturally. I would be grateful if you could attend to the cleaning, while I pack my belongings. You always keep the house spotless, so you need not do more than a quick tidy. Oh, and can you please tell Mr Palmer that Mr Arthur Postlethwaite will be here first thing tomorrow morning to pack up the book collection, which John left to Anne and me.'

'Very well, Mrs Godwin. Make sure you eat now. Miss Anne would like to see you when you are up to it.' She paused before adding, with deliberate emphasis, 'Mr Frederick has been in to see her.'

'Thank you. Tell Anne to come as soon as she wishes. And Mrs Palmer…' The housekeeper paused at the door, while Elisabeth framed her inadequate words. 'I… I'm sorry.'

When Elisabeth was alone again, she checked that her sapphire and diamond necklace was still nestled in the jewellery box, alongside the diamond hair-combs and cameo brooch, which had been gifts from her mother and aunt, and the little wooden owl her father had carved for her. With a vigorous swipe, she erased Frederick's fingerprints from the exquisitely crafted inlaid wood. She hugged the jewellery box to her chest before wrapping the box in velvet and putting it at the bottom of her trunk.

The only portrait she possessed of her mother was in the usual spot beside the bed, unsullied by his grasping fingers. Looking at her mother as a young girl was almost like looking in a mirror, except that her chubby child's face had grown longer and thinner with maturity. The unruly blonde waves of hair and the wide, blue-grey eyes were the same, as was the impish grin. She pressed the picture to her heart, wishing that there was a picture of her father to sit beside it. The thought of her parents gave her strength when she needed it most.

She, of all people, knew that nothing good lasted forever. Although she would give her soul to the devil himself if it would bring her loved ones back, in her heart she knew they were gone forever. The only solution was to be resolute, smart and fearless, just as her parents had taught her. With renewed resolve, she wrapped the portrait and tucked in down beside the jewellery box. She would write a note to a friend asking if she and Anne could stay for a few days. She would not – could not – spend a single day in this house with Frederick and his wife.

Suddenly, she felt ravenous. Within minutes, the tray was empty of even the tiniest crumb. Soon after, there was a knock on the door and Mrs Palmer came in. The housekeeper beamed when she saw the empty tray and promised to arrange for the note to be delivered straight away.

'Please tell Anne that I will be in the library,' Elisabeth said.

Elisabeth sat at her husband's desk for what might be the last time. Like all the furniture in the house, it spoke of a simple elegance and practicality, with its many pigeonholes and drawers for the correspondence and ledgers he had presided over. The walls were lined with books on all manner of subjects, from maritime history to poetry, and everything in between. She and John had loved reading together in the alcove by the window, with its view across the fenced garden in the middle of a cobbled square – a little patch of tranquillity close to the seething heart of the City of London.

When she had arrived, as a naïve girl of eighteen from rural France, Elisabeth had been shocked at the filth and smell and endless roiling humanity of the city John Godwin adored. Although she had come to enjoy the intensity of London as the years passed, her true happiness was reserved for their quiet evenings together in this solid brick townhouse, curtains closed upon the city, sitting side-by-side in front of the fire discussing literature, arguing about current events, or simply lying in each other's arms.

John had kept up his regular voyages, overseeing their fleet of ships, and gradually expanding his grandfather's business from coastal trading into the further reaches of Europe and the British Empire. His death at sea during a storm was a cruel blow.

Two months on, she still reached for him when she woke, still listened for his voice every time the heavy front door thudded shut. Most days, all she wanted to do was hide away in the library, where his presence lingered in the scent of his overcoat, the rows of well-thumbed books, and the dented leather of his chair.

But he had been a popular man and her days had been filled with a never-ending flow of visitors expressing heartfelt condolences, so many that the faces had become a blur. The Palmers had been wonderful, ensuring visiting cards were collected and noting down tokens received, while serving gallons of tea and mountains of cake.

To Elisabeth's relief, the stream of visitors had gradually dwindled to a trickle. And now, she had no idea where she would receive guests. Elisabeth had always known that Frederick and his wife, Clarissa, would want the house, and that she could never live alongside them, nor they with her. She just hadn't expected she would have to find a new home so soon. She got up and ran a finger along the spines of familiar books, feeling their imminent loss as a physical wrench.

Elisabeth picked up a portrait of John and set it aside with a small pile of items to pack. He was so like his sister – slim and understated, with a sharp-featured, intelligent face. His stern demeanour in the picture did not do justice to the generous heart within, although she felt his kindness radiating from his slight smile and warm eyes.

That reminded her of another task. She pulled John's personal bible from the shelf and placed it alongside the portrait, to ensure it went to Anne.

A gentle knock on the door signalled Anne's arrival, followed by Mrs Palmer and the welcome aroma of coffee. Anne slumped onto the settee by the table, as pale and silent as a wraith. Her sister-in-law had become a sister to her, so strong was their bond. Seeing Anne so lifeless added to Elisabeth's anguish.

Anne had only been twelve to Elisabeth's eighteen when they first met. She was a sensitive, studious child, who desperately missed her late mother. John had been protective of his younger sister, but Elisabeth saw that what Anne needed most was the support to feel confident of her abilities and the encouragement to find her own place in the world. Now she was an intelligent twenty-three-year-old who had already achieved more than most older people.

Until John's death, the only blight on Anne's life had been Frederick, who was pressing her to make a good marriage before she got 'too old', although Anne herself was happy in her charitable work and wanted to marry for love. Needless to say, Frederick felt Elisabeth was a terrible influence on his sister.

Elisabeth sat down beside her and poured the coffee. She handed a cup to Anne, waiting for her to compose her thoughts. She sipped her own coffee quietly down to the dregs, while Anne's drink went untasted. John had taught her the value of silence to draw out a problem, rather than rushing in, as she was wont to do.

Anne set her cup back down with a crack-inducing clatter and a splatter of coffee. 'Oh, Elisabeth, it's so unfair. John would have wanted so much more for you, especially after all you've done to build the business. He loved you with such a passion. I cannot understand how Frederick can be so mean. I won't even repeat what he replied when I said you deserved a proper share of John's estate to set up your own household.'

'Let me guess. That devious French peasant will never touch a penny of Godwin money?'

Red dots flared in Anne's cheeks as she fought between outrage and amusement. She settled on a wry grin. 'That was the gist of it. Am I missing something? I'm not sure I understood half of the undercurrents flowing around the attorney's office this morning. Why was Frederick so agitated?'

Elisabeth noted, with no surprise, that Anne's first thought was for her sister-in-law's welfare rather than her own. She reached across and squeezed Anne's hand. 'You are very perceptive. There are things John did not wish you to know. Frederick has not proved himself worthy of the respected Godwin name.'

'How so?'

'Anne, will you trust me a little longer? John and I have done everything possible in the circumstances to ensure that you will be looked after. Will you believe me when I say that we will be fine? We will have to leave this house, unless you can stand to live here with your brother and his wife.' She paused long enough for Anne to shake her head in a vigorous no. 'I promise we will have enough to make a good life for ourselves.'

'Dearest Elisabeth, of course I trust you. And John too. I put some money aside regularly from the generous allowance he gave me. You could survive on that for a few months at least until you find a better situation.'

'You're so kind, as ever. But we will be together, won't we?'

To Elisabeth's astonishment, Anne began to shake as if taken with a sudden fever. With a plaintive howl, she flung herself into Elisabeth's arms and burst into tears. All she could do was hold her tight and stroke her hair until the tears subsided.

'Is it something Frederick said?'

Through gulping sobs, Anne said, 'He's sending me away.'

'What? Away where?'

'He has arranged for me to marry the son of a business acquaintance in the Province of Canada. A fur trader. The son lives in the middle of nowhere, buying furs from trappers and sending them to his father to ship to England.' Anne collapsed into tears again, curling into a miserable ball on the settee.

Elisabeth sat back in stunned silence until anger overwhelmed shock. She jumped up and paced the room, barely holding herself back from the urge to fling something breakable at the wall. 'Monstrous! Slavery has been abolished, yet women can still be treated like sheep. This man sounds no better than a savage. I would not have thought even Frederick capable of this.'

Anne took a few hiccoughing breaths. 'The father has agreed to give exclusive shipping rights to Godwin and Sons. Frederick told me the wealth of Canada flowed through their hands and one day I would have a mansion to live in. He honestly thought I would be grateful for his intervention, given my lack of suitors in England.'

'There are thousands of decent English men who would be thrilled to marry a wonderful woman like you, if and when you are ready to marry.'

'Elisabeth, I…I don't know what to do.'

'Well, for a start, you will not be marrying this man while I have breath in my body. John would never have condoned this outrageous proposal.'

'More than anything, I want to stay with you. Frederick suggested you could come with me to Canada, but of course you must choose for yourself.'

'And when did he plan for us to leave?'

'He has already bought two tickets on a ship leaving in four days.'

Words failed her. Elisabeth closed her eyes and tried to think, but her head was throbbing. 'Let's go for a walk in the park. The fresh air will do us both good. We will need clear heads to plot our escape.'

Neither said a word until they had walked a good mile of gravelled paths in leaf-dappled sunlight. Elisabeth was wearing the mourning dress again, but this time she had left the satin robe on underneath. It felt sensuous against her skin and served as a reminder that there was always a subtle way around every problem.

The earthy smell of freshly turned soil and the heady fragrance of the few remaining roses soothed her anger, allowing her to think rationally. They reached a pond and sat on a park bench by a bed of bright orange and pink dahlias, watching children sail model yachts and throw sticks off the bridge.

Their joyful games brought a smile back to her face, even if her heart was heavy with the thought that none of this would have happened if she had been able to give John a son. They had both desperately wanted children, but – as Clarissa had so tactlessly summed up at dinner two weeks ago – Elisabeth had 'failed in her duty'. The dinner had been held to celebrate Frederick's triumphant announcement of his wife's pregnancy.

The walk had boosted Anne's spirits too, and she was able to smile wryly as she said, 'Frederick was generous enough to offer me my mother's emerald and diamond necklace if I agreed to go to Canada.'

'But that necklace was always intended for you. Your mother left it to you specifically.'

'Frederick felt it should rightly go to his wife, as he is now the head of the Godwin family.'

Elisabeth felt the blood rising in her cheeks again and wondered if she would ever again feel happy and at peace. 'Please, Anne, don't tell me any more of what he said, or I swear I'll not be responsible for my actions.'

'Oh Elisabeth, I can't imagine you hurting a flea.'

'You might be surprised what I am capable of when pushed beyond reason.'

They sat in silence for a few minutes, basking in the warmth of the late summer's day.

Fresh air and a change of scene was such a tonic, Elisabeth thought. 'Anne, this might sound crazy, but what if we were to take those tickets and go to Canada? Not to marry a disgusting fur-trapper, but to make a fresh start. We could go on to New York, perhaps. Anywhere we wanted to, in fact. Or come back to England again if we didn't like it. A first-class sea voyage, with fresh air and new sights – our little adventure, far away from Frederick. What do you think?'

'Just the two of us, without an escort?' Anne looked at her as if she had truly gone mad. Then, gradually, her astonishment faded to contemplation, and finally to excitement. 'Wonderful! Let's do it. I long to see the world beyond the grimy streets of London. I'd love to visit New York. And Rome. Maybe the Taj Mahal and the great pyramids of Giza.'

They looked at each other and burst into helpless giggles, causing a flock of waddling ducks to fly off in fright.

When decorum had been restored, Elisabeth said, 'Frederick and Clarissa are moving into the house tomorrow. Shall we go home and pack, so we are ready to leave as soon as they arrive? I've asked a friend if we can stay for a few days.'

Anne stood up and held out her arm. 'Perfect. We have a plan and we have each other. What more could we want?'

The next twenty-four hours were frantic with activity, allowing them no time to dwell on their fears. Elisabeth and Anne rushed around, packing only the essentials for the voyage and setting aside the rest for storage or charitable donation. The Palmers looked on with open mouths at first, but soon joined in to hunt out warm clothes from winter storage and get extra trunks down from the attic.

Elisabeth's friend sent a note saying she would be delighted to have her and Anne to stay for however long they wished. Elisabeth sent back a reply that they would arrive the next afternoon, for a couple of days only, if that was acceptable. Both women spent the evening writing farewell notes to their friends. Elisabeth also sent a letter to Mr Price, the attorney, explaining their decision and assuring him she would write again as soon as she could.

The book dealer arrived early the next morning with a large cart, dozens of boxes, and a group of strong lads. John had already had the books appraised, under a long-standing agreement to offer first purchasing rights to Mr Postlethwaite, who was giddy with excitement at getting his hands on the collection at last. The two men had agreed a sum, but Mr Postlethwaite insisted on paying a higher amount, in consideration of the increase in value since the appraisal.

Elisabeth was delighted to accept and pleased to be doing business with a man who loved books and traded with such honesty. She felt a sense of guilt at seeing the books being packed into boxes, after all the years of dedication that had been put into building the collection, but pushed it aside for more practical concerns.

Frederick and Clarissa arrived as Mr Postlethwaite's heavily laden cart pulled away.

Frederick hurried inside, finding Elisabeth in the library. 'What is the meaning of this? What has that man taken?'

Elisabeth sat down swiftly in an armchair, her voluminous skirt covering the bags of money the book dealer had given her. 'Calm yourself, Frederick. As you can see from the empty shelves, he has only taken the books, which John left to us.'

'But I expected you to leave those books in my library, where they belong. Not that I can abide people who waste their time reading, but a wall of books presents a picture of a solid business and a distinguished home.'

'As Anne and I are leaving, we felt it appropriate to remove all our possessions from your new home. We wanted to have the house completely ready for you to move in, with no inconvenience to you or your wife.'

Frederick stood nonplussed. 'You're leaving today?'

'Of course. You have arranged for us to go to the Province of Canada, or am I mistaken? We will stay with friends until the ship sails.'

Frederick stared at her, no doubt seeking signs of a trick. 'We were not sure you would agree to go.'

Elisabeth allowed her eyes to widen a little. 'But of course I must go. My dear Anne cannot travel unchaperoned. Now that you are here, Frederick, perhaps you could give me the tickets, as we may not see you again before we depart for our new life.'

Frederick mumbled something about going to get them and left the room, his brow still furrowed. Elisabeth hurried to her room to hide the money and finish her packing. She was taking only two trunks with her. The everyday trunk, plainly wrought in oak, contained the more practical garments in heavy cotton, linen and muslin that she was likely to need in her new life. The special items went into a magnificent mahogany trunk, which John had given her on their wedding day.

Two trunks – her entire future in such a small space. But possessions meant little. She would have swapped any amount of finery in a heartbeat for one last loving glance from John.

By the time Frederick returned with the tickets and travel documents, she was busy folding the last of her favourite silk and velvet dresses into the mahogany trunk. She checked the tickets – a first-class cabin for two from London to the Port of Quebec. 'Thank you, Frederick. Most kind of you to look after us.'

When she looked up, Elisabeth saw Clarissa had noiselessly entered the room and was standing by Frederick's side like a classical Greek statue carved from cold white marble. Her tall, slim figure was a picture of elegance in a silk gown, which would have graced any high-society tea party. Her hat alone probably cost more than the entire contents of Elisabeth's oak trunk, as the elaborate silk creation was festooned with enough feathers, ruffles, ribbons and bows to grace a dozen normal hats.

Clarissa whispered in her husband's ear, but her eyes remained on Elisabeth, with an expression that managed to combine disdain, annoyance and suspicion.

Frederick turned to Elisabeth. 'Clarissa says the cart belonged to an antiquarian book dealer. If there were any valuable books, I need to know so the money can be properly distributed to the estate.'

'John bequeathed the books to Anne and me. Surely you wouldn't begrudge us a few measly pounds for a dozen boxes of dusty old books? The dealer was a man John knew, who agreed to do us a favour by taking them away.'

'I need to know exactly how much he paid you.'

'Enough to buy your sister a wedding dress. Unless you have given Anne enough money to get her started in her new life?' Elisabeth could see that he had not even considered the needs of his sister, so she turned to leave before she said something she wouldn't regret. 'If you'll excuse me, I must finish packing.'

Frederick followed her out into the corridor and yelled after her. 'Come back here. You didn't answer my question.'

Mr Palmer appeared at the top of the stairs. 'Mr Frederick, there is a man waiting to see you in the drawing room. A Mr Kingston. I'm sure that gentleman would be appalled to hear you yelling like a fishwife at Mrs Godwin.'

Frederick stared at the butler in utter disbelief. 'How dare you! I will not be spoken to like that by a servant in my own home.'

Mr Palmer didn't budge. 'Just as well I'm not your servant then, isn't it? I quit, and so does my wife.'

Frederick bunched his fists, his eyes blazing. Mr Palmer continued to stand firm, his muscled forearms crossed over his broad chest. He may have been twice Frederick's age, but Elisabeth would have placed her bet on the older man any day if it came to a fight.

Frederick pushed past him and stomped down the stairs. 'Pack your possessions and leave immediately. And don't expect a reference.'

When he was out of earshot, Mr Palmer gave Elisabeth the merest hint of a wink. 'We packed yesterday. Are you ready to leave, Mrs Godwin?'

'Another ten minutes? If you are ready, could you arrange to have our trunks taken down to the carriage? I'm sure we will be able to squeeze you and Mrs Palmer in as well, even if it takes two trips to take all the luggage.'

By the time she had packed the last of her belongings, Mr Palmer had arranged for an extra cart and he and the carter were stacking boxes and sharing jokes. Anne and Elisabeth did a last sweep through the house, feeling rather overwhelmed and under-prepared due to the speed of their departure. Mrs Palmer was looking equally dazed as Anne helped her into the carriage.

Anne walked over to where Elisabeth was standing, staring up at the window of the library, as if she could conjure up John's face at the window one last time. They linked arms and returned to the carriage, where Mr Palmer was waiting to ask them for an address. To Elisabeth's surprise, Clarissa joined them. Before Elisabeth could stop her, Anne had given their address, which Mr Palmer relayed to the drivers.

Clarissa kissed them both. 'My dear sisters, I know the past two months have been difficult for you. My Frederick is not always as tactful as he should be. I want to wish you the best of fortune from us both. You will always be welcome here.'

'Thank you, Clarissa, that is very kind. I'm so glad we have not parted on ill feelings.' Anne clasped Clarissa's hands and returned her kiss.

'I wish you and your child well,' was all Elisabeth could muster.

Mr Palmer handed them into the carriage, then took a seat beside his wife.

Clarissa watched on with obvious annoyance. 'I'm sure there is no need for you to accompany the ladies, Palmer. Mr Godwin and I will need your assistance here.'

'My wife and I are no longer employed by this household,' Mr Palmer said, with a quiet dignity edged with a tinge of relish.

He nodded to the driver, who flicked a whip with a crack in the air above the horses. The harness tightened under their muscles and the party rolled out of the courtyard, across the square and away from the only house that any of them had called home in London, leaving in their wake a speechless Clarissa, standing with her jaw dropped and her hands on her hips.

Elisabeth shook herself out of her trance when they bumped onto the main road. 'I'm sorry you lost your job by defending me, Mr Palmer. I will write you an excellent reference as you both deserve.'

'I'm not sorry at all, ma'am,' Palmer replied. 'We wouldn't have lasted a day with the new lot. Truth to tell, me and the wife have our eye on an inn in our home county of Norfolk, which has just come up for sale. We would never have left you and Mr John Godwin, but now … all's well that ends well, as they say.'

'I'm delighted to hear it.' Elisabeth handed him the silver cigar box. 'John left you this in his will.'

'My goodness, Mrs Godwin, this is most unexpected. Thank you.'

'It is you and Mrs Palmer who are owed the thanks for looking after us so well all these years. You'll find six months' wages under the lining at the bottom, as a mark of our appreciation.'

Mr Palmer couldn't help but peek. 'Lordy be. I don't know how to thank you. This'll set us up very nicely indeed in our wee life, won't it, my love?' He held his wife's hand as she nodded and dabbed her eyes with a neatly pressed handkerchief.

Mr Palmer, the carter and the staff of Elisabeth's friend made quick work of unloading at the other end of the journey.

Elisabeth stood aside with Mrs Palmer and left them to it under Anne's supervision. 'I will miss you, Mrs Palmer, and not just for your wonderful cooking.' She couldn't help herself – she flung her arms around the housekeeper, who had been almost like a second mother to her when she had landed in London as a wide-eyed young woman.

'Oh dear, Mrs Godwin – Elisabeth – it's so hard to say goodbye. You and Mr John were so happy together and you always treated us like family. I'll miss you something terrible. If you're ever passing the Old Goat Inn in Norwich, please look us up.'

'I promise you we will visit, if we ever make it home to England.'

'You look after yourself, my dear. I overheard Mr Frederick and Mr Kingston as we were packing. Something about documents and a pearl necklace they wanted and thinking you had them. I didn't hear much, but I didn't like their tone. All shouting and angry, as if you had tricked them. In my experience, it's only the devious wrong 'uns who suspect tricks from decent folk.'

'Thank you for the warning. Thankfully, we'll soon be gone and they will trouble us no more. Here's Mr Palmer back. I wish you both the very best.' She gave Mrs Palmer another quick hug and waved as they and the cart disappeared around the corner.

Escape

Elisabeth was looking forward to a peaceful day of much-needed rest at her friend's house, but she had not even finished savouring a second cup of thick French coffee with a late breakfast when a messenger arrived. The maid handed her a note from Frederick saying he would be busy in meetings most of the morning, but they should not leave the house, as he would call on them before noon.

She had been feeling a twinge of guilt that they had left Frederick on bad terms without a proper goodbye, but that feeling vanished under the arrogance of his demands. Ordinarily, she considered herself a tolerant person who got along with almost everyone, but the events of the past two months had worn her good cheer to a sliver.

As she threw his note aside, the door-bell chimed. The maid showed Mr Price in, with a glance at Elisabeth that was part curious and part outrage at this uncivil level of disturbance to her routine at barely nine o'clock in the morning.

Mr Price strode into the room with unaccustomed haste, his tie and hat askew. 'Mrs Godwin, please accept my apologies for calling at such an early hour and disturbing your breakfast with unpleasant news.'

Elisabeth took one look at the deep frown lines on the normally imperturbable attorney, before guiding him to a chair and plying him with strong tea with an extra lump of sugar.

'I regret to say that my office was burgled last night.' Mr Price paused to run a handkerchief over his forehead and drain half the teacup at a gulp. 'The perpetrator left rather a mess, but, as far as I can ascertain, the only item taken was your husband's sealed packet of documents.'

Elisabeth looked up sharply in mid-reach for the toast rack. 'Good heavens. I hope you were not present at the time, Mr Price.' She spread butter and jam on two slices of toast and slid the plate in front of him.

He shook his head but reached for the toast anyway. 'I wish I had been there to teach the scoundrel the error of his ways.'

'This is disturbing news indeed. Did John say anything to you about what the documents contained?'

'Not the specific details. Mrs Godwin, I believe you know your husband was looking into some concerns he had about Fredick's dealings in the family business. My understanding is that the documents relate to that.'

'Yes, I'm sure you're right. Do you have any idea where the originals are?'

He shuffled uncomfortably in the chair. 'I rather gained the impression that he had given the originals to you, Mrs Godwin, but clearly that is not the case. Perhaps they are held at the bank or in his office?'

'I wish I could have searched our house more thoroughly before we left, although Frederick had already done a good job of that by the look of the mess in the library. My brother-in-law appears to think that I have the documents too, and he is furious about it. His behaviour yesterday was odd, even threatening.'

'I'm afraid there is more to tell. I also had a visit from a Mr Postlethwaite late yesterday afternoon. Mr Frederick visited him after you left the house and demanded to know the value of the books he bought from you. I could see that the poor man was shaken by the encounter. Indeed, he felt threatened to the point of revealing the sum paid. By good fortune, another customer entered the shop, saving him from your brother-in-law's wrath. He closed up the shop and came to see me immediately. I'm afraid I did not think the matter was as serious as he implied, until my office was burgled. Hence my haste to see you this morning.'

'Oh no, poor Arthur. I told him to refer any request for information to you, but it seems Frederick is more desperate that I thought possible, if he is willing to threaten a frail old man who had done nothing more than buy our books.'

Mr Price looked down at the empty plate and cup in front of him in surprise. 'I am most concerned about you, Mrs Godwin. I trust Mr Frederick does not know where you are?'

'Unfortunately, his wife was present to farewell us and overheard our address. He has sent me a note to say he wishes to see me this morning.' She noted the look of alarm in the attorney's eyes and added, 'Don't worry, Mr Price. I assure you that we will not be here to see him. But thank you for your concern.'

Soon after Mr Price left, Anne came into the breakfast room and helped herself to kippers and poached eggs from the metal chafing dishes on the sideboard. 'Mm, I'm starving. Sorry I slept late.' She sat down at the table and reached for the coffee. 'Goodness, you do look pale, Elisabeth. Are you unwell?'

Elisabeth gave her an edited account of Mr Price's visit and handed her Frederick's note.

'I don't want to see Frederick,' Anne said, 'and I can see from your face that you do not want to see him either. Should we go out to visit friends instead?'

'I think it might be best if we move to other lodgings, otherwise he will find us here eventually.'

'You sound worried.'

'I have a very bad feeling about this business. Frederick's odd behaviour, searching my room and threatening me, demanding my pearl necklace. And later, Mrs Palmer warning me that she overheard him and this Kingston fellow getting angry at me for hiding the documents. She is not one to worry for no reason, so yes, I feel unsafe. And Frederick knows where we are, thanks to Clarissa.'

Less than an hour later, they loaded their trunks onto another carriage and waved farewell to their bewildered hostess. As they turned from the quiet side street into a busy London thoroughfare, Elisabeth noticed that a hansom carriage had pulled out behind them, drawn by a skinny bay horse with one white sock.

When they arrived at the office of Godwin & Sons' Shipping, the bay horse with the white sock was nowhere to be seen. She chided herself for letting her imagination get the better of her common sense. All the same, she would be relieved when she and Anne set sail.

Her final task was to deliver the model ship bequeathed by John to Mr Rivers, who was a loyal employee of some forty years, and check if the missing documents were in John's office. Then they would disappear.

They found the office in disarray. Mr Rivers was slumped behind his desk, his face dribbling blood from a cut over his eye.

Anne rushed to his side. 'Fetch me some water, Elisabeth.'

Elisabeth hurried into the inner office. There were drawers pulled out and papers strewn everywhere. Fortunately, her brother-in-law was not there. This was the first time she had been into John's office since his death, but there was little sign of him left now that Frederick had taken over. She found an undamaged carafe of water and hurried out again.

Anne had Mr Rivers sitting in a chair, while she pressed a handkerchief to his cut. She took the water and raised an eyebrow at Elisabeth.

'Frederick's not here. The robber left such a mess that I have no idea if anything was taken.' Elisabeth sat down beside her old friend and ally, whom she had first met on her voyage over from France. 'I am so sorry you have been caught in the middle of this, Mr Rivers. How are you?'

In pain, judging by the way he was wincing as he pushed himself to his feet. 'Nowt to worry about, Mrs Godwin, merely a scratch.' Rivers swayed slightly.

Anne gestured for him to sit down again. 'Cut and bruised, but thankfully no broken bones.'

Mr Rivers eased himself back down like a man twenty years his senior. 'Mr Frederick Godwin were out o' the office when the man arrived. Just the one man, but as big and strong as a dock-worker. But he seemed a polite gentleman, at first.'

'What did he want?'

'You, Mrs Godwin. Told him straight out he was welcome to conduct his business here, but I would not give out personal information. He said he would wait for Mr Frederick, then had the brazen cheek to go through to his office rather than waiting out here. I heard him rummaging through the desk and confronted him. That's when he hit me.'

'We owe a great deal to your loyalty,' Elisabeth said. 'Are you quite certain he asked specifically for me at first?'

'Absolutely sure, ma'am. I'm terribly sorry, but I gave him your home address. He were very hard to say no to, but at least that made him leave.'

'I'd rather you had given the address to him without being hurt, Mr Rivers. Can you tell me, was the man English or foreign?'

'Well, I'm not sure I can rightly say as to that. He spoke English perfectly, but his manner and the cut of his coat seemed a bit foreign. Although that is often the case with Mr Godwin's customers, who naturally travel a great deal. He must have been feeling the cold, for he had a scarf wound around the lower part of his face.'

'Did he give a name?'

'No, Mrs Godwin. I asked, but he ignored me. I've seen him in the office before and he clearly knew Mr Frederick, but I can't recall ever hearing his name.'

'Thank you, Mr Rivers. Do sit down and rest while we decide what to do.'

Elisabeth took Anne aside, out of his hearing. 'I think it would be best if we continue to our ship, without delay. With luck, we can leave before this ruffian figures out where we have gone.'

Anne gathered her travelling bag. 'Mr Rivers, would you be so good as to accompany us to the docks? I would feel safer with you at our side until we are away from here.'

Elisabeth smiled at this, sure that the resolute Anne was less afraid for herself than wanting him to regain his dignity. Whichever it was, the diminutive Mr Rivers set his aging shoulders back, as if lining up for battle. He locked the doors and helped them back into the carriage, which was waiting outside with their luggage.

On the short trip to the docks, Elisabeth thanked Mr Rivers for his long service and handed him the model ship. 'John wanted you to have this as a memento of your time together. I'm told John's father made it.'

'He did at that. I remember it well, for I made the rigging myself when I were a lad. Well, that's very kind of your husband to remember me. I'll think of it as a retirement gift, as I handed in my notice last week. It's not the same without Mr John here and I've a widowed sister in Devon who would be pleased to have company and a hand with the gardening.'

She slipped a purse into his hands, against his protests. 'John wanted to be sure you would receive a fair reward for all your years of dedication. I hope it makes your retirement more enjoyable.'

The clerk wiped a tear from the corner of his eye. 'It were an honour to work with Mr John and his father. And you, Mrs Godwin. Never known a lady with a head for numbers like you, though, now I think on it, my late wife did all the household accounts and ran a charity for wounded soldiers. Times are changing and the old ways must always give way to the new.'

At the riverside, he talked to some contacts and within ten more minutes had arranged immediate passage downriver on a fast steam ferry. He was not the sort of man to welcome an embrace, but he did shake Elisabeth's hand with such vigour that she was relieved to disengage and step aboard the boat.

And even more relieved when the ferry cast off. Their ship was not due to depart until the day after next, but they would be able to find a secure place to stay overnight, far from the centre of London.

Anne retreated into the shelter of the cabin, curled up on the wooden seat, with her head between her hands and her shoulders hunched. Elisabeth lingered on deck for a moment to wave goodbye.

As the boat pulled out from the dock with a belch of black smoke, a hansom cab pulled up at the dockside with a clatter of hooves, the horse steaming in its lathered harness. A large man leapt out, tossed a coin up to the driver and sprinted towards the waving figure. She watched in dismay as their employee was grabbed roughly and in despair as she saw his hand pointing downriver at them. Mr Rivers was shoved aside roughly. He managed to grab a bollard at the last moment with one hand, while clutching the model ship in the other, just when it seemed he would fall into the stinking cesspit of the Thames.

The man must have found out they had left and come back to find them. He turned his head toward them, but he was too far away by now for her to make out his features, other than the impression that he looked massive and threatening next to Mr Rivers. Seconds later, their ferry wove itself into the moving tapestry of traffic that clogged the world's busiest waterway, and he disappeared from sight.

Elisabeth's heart did not stop pounding until well after they had rounded the next bend in the river. She retreated to the cabin only when she had regained control of her shaking hands. In the cabin, she sat close to Anne and wrapped her own woollen cloak around Anne's shivering shoulders. Though not yet the end of summer, the wind had a blustery chill and the sky was as leaden as her mood.

'How are you feeling, Anne?'

'Shaken by the suddenness of it all, as if I've been tossed into a torrent and haven't been able to come up for air. I'm not brave like you, Elisabeth.'

'Oh, Anne, I'm not brave, or at least only when I absolutely have to be. Inside, I feel just like you, shaken and scared and angry that our lives have been turned upside down. If I haven't shown those feelings on the outside, it's only because I'm trying to make the best of a bad situation.'

'I know you are. Part of me is excited by the prospect of seeing a little of the world, although it's dreadful to be leaving my friends and my home behind. London was a happy place for me when John was alive. He always looked out for me, even though he was older. When you arrived from France, it was as if sunshine had flooded into our lives. But I know everything has changed and it wouldn't be the same living with Frederick and his awful wife. We've made the right decision.'

Elisabeth hugged Anne to her side. 'Thank you, Anne. John was always so proud of you. We'll find a way to make a good life together. And I promise you faithfully, I will either find a wonderful husband for you or leave it entirely to you.'

'I shouldn't worry about that. I shall be perfectly content to settle somewhere and continue with my charitable work. Unless I can find a husband who makes me as happy as you were with John.'

Elisabeth gave Anne's shoulders a final squeeze. 'I'll check with the captain to see if he knows where best to drop us.'

It turned out he knew a great deal more than that. He had only been available for hire that day because he was no longer required to ferry passengers to the very ship they were booked upon. Unfortunately, a passing vessel had returned with news that their ship had struck foul weather in the mid-Atlantic and was now to be several days late due to a broken mast.

He dropped them at a dock lined with passenger ships and arranged for a couple of porters to take their luggage to the shipping office. Elisabeth was thankful they had a guide, as the embarkation dock was chaotic in the extreme.

The dock thronged with people – porters wheeling stacked trunks on handcarts, passengers dashing this way and that, crying children lost in the crowd, provisioners delivering casks, crates, and coils of rope. The air was bursting with a deafening cacophony of livestock wailing, people shouting, carpenters hammering the last partitions into place between decks, and barrow boys loudly proclaiming their wares. And worst of all, the place was awash with the nauseating stench from sweating bodies, animal dung, rotten vegetables, and the sewage in the river.

Elisabeth had scarcely become used to the bustle of the City of London, which now seemed an oasis of calm compared to the hideous sensory overload of the docks. Still, she was pleased to see that there were several vessels docked, so perhaps their ship would be there after all.

The shipping office was relatively ordered compared to the atmosphere outside, albeit busy with passengers. Anne waited outside with the baggage while Elisabeth joined the queue. When her turn came, the clerk confirmed that their ship had turned back to Canada and, therefore, would not arrive in London for several weeks. She could take a refund on their tickets or wait for its uncertain arrival.

The desire to leave pulled strongly within her. 'A refund please. Could you tell me which other vessels are departing sooner?'

As he handed over the money, he was already looking past her to the next person in line. When she didn't move, he waved a hand in a loose arc. 'Try the office over there. Next please.'

In the adjacent building, she joined another line behind several passengers with tickets in their hands. The woman in front of her nodded her head towards the counter and rolled her eyes. A stocky man of military bearing was engaged in a heated discussion with the clerk, who looked unmoved by his belligerence.

'I am sorry, Major Carruthers, but I cannot provide a refund on tickets already purchased, most especially when the vessel is due to set sail on the next tide.'

The Major's magnificent moustaches quivered atop his ruddy face. 'But my wife is extremely ill and we are cannot leave. I sent my man down two days ago to inform you of this, with a waiver signed by the Colonel himself.'

'Yes, sir, I recall. But we cannot refund passages with two days' notice.' He raised a hand to forestall the objection. 'Not even for one who has served his county so valiantly as yourself.'

The Major swished his cane within an inch of the clerk's nose. 'I demand to see the man in charge.'

Elisabeth realised she had arrived in the middle of a protracted argument. Feeling brave, or perhaps just reckless, she stepped forward. 'Sir, please forgive me for having overheard your conversation. My sister-in-law and I were hoping to leave immediately, as our own ship has been delayed by some weeks. Perhaps we might come to an arrangement?'

'Well now, young lady, that might indeed be acceptable on the right terms.'

She turned to the clerk. 'If that is acceptable to the shipping company, of course.'

The clerk's expression brightened at this opportunity to break a deadlock that had appeared to be heading for a painful end. 'You have all the documentation, identification, and so forth?'

She handed over the paperwork, which the clerk flicked through with the barest minimum of scrutiny. 'It's highly irregular, but I see no problem as long as you ensure the ship's passenger list is corrected and you pass the health inspection. You will have to board within the next three hours.'

'Thank you.' She turned to the Major. 'Perhaps we could go over the details?'

Elisabeth and Major Carruthers moved into a quiet corner, away from the curious, but relieved, stares of the waiting queue. To her annoyance, a man who was standing nearby, reading a newspaper, chose that moment to sit down on the bench closest to them. Some people were just too nosy, as if there weren't better things to do. His hat was an at an angle, so she couldn't see his face, but she was positive it was not the bulky man who had accosted Mr Rivers on the wharf.

Major Carruthers waved his hand towards the door. 'Don't you have a husband or father I could speak to?'

'I am afraid you will have to deal with me or not at all, sir. I am used to transacting business.'

'Are you indeed? Most irregular.' The Major harrumphed but had little choice other than to proceed. 'I have the best cabin on the *Lady Rosalind*, a fine new ship heading to Wellington.'

'If you'll pardon my ignorance, where exactly is Wellington? It was not our intended destination, so I must be sure we can arrange onward travel.'

'Wellington is the latest settlement being opened up by the New Zealand Company. Had you intended to go to Auckland? I believe there are vessels on the coastal route around New Zealand that would take you.'

Elisabeth hardly knew what to make of this, having no idea where any of these places were. She was going to be very embarrassed if they had to turn down the tickets after being so bold as to drag him out of his argument to make her offer. 'Would you be so kind as to wait for me for a few minutes while I consult my sister-in-law?'

She hurried out to where Anne was sitting on a trunk, chatting with several other women clustered around a pile of luggage. 'I can get us tickets leaving almost immediately on the *Lady Rosalind*, but it's going to a place called Wellington in New Zealand. I've never heard of it. Or we could wait a few days in the hope of finding another berth.'

A woman sitting nearby leaned over. 'We're all off to New Zealand too. As far away from 'ere as possible, without falling off the other side o' the world. A new colony where ordinary folks can get ahead, so they say.'

'Is it part of Canada or the Americas?'

'Nay lass, it's in the middle of the ocean, near nowt but Australia, where the thieves and sinners get sent. But don't you be worrying 'bout that. Ain't no prisoners in New Zealand, just hard-working free folks like us. Darn sight warmer than Canada too.'

'Any fur traders?' Anne asked.

The woman looked at her in astonishment. 'Fur traders? Not so I've heard, ma'am. Whalers and sealers in some parts, but mainly farmers and builders in Wellington.'

A kindly looking, plump-cheeked woman in black looked up from a bible. 'New Zealand may be a completely new colony, but it has been designed by the New Zealand Company to be a southern version of an idyllic Britain. According to their advertisements, at least. I expect the reality is rather more rustic than you ladies may be used to.'

Anne looked at Elisabeth, a sudden smile crinkling around her eyes. 'Let's go. Can't be worse than my fate in Canada.'

'You're sure? It seems completely reckless to launch into the unknown like this.' On one hand, Elisabeth was reassured by the kindness of the women around them, but on the other … well, the phrase 'out of the frying pan, into the fire' might never be more apt. Her sense of urgency to leave London, combined with the ticking clock as Major Carruthers waited, tipped the balance. If it was too awful, they could always come back. It couldn't be much further away than Canada, surely.

'Where's your spirit of adventure, Elisabeth? We wanted to get away from here, didn't we? Sounds like we couldn't get much further than New Zealand.'

Elisabeth went back inside to complete the purchase of the tickets from the Major, negotiating a deep discount on the original price.

He accepted the deal with good grace. 'I can see you'd be a fine asset to any business. Truth is, I'm glad to get anything at all back on the tickets. More than I'd have got from the shipping company at any rate. May I see you ladies onto the ship?'

'That would be most kind of you.'

As they walked out of the office, Elisabeth noticed the man with the newspaper had re-joined the queue, alongside another man of similar age and type, to whom he was chatting amiably. He must have been waiting for a friend. She really would have to stop mistrusting every person who passed.

Setting Sail

And so it was that the Godwin sisters boarded the *Lady Rosalind* under the name of Major and Mrs Carruthers. The Major was kind enough to oversee the carrying of trunks aboard. He barked out orders, summoning porters like magic, and directing them with a determined swish of his cane. They beat a path through the crowd as if cutting a swathe through enemy soldiers on a battlefield.

Elisabeth nudged Anne. 'No wonder the English won at Waterloo.'

At the far end of the docks, the ship sat in all her glory, stretching around a hundred feet from her tapered bow to her high square stern. The *Lady Rosalind* was freshly scrubbed and magnificent – a barque with three masts reaching for the clouds amidst a dense web of stays, ratlines, pulleys and spars. She was enormous from the perspective of the wharf-side, with her black hull looming over their heads, cut through by a white line and a row of scuttles mid-way to the waterline.

Once up the gangplank, the vessel appeared smaller. Too small for such a long voyage across the ocean. The longboats suspended along her sides gave little assurance of a safe escape route if disaster struck. Almost every inch of the teak deck was crammed with barrels, crates, pens and hen coops, winches, hatches, and coils of rope. A throng of people added to the mayhem, with carters delivering last-minute supplies, sailors intent on their allotted tasks, and passengers saying their final tearful farewells to loved ones, perhaps forever.

The captain strode aboard ahead of them, paperwork in hand and gangplank shaking under his heavy tread. As soon as his boots hit the deck, he bellowed for the chief mate to prepare the vessel for departure as soon as the tide turned.

The Major commandeered the chief cabin steward, ordering him to give them the very best of service, before dismissing the poor man to dash about his work. Elisabeth repeated her thanks and wished his wife a rapid recovery from her illness, before heading off after their disappearing trunks.

Anne stood at the rails, waving their thanks as the Major stepped ashore. As he turned to wave back, he was almost tipped backwards into the sludge of the Thames by a man pushing past in haste. A very rough-looking character, Anne reported to Elisabeth later, bereft of manners. With her habitual fairness, she allowed that perhaps he could not see properly because of the large canvas bag carried across his broad shoulders.

Elisabeth caught up with the cabin steward at the stern of the vessel underneath the elevated poop deck. The steward, a man of slight build, was cowering under the verbal assault of a tall, strong-jawed lady, who was standing with her hands on her hips and chin thrust forward. On each side of a ruler-straight centre-parting, her brunette hair was pulled back so tightly into a bun that her eyes were pulled to a slight slant. In sharp contrast, the elaborate ringlets framing her face quivered as loosely as spaniel ears as she shook her head at the steward. A large number of trunks were piled at her feet, obscured behind a skirt so wide it must have had at least six petticoats.

'No, no, no. Perhaps you do not realise who we are. Sir Julius Maynard and myself are accustomed to the very best of service and will not settle for less than the very best cabin.'

'But your ladyship,' replied the steward, in a carefully neutral voice, 'Major Carruthers booked this cabin some months ago and was adamant that this particular one be his. I'm sure you will find the allocated cabin more than meets your needs.'

'It most certainly will not. There's scarcely room to turn in it. And we must be at the back of the boat, for we have been informed that is the best place to be.' Lady Maynard turned to face Elisabeth as she came up behind them. 'And who might you be?'

'These ladies are to have the Major's cabin. He was most insistent on it and of course he paid extra for the privilege of having the best cabin.'

Elisabeth felt almost too exhausted to stand after the events of the day. In fact, she had hardly slept since John's death. All she wanted was to sink onto a bed and shut out the clamorous world before her head imploded. The steward turned to her and swept his hand forward, indicating the cabin she was to be in.

Lady Maynard barred the way. 'I must insist upon this cabin. You will swap with us. Naturally we will pay the difference, if it is a matter of money.' The last word was snapped out with a level of scorn possible only to the rich.

Elisabeth turned to the steward. 'Perhaps you will show me both cabins. I cannot promise anything, but I am willing to consider the matter.'

The steward opened the door in front of him and showed her the cabin that should have been theirs, or rather the Major's. It was spacious for a ship, more than she was used to when she had travelled with John. In many a cabin on their coastal traders, she could touch the walls with outstretched hands, but this cabin was closer to the size of a small sitting room. The cabin that had been allocated to the Maynards was smaller, but still more than adequate for herself and Anne. Aside from the two narrow beds, with several drawers underneath, there was a narrow washstand, a small writing desk, space to lash trunks, and two narrow chairs. Elisabeth was pleased to see that there was a porthole, to let in light and fresh air.

The steward lowered his voice to a whisper. 'This one is smaller, but I think you'll find that when the weather gets warmer, this cabin will be far nicer. The larboard side gets more breeze and still has an excellent view. I cannot ask you to change, but if you are willing, I would be grateful indeed to have this situation resolved.'

Elisabeth considered the smaller cabin more than acceptable. 'Then please have our baggage moved in here straight away. I feel I must lie down soon or I shall faint clean away.'

The steward hurried off and soon had their trunks neatly stowed. Anne arrived moments later and closed the door on the shrill voice of the woman in the corridor, who had evidently received the news of her triumph with impatience rather than gratitude. Both women collapsed onto the beds with sighs of relief. Their own dresses were less elaborate, but far more practical, than Lady Maynard's gown. They were so exhausted – physically and emotionally – that they simply loosened the fastenings of their clothes and took off their boots before lying down.

Elisabeth was sure she would not be able to rest, given the depth of her unease at the hasty decision that had been forced upon them, but the next thing she knew, she was jolted out of a deep sleep by a rap at the cabin door. The cabin steward had brought a tray of tea, with a generous plate of sandwiches and cakes, which made Elisabeth's mouth water. She realised they hadn't eaten since early that morning and now it was almost dark. Behind the steward was a skinny little lad, surely no more than twelve years old, struggling under the weight of a steaming jug. He left it by the washbasin before scampering away again.

'Thank you, sir. I cannot tell you how welcome the sight of that tea is. I realise now I am faint with hunger, and much in need of a wash.'

'A mark of my gratitude, ma'am,' the Head Steward said. 'Her ladyship was most insistent on changing cabins, although she had no right to. Please do not hesitate to ask if there is anything at all I can do to assist you ladies. Ask for Thomas and I shall be there directly. Oh, and here is the difference in fares, which you are owed for moving to a smaller cabin.'

'Well, Mr Thomas, it was no great problem for us and it seems we are already ahead on the deal. I thank you for your trouble.' Elisabeth handed Thomas a substantial tip, which startled the man into making a rather formal bow.

A useful ally thus secured, Elisabeth and Anne washed their grime-coated faces and arms in hot soapy water with purrs of delight. Outer selves refreshed, they set to on the inner, demolishing the offering down to the last crumb and tealeaf.

'I could sleep for a week. But I do want to write a few words in my diary.' Elisabeth felt that a new diary should start with words of wisdom, or at least optimism, but her mind was a complete blank. She picked up the pen, dipped it in ink, and wrote:

Diary of Elisabeth Duchamp Godwin, 14 August 1841

Our journey to an exciting new future begins aboard the 'Lady Rosalind'.

Elisabeth put the pen down again. Her heart was filled with words that were more apt to express her true feelings. But the diary would have to be like her face, a passive facade to a judgmental world. She puffed the ink dry, snapped the diary shut, and slipped it into the high-sided shelf above her bed, alongside the portrait of John. She was asleep an instant after her eyelids closed.

Hours later, she woke to the familiar see-saw rolling and frenetic activity of a ship getting underway. A steam tug came alongside, then disappeared amid sounds of hawsers being attached and directions shouted. With a jerk, they were underway, being towed to the mouth of the River Thames to wait for a fair wind.

With an unexpected sense of excitement, Elisabeth watched the dark riverscape pass by the porthole. The pleasure of being safe, comfortable and having a sense of purpose was enough to keep a lid on her doubts, for the moment at least. John seemed to be watching over her from the portrait, his steadfast gaze reassuring her that all would be well.

15 August 1841

Elisabeth was up before dawn, as was her long-ingrained habit. It was impossible to dress without disturbing Anne because of the small space and the layers of garments. She apologised to Anne as she slipped out, but her sister-in-law had already dropped back into a deep sleep.

Their cabin was conveniently placed to ascend the steps to the poop deck. The day was a fine one, with a light breeze and an early morning chill. The anchor, which was taller than a man, had been raised and now sat snug against the starboard bow, where it would likely remain for the rest of the voyage. A full set of sails billowed on the three masts, from the slim triangular gibs attached to the long bowsprit, to the four enormous square sails stacked in increasing size down the main mast. A dozen or so sailors tended the mass of canvas and rope to the shouted commands of the mates, who were manning the helm and keeping a sharp watch out for the host of other vessels sailing all around them.

Her hairpins, bonnet, lace cap, and gloves lay forgotten in the semi-darkness of the cabin. It was, no doubt, a breach of etiquette to be on deck without them, but the wind blowing through her roughly plaited hair felt wonderful and brought back happy memories of her many voyages sailing at John's side.

The creaking of rigging under sail was almost hypnotic. Elisabeth leaned on the salt-encrusted stern rail and closed her eyes, drawing in a deep breath of crisp air, and relishing the peace after the chaos of the docks and the trauma of the last two months.

Somewhere out there, deep in the English Channel, John's body lay in its watery grave. She no longer feared her own death, knowing her soul would join his in heaven. But, if she was fated to survive, then how wonderful it was to be heading for a fresh start, leaving their troubles behind them in the foamy curls of the wake.

'Best hold on, ma'am. Wouldn't want to lose you over the side in a rogue wave. Least ways, not on the very first day.'

She looked up to find the owner of the deep voice, with its deeply rolling Rs and gentle humour. A brawny sailor turned his wind-etched face and nodded at her.

'Good morning,' she said. 'A rare favourable breeze for this part of the channel.'

'Aye, 'tis a rare pleasure to set sail so soon, instead of waiting days or weeks for a fair wind, as we often must.' His ocean-blue eyes flicked to her before returning to their relentless scan of sails and maritime hazards. 'You've sailed before then, ma'am?'

'My husband's family is in shipping. I joined him when I could. I love the fresh sea air after London.'

'Don't know how folk can live in the city, what with the smoke and fog an' all.' His fingers flicked up to his cap in an instinctive salute, as clear a sign of his navy past as the tattoo on his forearm. 'Chief Mate Enys at your service, ma'am.'

'Mrs Elisabeth Godwin, at yours.'

'Lucky you're a good sailor. You mark my words, it'll be a rough time for most of the passengers in the first few days. Things tend to settle down a bit after that until we meet the big waves down south again for the last few weeks. Might even see some icebergs in the Southern Ocean.'

Elisabeth hadn't given a moment's thought to the voyage itself, merely the destination. Icebergs? Hadn't the woman at the docks said New Zealand was warm? 'How long is the voyage expected to take, Mr Enys?'

'Three months if King Neptune smiles on us, four months or more if we get becalmed in the doldrums or hit by foul weather. New Zealand is about as far from home as you can go.' He paused to bellow out a command to the crew. 'Not sure meself why anyone would want to set up a colony at the end of the earth on an island full of ferocious natives and volcanoes, except maybe to stop the French doing it first.'

Elisabeth could think of nothing to say. Four months! Ferocious natives? Volcanoes? What on earth had she gotten them into? It was as if she had been in the grip of some form of madness since John's death, driven by Frederick's goading and her own utter despair.

The chief mate was still talking. 'Course I ain't surprised they get emigrants to go there, despite the voyage. The New Zealand Company makes it sound like some sort of wonderful opportunity. Truth to tell, it probably is a sight better for some of the poor folk in steerage than what they're used to. Plus, they don't have to pay, of course.'

'Why not?'

'The new colony desperately needs tradesmen and labourers, so they pay for them to emigrate. Creating a new class of serfs for the colonist's estates, if you ask me.'

The pilot and captain came on deck, heading for the helm at the rear of the poop deck. Elisabeth thanked the chief mate and hastened down to the cabin. How was she going to tell Anne that their destination was four months away and fraught with danger? Unless the mate had been spinning a tale, which was more than likely in her experience.

Anne's reaction was as startling as the news. She burst into laughter. 'The voyage may be a long one, but I, for one, am delighted that there won't be a smelly fur-trapper waiting on the wharf. We can be free!'

'But we know nothing about New Zealand. It might be full of fur-trappers. Not to mention ferocious natives.'

'If the passengers are mainly farm workers and tradesmen, that suggests some level of civilisation.'

'Are you sure about this, Anne? We could still go back to London when the pilot leaves.'

'It'll be an adventure. A chance to make a new life.'

Elisabeth felt herself being swept up in Anne's enthusiasm. A new life where no one knew them or had any expectations of them? Why not indeed. 'Well, it seems we are to be the female heroines in our very own swash-buckling adventure story.'

The decision was no sooner made than the ship's bell started ringing. The cabin boy ran around knocking on doors and summoning all onto the deck. Elisabeth tamed her windblown hair, found her bonnet, helped Anne with her dress, and then they went to meet their fellow inmates. The cabin passengers assembled on the elevated poop deck, while the steerage passengers crowded the main deck below them.

The chief mate bellowed for silence. He introduced the ship's surgeon, Mr Penrose, who was in charge of all things to do with the passengers, including establishing and maintaining order on the ship. The doctor's first task was to take a roll-call. After a moment of confusion, because of the last-minute substitution of one man for another, the roll-call was followed by a reading of the Ship's Rules in a suitably stern voice.

The chief mate and captain stood beside the ship's surgeon, their muscles bulging in crossed arms, to reinforce the message. Next came a lecture on the vessel, the voyage and the detailed expectations of the New Zealand Company, after which the cabin passengers were allowed to go down to breakfast.

Elisabeth and Anne stayed up on deck, as they were keen to find out about all aspects of life on a passenger ship. The doctor proceeded to sort the steerage passengers into messes, which would form their cooking and cleaning groups for the rest of the voyage. He was by no means a large man, nor the least bit intimidating like the chief mate, but he had a very effective sort of quiet authority. He chose an assistant and four constables from the emigrants to help him keep order and distribute rations.

They could not believe that nearly two hundred steerage passengers were squeezed between the decks of the *Lady Rosalind*. The poor souls must be jammed into their quarters like a herd of penned sheep. Unlike the cabin passengers, steerage passengers had to cook their own food, attend to the cleaning of the ship, share the watch, and many other tasks.

Naturally, several passengers grumbled loudly at these expectations. The chief mate banged a belaying pin on the rail and barked that they would do their duties or find themselves swimming back to England.

Anne gestured to the chief mate. 'I don't imagine anyone would give Mr Enys an ounce of trouble. One look at those bulging arm muscles, not to mention his broken nose and scars, is enough to frighten me. His voice is louder than a foghorn.'

'It was him I talked to him this morning about New Zealand. He may look scary, but he's gentle on the inside and has quite a sense of humour. A sharp mind and a lot of experience too.'

By mid-morning, the breeze had swung around to the south-west, directly opposing their direction of travel. Soon, it had risen to a gale. The *Lady Rosalind* pitched and rolled and yawed in the unpredictable waves of the English Channel, while tacking back and forth with little discernible forward motion. A dozen sailors climbed up the ratlines to reef the sails as the storm intensified. Looking up from the deck far below, they looked like tiny spiders as they clung to a giant web of ropes and spars. They were singing to coordinate the task, an eerie sound against the roar of the waves and the keening of the wind through the rigging.

All around the sides of the ship, passengers were weaving around on unsteady legs and heaving their stomachs into the swell, misery writ large on their faces. Dress standards were soon forgotten, in favour of a shawl or cloak hastily pulled around whatever clothing was to hand. Even some of the sailors looked green, although that did not spare them from their relentless tasks of furling and unfurling sails as the conditions changed.

Thomas, the steward, was busy directing the cabin boys, who dashed back and forth with basins and buckets. One sailor, who had disgraced himself by coming aboard drunk on the first day, has been assigned mopping duty to keep the decks clean. He became quite forceful at ensuring the sick were directed to the leeward side, after several mishaps on the windward.

Anne and Elisabeth had sailed before within the confines of the Channel and Bay of Biscay, so were spared the worst of the ill effects of seasickness. The helmsman banned them from the poop deck, which was flecked with sea-foam, so they retreated below, using the time to get their cabin shipshape. Elisabeth hung John's picture more securely on a nail above her bed, to watch over her. She wrapped her rose satin dressing-gown around the prickly linen covering of the pillow, tucking mother's portrait under her pillow, so she could be close to her in her dreams.

All they heard of their fellow passengers was groaning and the frequent thudding of feet down the corridor as they hastened to the side of the ship.

New Beginnings

By the time the dinner bell rang, their stomachs were rumbling, having missed breakfast. They were looking forward, with some trepidation, to meeting their fellow cabin passengers, with whom they would spend the next several months.

At first, they were alone in the saloon cabin, which Thomas called the 'cuddy', a combined lounge and dining room with a long table, centred under the poop deck and lit from above by a skylight. They sat at the aft end of the table, away from the incongruous pillar of the mizzen mast, which went through the forward end of the cuddy table. The steward started serving them, without waiting for the others, as he said most passengers had taken to their beds with seasickness.

A short, plump woman with rosy cheeks bustled in, wearing a high-necked dress in black cotton, with a touch of lace around the sleeves. They recognised her as the woman they had talked to on the dock.

'Hello again, ladies. Glad to see you made it aboard. What's on the menu? I'm so hungry, I could eat a whole peacock, feathers and all.' She looked behind her, frowned, and went back to the door. 'In here, Matthew. Goodness man, how can you get lost on a ship, yet find your way around the back alleys of London?'

A tall, gangling man wandered in, dressed all in black but for a white collar. He tripped over the sill as he entered, as if his legs had an extra joint that he hadn't quite accounted for. 'Just thinking about my first sermon, dear.' He lifted his nose out of his bible before he tripped over them as well. 'Oh, hello. Robertshaw, Reverend, and this incomparable treasure is my wife. I say, that soup smells appetising.'

'Mrs Elisabeth Godwin and Miss Anne Godwin. Please join us.'

Mrs Robertshaw sat down beside Anne. 'Your name seems familiar, my dear. Not the Miss Anne Godwin of the Children's Benevolent Fund perchance?'

Anne, who was indeed part of that charitable group raising funds for child health and welfare, was soon deeply engaged in conversation about the dire state of the working classes in England. Soup bowls had been removed by the cabin boys and roast goose served by the steward, during an impassioned discussion of the inequities of labour and land laws, the shortage and price of food, and the plight of factory workers ousted by the new mechanical devices.

The Reverend Robertshaw's congregation at Bethnal Green included many silk weavers, whose livelihoods had been crushed by cheap imports and mechanisation, so they felt it was little wonder so many were willing to risk a voyage to the other side of the world to make a better life.

Elisabeth engaged a little in the discussion and was otherwise kept busy by rescuing crockery and serving dishes, which were slipping back and forth across the table with the lurching of the ship. The table had a lip to prevent items slipping right off, but it wasn't much of a barrier to a soup bowl. The others were so engrossed in their discussion, they seemed not to notice, even when another passenger arrived.

The young gentleman bowed to her. A sweep of dark-blonde, wavy hair fell over his face, giving his handsome features a boyish charm. He flipped the lock of hair back with practised fingers. 'Mr Walter Knight. How do you do?'

'Mrs Elisabeth Godwin. Delighted to make your acquaintance. Please, take a seat. You'll not get a word out of the others until they have righted the ills of the world.'

'No small task. I shall enjoy the pleasure of your company instead.' Mr Knight sat down opposite her, taking care to smooth out the long frock coat he wore with a waistcoat of gold-swirled, chestnut coloured brocade. He listened in briefly as the inequities of the Corn Laws were thrashed out. 'I had expected the colonists would be more sympathetic to landowners.'

'The colonists are all abed with seasickness. You sup with the reformists today, Mr Knight.'

'Fine by me. I have little sympathy for those who simply inherit privilege, especially those who squander it. A man has to make his own way in this world.' His hazel eyes looked into her eyes with youthful candour, helped along by a wide, off-centre grin, which was swallowed at the edges into deep dimples.

She diagnosed a born charmer. But one with a passion to lend him substance, she suspected. 'You are not a landowner yourself, then?'

'My father owns a modest estate, but I am the fourth son of nine children. I decided to train as a surveyor, rather than spending my life living off the table scraps from my father and eldest brother.'

'Why a surveyor?'

'I hope to make my mark by exploring the wilderness. Map-making in uncharted terrain and discovery of new resources. What could be more exciting?'

'Goodness, that does sound adventurous. I believe I am a little jealous.'

'Then you are welcome to join me, for pleasant company is always to be desired, especially in the middle of nowhere. I would head for the mountains as soon as we drop anchor if it was up to me, but I was engaged by the government to extend Wellington's boundaries. I am bonded for two years, or I'll be required to pay back my passage.' At this, he let out a small sigh, before rallying his good humour. 'And you, Mrs Godwin, are you a colonist or a reformer?'

'The latter by inclination. But keeping the accounts for my husband's business has kept me too busy to be an active participant. My sister-in-law, Anne, is the true reformer. She looks after the health of workhouse children, as well as raising money for their needs.'

'I applaud you both for using your time constructively. My sisters seem to do little but drink tea, attend dances and embroider more cushion covers than a sane world would ever need.'

'My brother-in-law would approve of their choice.' Many arguments had raged over Anne's choice of occupation, with herself and John in support and Frederick vehemently opposed. Nor had he ever reconciled himself to Elisabeth working in their business, even discreetly from home, and so had banned her involvement after John's death. She wondered how long the business would survive without either John or herself taking an active role. Not that it was her problem anymore.

The sound of laughter broke over the chatter around the table as the door opened and a tall young man blocked the entrance with his broad shoulders. He hesitated for a moment, giving the impression that he was pausing to show off his striking good looks. But the would-be Narcissus was merely being polite – he removed his top hat and stepped back to hold the door for his friend. Judging by their dampness and the smell of tobacco, they had come down the stairs from the deck. Both were impeccably dressed in tailored dark frock-coats and white cravats.

'Mr Edgar Amberley,' the taller man announced, with a contagious smile, which curved up towards lightly freckled cheeks. 'And this fine fellow is my friend, Mr William Templeton. How do you do? Please excuse our tardiness.'

After a round of introductions, Mr Amberley launched into animated conversation, taking care to bestow his attention equally on all the company. Within a few minutes, he had command of the table. 'I admit to being addicted to poetry. Why, only last spring, I was wandering the estate reading Wordsworth. I felt I was right inside his poem, wandering lonely as a cloud through a host of golden daffodils dancing in the breeze, when I looked up and saw an enormous and very angry bull charging towards me. Quite broke the reflective mood, I can tell you.'

Anne was blushing and staring into his twinkling blue eyes, the plight of the poor forgotten for the moment. 'Good gracious, Mr Amberley. Whatever did you do?'

'Sprinted like a greyhound and hurdled the gate in a bound. Landed in the mud with a daffodil up my nose, nothing damaged but my dignity. Serve me right for not keeping my wits about me.'

Mrs Robertshaw laughed so hard she choked on her roast goose, requiring a swift slap on the back from her husband. When she recovered her breath, she said, 'In India, I always carried a bright pink parasol to ward off the bovines. Cows are absolutely everywhere in the streets and revered by the Hindu people.'

'Thank you for the advice, Mrs Robertshaw,' said Amberley. 'I shall carry one on future rambles. Perhaps not in bright pink, though.'

'I can vouch for the efficacy of the ice-axe as a more manly alternative,' Mr Knight said. 'I was attacked by a mountain goat once while climbing Snowdon. The devil trapped me with a cliff on one side and a sheer drop on the other.'

'You didn't hurt it, I hope,' said Anne.

'Not at all. I charged at the beast, bellowing like a lunatic and fending it off with the rounded top of the ice-axe. It was so surprised, I swear it jumped three feet in the air and straight off the side of the bluff. But when I looked down, it had landed on its feet on a narrow ledge and was happily browsing on a prickly bush as if nothing had happened.'

Elisabeth wondered just how long it had been since she had laughed like this, until her belly hurt.

Lively conversation and laughter were a tonic they could all do with. If this was a fair sample of the ship's company, she felt the long voyage might be a great deal more enjoyable than expected.

The man beside her had not said a word, and it looked as if this was very much the usual state of affairs. Templeton was almost as tall as Amberley, but lanky and angular, with a lop-sided face and a narrow moustache, which gave him a rather melancholy air.

She turned to him to bring him into the conversation. 'And you, Mr Templeton, do you have a favourite method of fending off wild beasts?'

Mr Templeton gave a little start, dropping his knife with a clatter to his plate. He wiped a splatter of gravy from his cuff with a linen napkin before composing himself. 'I'm pleased to report the occasion has never arisen. We do have bulls on the estate, of course, but I have found them to be good-natured creatures, if treated with respect.'

'I would have to agree with you. I have little experience with bulls, but I always found our dairy cows to be sweet-natured, especially if I sang to them while milking.'

Mr Templeton looked at her in surprise, before leaning in to whisper, 'I would never admit it in general company, but I often sang to our animals too. Does wonders to calm them.'

'I'm sure it does. Tell me, what are your plans for New Zealand?'

'Amberley and I have both purchased land from the New Zealand Company, which we hope to develop into profitable estates.'

'What type of farming do you have in mind?'

'I am a great believer in scientific method, Mrs Godwin. What little information is available on farming prospects in New Zealand suggests sheep may be the best option, so I have brought a small herd of Horned Dorsets with me and a man to look after them. They have the hardiness of the Welsh Horned, cross-bred with the wool quality of the Merino. But I also have a dairy cow, two pigs, seeds of many varieties, and a small plough, so I can test what the land is best suited for. In fact, the milk in your tea comes from my Mabel, so let us pray she doesn't dry up with the shock of the voyage. Perhaps I might get you to sing to her?'

She smiled at his joke, feeling pleased to have drawn him out of his silence. 'I will leave the singing to you. My voice is adequate for a milking shed, but not for refined company. Do tell me what type of seeds have you brought along.'

'A variety of vegetables and fruit, so I can establish a kitchen garden beside the house. Also, wheat and barley, though I fear they may not do well in Wellington. Still, I can always trade them for something else. An investigation of soil quality will be–' He seemed about to launch into further detail, but he checked himself. 'But that is no doubt of limited interest to a lady, although it does appear that you have some knowledge of agriculture, Mrs Godwin.'

'I grew up in the country. We had an orchard of apples and stone fruit, a large vegetable garden, chickens, a few pigs, and two dairy cows. I too have some seeds with me, in hopes of establishing a small garden. Though they have been sitting dormant for over a decade while I lived in London, so perhaps I am being overly optimistic. Do you know much about the available housing in New Zealand, Mr Templeton?'

'The standard is rather basic, I hear. Simple mud and reed huts for the working class, with a few sturdy wooden and brick dwellings. I understand there is a great deal of construction underway, but I felt it was wiser to trust in myself, so I have brought a basic cottage with me.'

'A whole cottage! However did you manage that?'

'Only the makings of a small cottage, not the whole. The wood is pre-cut to length and I shall assemble it on site. I also have all the required nails, hammers, saws, and so forth, not wanting to leave anything to chance. Fortunately, I was able to purchase some additional storage in the hold from one of the other colonists, who did not require all of their allocated space.'

'Well, Mr Templeton, I must congratulate you on your ingenuity and forethought. I expect you will do very well for yourself with such an intelligent approach.'

The young man blushed with the compliment and stammered his thanks, as if unused to receiving such attention and praise. And she meant it sincerely – his planning was impressive. The combination of Amberley's charm and Templeton's scientific application boded well for their futures.

Her thoughts were interrupted by Thomas, who was standing at her side and offering pudding. She waved him away with thanks, suddenly feeling overwhelmed with exhaustion.

Before she slept, she took down the picture of John that she had hung over her bed, kissing her husband and renewing her promise to look after his sister. She didn't like to admit it to Anne, who seemed to view their voyage as a grand adventure, but the prospect of arriving in a country that she knew so little about was more than a little terrifying.

Talking to Mr Templeton had only reinforced her concerns at their own foolishness and total lack of preparation or planning. The future loomed like the mouth of a dark tunnel into the unknown. She pulled her shoulders back and dismissed the doubts. Teaching, a small orchard or market garden, even a shop or trading business – there were many options open besides a marriage of convenience.

And anything was better than a marriage of inconvenience. The love she had shared with John made her determined she would not part with Anne to any man who could not bring her the same joy. As for herself, she would have to hold her grief tightly inside, as a hard knot within her heart, and focus on cherishing the many happy memories.

16 August 1841

Elisabeth and Anne watched the white cliffs of the English coast slide slowly past. Sometimes the ship made gradual headway, while at other times the headwind and currents undid what little progress they achieved with the endless tacking back and forth.

She asked the captain how far they had come, but he was not inclined to talk. Mr Enys told them later that the captain could not stand the constant questions of passengers and often resorted to eating in his cabin for the first few days until the passengers gained their sea-legs and became resigned to the long voyage ahead.

By mid-morning, the wind dropped away. The ship heaved up and down in the swell, its vast swathes of canvas flapping uselessly against the swaying masts. Several other ships were visible around them, all bobbing up and down like toys in a giant bathtub. The sight and smell of a line of seasick passengers at the rail was enough to make Elisabeth and Anne feel nauseated as well.

'Why don't we go back to the cabin, Anne? I have something that will cheer you up.'

Back in the cabin, she reached for the bible that John had left to Anne, which was sitting in pride of place on the shelf above Anne's bed.

'You wish to cheer me up with a bible reading? To be honest, I can't think why John left me his bible collection. I'm a good Christian, of course, but he knew I preferred to show it through good deeds rather than Sunday scriptures.'

'Ah, my dear sister, you underestimate the cleverness of your brother. The truth is, he was well aware of Frederick's deficiencies, but the law left him no choice other than to leave the house and business to his male heir. He wanted to ensure we would have some money to do with as we pleased and was astute enough to realise that books were the last thing Frederick would have coveted, especially the bibles.'

'But didn't I hear you say to Frederick that the books were only worth enough to buy a wedding dress?'

'I did. But I may have failed to mention that it would have been a wedding dress to rival Marie Antoinette's and Queen Victoria's combined.' While she was talking, Elisabeth had pulled out her mahogany trunk and laid the contents on her bed. When it was emptied, she removed the false bottom of the trunk and pulled out two bags of gold coins and two rolls of banknotes.

Anne's eyes almost popped out. 'Good Lord! That's a fortune!'

'Good Lord is an apt expression, in the circumstances.' Elisabeth held out around half of the stash. 'This is your money from the sale of John's bible collection.'

'I…I don't know what to say! I had no idea that books could be worth so much.'

'They weren't just any old books. The Gutenberg Bible alone was worth more than a year's keep for a modest household. Our dear friend, the book dealer, was positively trembling with excitement. Forgive me for not telling you earlier, but you are too honest a soul to have kept it from Frederick.'

'You seem to know a lot about book collecting.'

'I was the one who started the collection. I saw it as a way to help fund the French émigrés who had lost their homes. Often all they had left were the valuables they could carry, like jewellery and a few precious books. Sad to say, family heirlooms are no longer a priority when one is homeless and hungry.'

'I thought all those outings were visits to friends. How did you know what to buy?'

'Arthur Postlethwaite was a fine teacher. You know how I love books and I'm good at remembering figures, so it came naturally. To be honest, it was tremendous fun. We always gave them a fair price and the option of buying the book back if circumstances improved. All too rarely, I'm afraid.'

'So, it was really your book collection, not John's, all along?'

'Not at all. He funded it and we had a lovely time going to auctions together, poking through the lots to find the bargains. We both loved the hunt and the chance to read great works.'

'Goodness, Elisabeth, you never cease to amaze me. Did he always intend to leave the books to us?'

'That came later. At first, John saw the collection as a good way to diversify the business. Shipping can be so fickle. War, plague, storms – any of them could have been disastrous.'

Anne nodded her understanding, having grown up around stories of maritime disasters. 'When I was little, we lost three ships in one storm. I remember being frightened by the anxiety in my parents' voices when they thought they would lose everything, even the house. The debt wasn't cleared until John took over when our father died, as you know.'

'John felt the same anxiety. Later, he wanted to ensure we would be taken care of if anything happened to him, so he changed his will. Arthur appraised the collection and entered a written agreement with us to purchase the books at any time for an established price.'

'My dear brother, how kind and clever he was. He certainly knew that Frederick would not want the books. Especially not the bibles.'

'The bible collection was always intended to fund your marriage and your charitable work, or whatever you wished. It was his little joke – the Good Book funding good works.'

Anne took John's bible from her and absently stroked the thick leather cover with its lettering embossed in gilt. 'Frederick did something to upset John, didn't he? They were so tense together before John's death.'

'There are things that John did not wish to burden you with, but I think it's best you know. Frederick took out an extremely large loan secured against the business a few months ago, using a forged signature so it looked as if John had agreed. John was angrier than I have ever seen him when he found out. The business and even the house were put at risk. Now that John is no longer here to rescue the business, we may well have ended up with the most valuable part of the Godwin estate.'

Anne sank back onto her bed, clutching the bible to her chest. 'Why would Frederick do such a thing? To put everything the family had built at risk. I know he lacked John's business sense, but still … it's shocking.'

'John never told me why Frederick did it or where the money went, but I heard them arguing about it once. Frederick insisted he would make a colossal fortune with the money, but John told him he was a fool, so I assume it was some type of speculative investment. I know John spent several troubled weeks before his death, agonising over what course to take. He was not at all himself. I fear the distraction may have been the reason he was careless on his last voyage and went overboard in the storm.'

Both sisters closed their eyes tightly to stem the tears triggered by the mention of John's death.

Anne stiffened her spine and took a few deep breaths. 'Best to put all that money away in the safety of your trunk. This is all too much to take in.'

Elisabeth sat down beside her and put an arm around her shoulders. 'I know how hard this must be for you. Our safe and happy little world seems to have fallen apart in the space of a few weeks. But at least we know that the future is more secure than it might have been. It's not really a fortune, but we will be well provided for until we can set up some enterprise to earn our own living.'

She handed Anne a small box. 'One last surprise for you.'

'Pears' soap?'

'Look inside.'

Anne opened the box and let out a shriek at the sight of her mother's emerald and diamond necklace. Anne wrapped her arms around Elisabeth and squeezed the breath from her lungs. 'Truly, this means more to me than anything.'

'I have mine too.' She held up the sapphire and diamond necklace John had given her as a wedding present, in a matching style to the one bought by his father for his mother as a wedding gift. 'Let's put them away now and look forward to the day we can appear in matching jewels to dazzle an adoring crowd.'

Anne's dazzling smile was all the response she needed. Anne sat back on her bed and slipped off the gold ribbon holding John's bible closed. 'I've changed my mind. I do feel like reading some words of wisdom, given to me by my one and only wonderful brother and sister-in-law.'

When she opened the book, a letter fell out. Anne picked it up. 'It's from John.' As she read it, tears came to her eyes. She passed it on to Elisabeth.

Elisabeth skimmed through it. 'He loved you very much. How proud he was of you and your charity work. John told me several times that you were the best of the Godwin family.'

'It was always John who guided me, more like a father than a brother. Heavens, but I miss him like a physical ache in my heart.'

Elisabeth could only hold back her own tears and nod her agreement. She took a deep breath and finished the letter. 'I see he warned you against Frederick and that man, Kingston. I expect John was worried that Frederick would take advantage of your good nature. Well, it's all academic now. The past is disappearing behind us, just as England is. Nothing Frederick can do will harm us now. In fact, he need never know where we are or why we failed to turn up in Canada. I find that rather comforting.'

'Yes, indeed.' Anne laid a hand on her arm. 'And you no longer need to worry that your past will catch up with you from France.'

'You know why I had to escape France?'

'Don't look so shocked, Elisabeth. John trusted me with the story, in case you ever needed my help. You can be assured that I will tell no one else.'

'I have to say, I'm quite relieved that I don't have to bear the burden alone.'

'Lovely. Let's talk no more of it. I'm starving. I wonder what's for dinner?'

'I wish you hadn't mentioned food. This rocking-horse of a ship is making me feel quite unwell. I think I might skip dinner and try to catch up on sleep.'

When Anne had gone, she stretched out on the bed and tried to ignore the movement of the vessel by concentrating on happy memories of her life with John, and before that, of growing up on her family's farm in the Loire Valley. Despite the constant rolling and the thousands of miles of sailing ahead, she dropped off into the deep sleep of one who feels safe at last after a perilous journey.

The Class Divide

Elisabeth had never been seasick before, not even in conditions far rougher than this voyage. Her empathy for the other passengers increased tenfold as she battled through the vomiting and stomach cramps. Her head was hammering with dehydration, but no liquid would stay down. She felt exhausted for days on end, despite doing nothing but sleeping, attempting to sip a little soup, and dragging herself up to the deck for fresh air. She felt marginally better on the fifth day, well enough at least to tell a story to a miserable little girl, who was sitting alone on deck, tucked behind the skylight.

Anne remained as bright as ever. She had attached herself as an able assistant to the ship's surgeon, George Penrose. At first, the doctor refused to allow Anne to help him, as he said it was not proper for a lady to mop the brows of sick passengers. Elisabeth was not at all surprised that he soon gave in, as Anne not only had experience and common sense, but also a great deal of determination. And the need was great. The appointed Matron, who was supposed to assist him, as well as supervising the single women, was ill herself. Rumour had it she had been dipping into the medicinal brandy.

Elisabeth watched the doctor as he moved between patients, working swiftly, but taking time to talk to them as well. She thought if he didn't get some sleep soon, he might topple over the rails in exhaustion.

By supper time on the fifth day, she was feeling better and suddenly felt famished. She was also looking forward to catching up with their fellow travellers and ship's officers. The captain, mates and ship's surgeon had meals in the cuddy when they could. They had their own cabins, whereas the rest of the crew ate separately and kept to their quarters in the fo'c'sle, as they were strictly forbidden from consorting with the passengers.

Tonight, the second mate was at the helm and the doctor was still tending the sick and injured, but almost everyone else was present, including several people Elisabeth had not yet spoken to.

Anne took Thomas aside. 'Mr Thomas, might I take a plate of food to Mr Penrose? He has not been to any of the meals today and must be starving. In fact, I can't recall the last time I saw him eat.'

'A kind thought, Miss Godwin. I shall do it myself. He mostly just drops in to get food direct from the cook, so he is not missing out entirely.'

Sir Julius Maynard cut in, his voice slurred. 'Steward, more port here. We expect you to serve us, not go running after the crew. Miss Godwin, I shouldn't worry about the quack. I'm sure he'd rather eat with steerage anyway, from the look of him.'

This remark caused some murmuring around the table. Sir Julius was rarely seen during the day, except at meals. His principal activities seemed to be the consumption of prodigious amounts of brandy, wine and port, and gambling at cards. Although still a young man, his puffy face was already showing the first signs of broken red veins and sagging jowls, while his fashionable silk waistcoat wasn't quite wide enough to close at the bottom. Aside from these indications of an early slide into a dissolute middle age, he was a handsome man, who wore his hair in a side-swept wave identical to Prince Albert, with the same small moustache, full side-burns and proud posture.

'He hasn't eaten all day, Sir Julius, as he is looking after sick children. I think that warrants some small consideration on our part.' With that, Anne took the loaded plate from Thomas and marched out the door, letting it bang behind her.

Thomas poured a little more port into the glass. Elisabeth noticed he'd been trying to pour smaller and smaller amounts as Sir Julius became increasingly tipsy.

'Right-ho. Which of you men will join Knight and I for poker? Decent stakes mind. If we're playing for pennies, we may as well play bridge or bezique like a bunch of women.'

Two of the men present, Mr Gilbert and Mr Forrester, said they never gambled. Sir Julius looked down his nose at them with derision and turned to Amberley and Templeton. 'You two look like proper gentlemen. How about it?'

Mr Amberley nudged his friend. 'What do you say, William?'

Mr Templeton whispered back, 'I'm not much of a gambler and I feel we would be taking advantage of a couple of men who are the worse for drink.'

'We're in, Sir Julius. Modest stakes though. Templeton and I cannot afford to squander our wealth.'

The four men rearranged themselves into a cluster at one end of the table. Mr Gilbert retreated to the far end and engaged the Reverend Robertshaw in a loud conversation about the bible's teachings on vice.

Mr Forrester shook his head as he watched Sir Julius call for more port. He mumbled 'shameful, giving gentlemen a bad name' under his breath. Elisabeth, who was sitting next to him, could only agree. A drunken gambler with a fat purse bulging in his pocket was a disaster waiting to happen.

She was more concerned about Mr Knight, whose adventurous spirit seemed to extend to gambling and drinking. Perhaps he was hoping to win enough to buy off his bond period. Although Elisabeth had taken an instant liking to him, she had to admit he was only charming when sober. His superior, Mr Strickland, had already admonished him over boorish behaviour. She gathered from Mr Strickland's grumbles that he had been assigned the 'undisciplined young pup' by some anonymous government official without being given any choice in the matter, his own selection of an experienced surveyor having met with an accident just prior to departure.

She turned back to the man beside her, about whom she knew little, beyond his determination to become a successful merchant in Wellington. Like most of the gentlemen, he looked to be in his mid to late twenties. It was hard to judge his expression, as a huge walrus moustache and rampant auburn sideburns dominated his face. He had been courteous to her and seemed a serious sort, as he dressed conservatively and never joined in the constant banter between the other young men.

'I never touch spirits myself, Mrs Godwin. I aim to make something of my life, not drink it away.'

'A sensible attitude, Mr Forrester. What are your plans once you reach Wellington?'

Over the next half hour, she learned, in great detail, about the trading business Mr Forrester planned to set up in Wellington. He was the son of a merchant in London and had inherited his father's business acumen and enthusiasm.

She kept half an eye on the poker game as Mr Forrester ran through an inventory of haberdashery and the merits of various types of fabric. Sir Julius won several of the early hands and demanded a raise in the stakes, against Mr Templeton's wishes. Mr Knight looked worried, probably because he had little money to waste. But Amberley agreed, his expression shifting from his usual good-humoured grin to a benign blank as he dealt the next hand with professional dexterity.

From that point, it was all downhill for Sir Julius. He kept slapping down money and Mr Amberley swept it up in round after round. Elisabeth noticed Amberley had a tendency to bite his bottom lip – ever so slightly – when he bluffed, but she seemed to be the only one aware of it. Templeton played a conservative hand and rarely won or lost a large amount. She was relieved to see Mr Knight was winning enough to put him a little ahead of even.

Eventually, Sir Julius threw his losing hand down in disgust, lurched onto unsteady feet and declared the game over. 'Damn it, Amberley, you've the luck of the devil.'

'Beginner's luck, Sir Julius.'

Elisabeth very much doubted that Amberley was a novice at poker, based on the crisp efficiency with which he handled the cards and the calculating manner of his play. But she was pleased to observe that he was not only gracious in his success, but that he tucked his pile of money away discreetly, resisting the temptation to flaunt his winnings.

Sir Julius stomped off to his cabin with a light purse and a heavy scowl, slamming the door on his way out. Nobody said a word, perhaps because they were aware, as she was, that somehow they must all find a way to get along on this long voyage, for better or worse.

22 August 1841

Elisabeth rose early, as usual. She felt rather queasy still, so she went up into the fresh air. The storm had blown itself out and the vessel was surging ahead steadily on a light breeze. Most people seemed to be over the worst of their seasickness, so the only person leaning against the stern rail was the doctor, who looked lost in thought as he watched the horizon glow with the first light of a new day. She turned away to allow him his solitude, but he must have seen her.

'Good morning, Mrs Godwin. Are you are feeling better this morning?'

She moved up to stand at the rails. 'A little better. I can't seem to shake this sickness, though I have never had it before now. I'm usually better after breakfast.'

'Even experienced sailors get seasick in the Channel. Most people find it lasts only a few days. Make sure you keep drinking water or you will become dehydrated.'

She gestured out to the horizon. 'Fresh air and a beautiful sunrise certainly help to lift the spirits.'

'They do indeed.' After a moment's peaceful contemplation, he turned back to her. 'When you are feeling better, I need to talk to you about altering the passenger list. I believe you boarded in place of Major Carruthers and his wife?'

'Perhaps in a few days when we are settled in?' Elisabeth would have been happier to leave the Major's name in the official documents, but there was little she could do if the doctor insisted on correcting the error.

Mr Penrose nodded and turned back to the sunrise. 'No hurry, we have a long voyage ahead.'

His unruly thicket of coal-black hair flopped over his forehead and reached beyond his collar, as if it had been cut months ago by a person more experienced with hedge-trimming. But somehow it went with the sun-tanned skin, sharp cheekbones, dark stubble and fraying peacoat. He might look more like a fisherman than a physician, but she had seen the care and comfort he bestowed on every patient, regardless of class.

'There is one other thing.' He shuffled his feet and continued to gaze out to sea. 'It's about your sister-in-law. She has been a great help, but tending the sick is not appropriate work for a lady. Perhaps you could thank her from me and say that Matron and I can handle it from now?'

Elisabeth smiled to herself. Here was a competent man in a position of authority, overseeing two hundred steerage passengers, yet he wanted her to talk to Anne. Credit the man with some perception – Anne could be very determined. 'Well, I could try, but Anne is not one to sit idly by when people are in need.'

Dark grey eyes turned on her, as if wanting to ensure she understood the gravity of the situation. 'The conditions in steerage are appalling. No matter how rigorous our health checks are before boarding, disease and lice are always a problem and the smell is atrocious. The captain is adamant that she is not to be exposed to it.'

'I appreciate your point, but please don't be concerned for her sensibilities, as she has worked with the most desperate of people in the workhouses of London.'

One eyebrow shot up, ruining the illusion of stern command. 'Really? I have to admit that her medical skills are first rate. Far better than Matron. I couldn't have coped without her when we had so many people ill. But it's still not right for her to help.'

Elisabeth could see he was wavering between decorum and practicality, so she just smiled and left him to come to terms with the inevitable decision in his own time. The poor man looked as though he was about to keel over and was certainly in need of the help. 'When did you last sleep, Mr Penrose?'

'I had a few hours last night.' The sagging skin around his eyes crinkled with a smile. 'Thank you for asking.'

A decent man, she thought, although perhaps not one given to unnecessary speech. Surprisingly, she felt at ease in his company, watching in blissful peace as the sky turned from soft grey to burnt orange. The only sounds were the rhythmic creaking and sloshing as the ship carved its way through the rolling waves and the squabbling of the hovering mob of seagulls. The breeze blew in from the stern at last, so that even the reek of massed humanity and stock did not detract from the pleasure.

Elisabeth realised that this was the first time she had seen Mr Penrose standing still. Indeed, he'd hardly had time to gulp down his meals before returning to his duties. Mostly he was striding the decks, going from one patient to another, like a man used to walking open moors. A stark contrast to the slow, rolling gait of the sailors.

She had seen him lift a burly sailor with a twisted ankle, so he must have a wiry strength despite his lean frame. Not as tall and handsome as Mr Amberley or Mr Knight, and far more plainly dressed, but attractive in his self-possession. She thought he was probably in his early thirties, about the same age as or a little older than most of the colonists, but without the soft edges that come with a pampered upbringing. She wondered why he had chosen to be a ship's surgeon, rather than a well-paid doctor living in comfort at home.

He must have sensed her scrutiny. 'I'm sorry. I'm neglecting my conversational duties.'

'Not at all, Mr Penrose. It is a joy to stand quietly and watch the sunrise, after all the activity and noise of the past few days. I much prefer serenity over clamour.'

He looked at her again, as if seeing her for the first time. 'Too few of us share your opinion.'

'I grew up in the countryside, milking our cows as the sun rose over the fields. On a calm day, the river used to light up as if it was on fire and the birds would sing the glories to heaven. My favourite time of the day.'

'Sounds like paradise. Although I must say I cannot imagine you milking cows.'

'Well, it's true that over the last decade you would be more likely to find me tallying expenses in a ledger. Dairy herds and orchards are a little thin on the ground in the City of London.'

They sank back into companionable silence, as the sky faded from vibrant orange to gold, before settling into light blue. Behind them, the bustle of daily life was beginning.

The doctor cleared his throat. 'I'm afraid I must ask you to go below again, as the men from steerage are to bathe on deck this morning.'

She slipped away quietly so he could enjoy a few more moments of peace before supervising the activities of the day. The steerage passengers were kept busy with a strict routine – seven o'clock wake-up, sweep the decks before breakfast, then other chores such as scraping the decks with holystone, emptying toilet pails and sorting food rations for the day. Even without sick passengers, the work of the ship's surgeon seemed never-ending.

Everyone was present for breakfast, crowding the cuddy with bodies hungry for food after several days of illness. The seats nearest Anne were taken by a trio of well-dressed and attractive men, who seemed to be competing for her attention. Amberley, Templeton and Knight. Elisabeth knew that if Frederick was here, he would be sizing up the net worth of these gentlemen and checking for any undesirable traits in their bloodlines.

She paused to make sure Anne was not in need of rescue, but quickly concluded that she was enjoying herself immensely. Such a pleasure to see her sister-in-law coming out of her shell and having fun. Anne had always felt she lacked the beauty to be well received by society, no matter how often Elisabeth told her otherwise. Perhaps this journey was just what they both needed.

A booming voice erupted from the other end of the table. 'Come, sit here, lassie. Mr Enys tells me your husband in is shipping and you know a mizzen from a main.'

'Good morning, Captain.' Unable to ignore the stentorian summons, she slipped into the seat beside him, having to shuffle a little to the side to accommodate his muscled bulk. 'I've sailed a few times, but only on the coastal trade to France and Spain.'

'And where is your husband? I should have thought he would be reluctant to let two such lovely ladies out of his sight, especially on a voyage to the colonies, where ladies are in short supply.' He shot her a bold wink and a bark of laughter.

Elisabeth was taken aback at this forthright questioning. She had agreed with Anne that it would be best to present themselves as a married woman and her sister emigrating to join relatives, in order to avoid the unwanted attentions paid to unattached and unchaperoned women. Hence her decision not to wear strict mourning clothes on the voyage. But now that the question was asked, as it surely would be by others, she found it difficult to deceive.

'I am a widow, Captain. My husband was lost at sea.'

'Well now, I'm right sorry to hear it. The sea has a way of claiming the best of us without fear or favour.'

Fortunately, Mrs Robertshaw came to her rescue. 'Do have some breakfast, my dear. I am quite desperate to talk to you once you are done.'

'In that case, Mrs Robertshaw, perhaps I could just take some tea down to your cabin. I am not hungry this morning.'

In the relative quiet of the Robertshaws' cabin, a deck lower than hers, Elisabeth thanked the clergyman's wife for her intervention. The cabin was so tiny that Mrs Robertshaw had to perch on the narrow double bunk, while Elisabeth squeezed herself into the one slim chair by the tiny desk. Their knees were almost touching.

Mrs Robertshaw waved away her gratitude. 'The captain has as much tact as my Aunt Fanny's spaniel. But we're told he is a competent captain and that, lord knows, is by far the preferable trait when struck by a storm in the middle of the ocean.'

'Yes indeed. And Mr Enys is an excellent mate. Did you notice how our vessel was out-running the other sailing ships in the Channel with him at the helm? Now, did you wish to discuss something with me, or was it a ruse to save me?'

'Well, my dear, I did happen to hear you telling a tale to young Victoria Maynard yesterday. You have a lovely voice and a good ear for a story. It struck me that some schooling might not go amiss, to pass time gainfully on the long voyage.'

'For Victoria and Francis? I believe Lady Maynard already has a maid who also acts as a nanny. I have no teaching experience.'

'You are well educated and good with children, which is what counts. And I rather thought we could teach the children in steerage to read and write a little, to help them to a good start in a new land.' She must have seen Elisabeth's hesitation, as she added, 'I have some experience. My husband's ministry took us to India for several years. The little school we started there was well received. Taught my own seven children too and they haven't disgraced us, God bless them. The school was supposed to be for the colonials' inbred moppets, of course, but the local children had such a thirst for knowledge that we opened up the school out-of-hours for them.'

'Good for you, most impressive,' was all Elisabeth got in before the flow continued.

'Got away with it for years. Only got found out when the Colonel's wife caught her houseboy reading a recipe for Yorkshire pudding to the cook. Still, it was time to seek pastures new anyway.' Mrs

Robertshaw gestured vaguely in the direction of travel.

'With that experience, I shouldn't think you'll be in the least daunted by the challenges of New Zealand.'

'So, will you join me?'

Elisabeth could see that she was being watching closely for her reaction. Really, she hardly knew what to say at first, but the thought, once planted, grew quickly. 'I think it's a wonderful idea, truly. My hesitation was over gaining permission to interact with steerage. The rigidity of the class system on the ship seems almost worse than in England itself.'

'Or perhaps it is just more visible in close quarters?'

'Indeed. Will you speak to the captain?'

Mrs Robertshaw smiled that particular crusading smile of clergymen's wives across the Empire – the smile that sweeps all opposition aside, whether for flower-arranging rosters in the Cotswolds or charitable missions to the back streets of Calcutta. But with her sparkling humour and motherly warmth, there could scarcely be a victim of that smile who didn't walk away feeling honoured to be asked to help.

'Mr Penrose is in charge of passenger welfare. If your sweet sister can wrap him around her little finger, then he will certainly be no match for me.'

Elisabeth did not doubt that for a second. 'The doctor seems an educated and caring man. I'm sure he will agree without hesitation.'

'Yes, indeed, he is skinny enough without a turn on the rack.' She slapped her hands to her knees and gave a raucous chuckle. 'Poor love could do with feeding up, like most of the folks in steerage.'

The thought of food turned Elisabeth's stomach, even though she had not touched her breakfast.

'I say, Mrs Godwin, you're looking a little peaky. Shall we take a turn on the deck?'

The fine weather had lured a crowd to the deck, especially as it was rumoured that today might bring their last sight of England. The main deck was in a state of disorder as the steerage passengers had brought up their straw mattresses to air while they scrubbed out their compartments. Reverend Robertshaw was helping bring order to the chaos, his long limbs windmilling as he directed traffic. Elisabeth had already seen him mediate in a few minor disagreements to good effect. A useful man to have on a crowded ship on a long voyage.

No doubt there would be many more arguments arising from the close living conditions over the coming months. Anne had told her that the 'tween-decks space was divided into separate compartments for single women, families, and single men. Each was filled with as many bunks as could be squeezed in, leaving a central space for a long table. Elisabeth had heard their singing and dancing at night, but little interaction between the cabin and steerage classes was allowed.

Up on the poop, there was a little more open space to enjoy, or rather, fewer people to cram onto it. In the corner, Mr Penrose was fast asleep, with his cap over his face and his back against the ship's small skiff. Mrs Strickland and her daughter, Charlotte, were strolling the short circuit around the deck with Lady Maynard, while Amberley, Templeton, and Knight lounged by the rails and looked on. Mrs Strickland was a fine figure of a lady, with a stiff spine and immaculate tailoring, but little conversation. She reserved her words for those on her own level, which severely restricted her social circle aboard the *Lady Rosalind*.

Charlotte, who looked about twenty, was wearing a wide-brimmed coal-scuttle hat to shade her chalk-white complexion. She appeared to be so unwell that she had to lean on her mother's arm to stay upright. Elisabeth had not had a chance to talk to her yet, as she was as quiet as a ghost, floating in her mother's shadow. Mother and daughter were sharing the cabin next to theirs, along with most of the family luggage, as Mr Strickland had commandeered the larger cabin as an office. The Strickland's three sons had been left behind at boarding school to complete their education.

Around mid-morning, the call went out to farewell England. Elisabeth hurried down to rouse Anne from her diary. By the time they returned, all the cabin passengers were at the stern rail to catch a last glimpse of the Isle of Wight, while the steerage passengers leaned outward from the main deck. Women who had never previously travelled beyond their local villages were now openly weeping at the thought of leaving behind everything and everyone they had ever known. Elisabeth could not look at Anne, who she knew would be bravely trying to hold back tears.

Mr Knight offered a handkerchief, which Anne declined. 'Thank you, Mr Knight, but it is not necessary. I admit to being terribly sad at leaving my friends and work behind, but mostly I feel excitement for the adventure ahead. Who would have thought, even a month ago, that I would be voyaging to the other side of the world?'

'Well said, Miss Godwin. It's a great pleasure to meet two young ladies with such spirit. So many these days seem to baulk at the slightest of discomforts. No sense of adventure at all. And might I say, your medical skills are most impressive too. Are you a trained nurse?'

'Not at all. I've merely learned a few skills as needed. But I hope to put what skills I have to good use in Wellington. I am inspired by the wonderful achievements of the Robertshaws.'

Their conversation was interrupted by squeals from above. Several of the youngsters from steerage, who could not see in the crowd, had climbed the ratlines to get a better view, while some of the adults had ventured up the ladder to the poop deck. One of the lads – a skinny boy who looked about ten years old – was hanging upside down and cheering. Elisabeth was instantly reminded of her nephew, who had been a little monkey just like this lad.

A woman, whose patched dress hung off a bony frame, called out to him. 'Ned Bell, you stop that this instant. I'll not be having you dead from a cracked head if you fall.'

Lady Maynard looked on with a tightly pursed mouth. Before any intruders reached the top rung of the ladder, she summoned the chief mate to heel, one hand on her hip and the other gesticulating at the intruders. 'This is outrageous, Mr Enys. Please remove these people immediately.'

Mr Enys advanced on the offenders, waving them off. 'You know the rules – no steerage on the poop.'

Lady Maynard turned to Mrs Strickland. 'Really, one cannot rely on the lower classes to follow even the simplest of rules. Look at them, dressed in little better than rags. Probably covered in fleas and carrying God only knows what diseases.'

Mrs Strickland shook her head. 'I hope the ship's surgeon can keep them properly contained.'

'I have little hope of it. He seems little better than they are – a poorly trained village quack at best, I should think. Did you see his table manners? Appalling, positively gulping down his food like a dog.'

Her voice was stiletto-sharp and unrestrained. Elisabeth could see that Anne was glaring at the ladies with narrowed eyes and a sour-lemon pout. The doctor was awake, but unfazed. She saw Anne lean down and whisper something in his ear, causing him to grin. Mrs Robertshaw had turned puce and was puffing out her chest, ready for battle.

Elisabeth put a restraining hand on her arm. 'Let's not sink to her level. Your idea for a school will do a lot more good than exchanging crass insults.'

'I'm sure that dreadful woman will try to stop me with some twaddle about keeping the lower classes ignorant for their own good. I won't stand for it. That poor doctor has hardly had a moment spare to eat at all, let alone to lounge around the table chit-chatting about the latest fashion in silly hats.'

Lady Maynard's haughty display of class segregation was met with grumbles from the lower decks. Fortunately, the good-natured Mr Amberley broke the tension by loudly daring Mr Templeton to join him in a race to the crow's nest. Mr Templeton refused, but wagered that Mr Amberley could not do it in under a minute.

With a loud cry of 'tally ho', Amberley launched himself up the ratlines, to cheers from below. Templeton looked on with an expanding grin as the chief mate tipped a nod to the second mate. The latter was soon racing up at twice the speed, to a backdrop of chanting, cheering and side-betting from all quarters. The loudest cheers of all came from the sailors.

Amberley was no more than halfway up when he was dragged down by the mate and fined a bottle of brandy for breaking one of the Ship's Rules. The sailors erupted in cheers at their good fortune.

Mr Templeton roared with laughter. 'You owe me a shilling, Edgar. Serve you right for looking at pretty ladies rather than paying attention when the rules are read.'

'Ah, William, what is a man to do when he is surrounded by such loveliness,' Amberley replied, catching Elisabeth's eye and sending her a wink.

Speculation

Elisabeth escaped to the cabin but found herself too preoccupied to read. The voyage so far had been surprisingly busy, leaving her little time for reflection. She had welcomed the distractions as a means of shutting out the painful events of the past months, temporarily at least, but there were too many loose ends that chafed against her orderly nature to let it go entirely. Solving the mystery – or at least trying to – might help to stave off the waves of grief that swamped her when she was alone.

As she lay on her bed, staring up at John's picture, she considered the questions she had been trying so hard to suppress.

Why had Frederick taken money from the business? And why had he been so worried about the documents that John had left with the attorney? His determination to find them could not be doubted, after he had rushed straight to their house after they'd left the attorney and made a frenzied search of their library and even her bedroom. The burglary of the attorney's office could hardly be a coincidence, and indicated a desperation serious enough to resort to crime. If Frederick's only wrong-doing had been to borrow a large sum of money to invest in something risky, then such panic seemed unwarranted.

Unwilling as she was to accept it, the most likely conclusion was that Frederick had been involved in something shady or scandalous, possibly even illegal. Presumably the mysterious Mr Kingston was also involved, as he too had been angry about the missing documents. She would likely never know and it irked her.

None of it made much sense, including his plan to marry off Anne to a Canadian. She wished she could stop churning it over in her mind, but it was like a sore she couldn't stop scratching, even though there was nothing to be achieved by ripping the scab off, other than to upset herself all over again. She could only hope that John had been wrong, which seemed unlikely, and the investment might turn out to be a great success.

She was no further ahead with her speculation by the end of the day. Most of the passengers were tired out by the sea air and the emotion of leaving England behind, opting for a quiet supper and an early night. Sir Julius and Mr Knight disappeared to a poker game, brandy bottle in hand.

Elisabeth felt restless after a day of inactivity, so she stayed on in the cuddy, listening to the small group of men sitting around the table, sipping brandy and talking of what they would miss most about England.

Mr Forrester's flamboyant moustaches quivered as he put his view. 'I'm sorry to be leaving at a time of great technological change. As a merchant, it could hardly be more exciting. Faultless fabrics woven in a fraction of the time by mechanical looms, rushed to the shop on railways stretching from one end of the country to the other. There seems no end to the potential of Mr Stephenson's steam engines. You mark my words, it will transform our entire society.'

Mr Templeton shook his head. 'I'm sure you're right, but it may not be all for the best. What will become of all the workers who are put out of a job? As for me, I'll miss the grand houses and green fields. I'd far rather ride a fine thoroughbred down the leafy lanes of Somerset than sit in filthy coal smoke in London. What about you, Amberley?'

'I too shall miss the green fields of England, as well as the entertainments of London. I doubt they have opera or theatre of any sort in New Zealand yet. But I did come down to London on the new London and Birmingham Railway and I have to say it was a marvel. So fast, no need for constant changing of horses at squalid inns, and a first-class compartment to myself, instead of being squashed in with any old vagabond. On the other hand, I did find my travelling suit was covered in soot by the end of the journey and my face and gloves were filthy. And it is a shame to see the countryside being turned over to railway tracks and vast industrial estates.'

'One cannot hold back progress.' Mr Forrester said. 'Think of the gains – goods coming into England from all over the world. New types of cloth, new foodstuffs, new ideas. Railways will open up the vast resources of the Americas and all the other great continents.'

'But surely the railways will put the shipping companies out of business, on some routes at least. What say you, Mrs Godwin? Your family is in shipping, I believe?'

'Well, Mr Templeton, it is true that some of the coastal routes might suffer with an extension of the railway lines. But Mr Forrester is right too. There will be so much more trade, so many new types of goods, that shipping companies can only benefit. After all, a railway in America or Africa is of no use to us, unless we can ship the goods back to England.'

'If the development is done right, I suppose I would have to agree,' Mr Templeton said. 'But it seems to me that most of these schemes to build railways across England – let alone across a vast continent like America – are no more than grandiose notions or out-and-out frauds, no doubt set up to separate foolish rich people from their money.'

'My husband would have agreed with you, I suspect. He was in favour of innovations but despaired at man's greed to exploit the mania. One reads of lost fortunes sunk into such schemes, but it seems to make little difference when the next scheme is promoted.' In fact, John had talked about the issue just before his last fateful trip. That was probably just a coincidence, as railways and steam inventions were a constant topic of conversation around dinner-tables throughout the Empire. Nevertheless, it was worth dropping a fishing-line into the conversation to see if it came up with anything. 'I don't suppose any of you gentlemen have heard the name Kingston associated with such an investment company?'

'I rather think that does ring a bell,' Templeton said. 'My father mentioned a charismatic young fellow who was doing the rounds at a London club, selling shares in a railroad company. North America, if I recall right. I thought he mentioned the name Kingswood, but it might have been Kingston.'

'Would that be the United British Canadian Railroad?' Mr Forrester asked. 'I heard the name mentioned not so long ago at my club, though I know nothing about the particulars. Some of my fellow members thought it would be a huge success as an investment, but I prefer to invest my money in my own business, not someone else's.'

'Could be the same one. The name sounds vaguely familiar.'

'And did your father invest in it, Mr Templeton?' Elisabeth asked. She tried to keep her voice light, but Canada seemed all too plausible as a lure for Frederick, who had managed the Canadian shipping route for Godwin & Sons. He had often talked of the rich resources to be plundered there, to their benefit. A railroad to bring those exports to the coast would certainly have appealed to Frederick's desire to make a success of the route.

'Good heavens, no. My father has a firm rule never to invest in anything he can't see with his own eyes, especially anything being sold by charming young men. But I believe a number of his acquaintances were persuaded of the merits. Canada certainly sounds like a better bet in my view than, say, a railway across the wilds of Africa. Who knows, it could be a splendid success. I've even heard talk of gold there, or is that the United States of America? Have you heard anything, Amberley?'

'I plead total ignorance of geography and railways. The only Kingston I recall was a boy at my boarding school who played the most marvellous pranks on the masters. Switched their port for cough medicine once. Same colour, not sure half of them even noticed, but we lads enjoyed a good drop that night. Eventually got the push, after filling the headmaster's carriage with goats.' Amberley drank off the rest of his port, allowing just the right length of pause for the punchline. 'Might have got away with it if he hadn't put a buck in with the nannies. The head's wife and her lady friends were not amused.'

Amberley stifled a half-smile, half-yawn as laughter rang around the table. 'Almost time for light's out. I'm off to bed.' He bowed to Elisabeth and strolled out.

To Elisabeth's annoyance, Mr Amberley's anecdote ended what was proving to be an interesting discussion. On his departure, the group broke up and they all headed for their cabins.

She found sleep hard to come by, as her brain was churning with the many ways men found to be wicked – fraud, violence, theft, tyranny over women, and that was only the vices she had been exposed to in the past month.

But, in fairness, there were many wonderful men in the world too – kind, clever, caring, and willing to stand up for what was right. John had been one such. She was sure she could put the Reverend Robertshaw and Mr Penrose into that category too. Messrs Templeton, Amberley, Forrester and Strickland seemed like good men as well, and Knight, if he could keep his vices in check. As to the rest, who could really tell what lay beneath, and who was she to judge?

Elisabeth had only just dozed off when she was awoken again by Sir Julius lurching along the corridor and swearing. She mentally added drunkenness and gambling to her list of infuriating male vices, before dropping into a fitful sleep.

Medical Matters

23 August 1841

As the weather remained fine, most of the company was in favour of a joint service on deck, as proposed by the Reverend Robertshaw. Naturally, it was Lady Maynard who was opposed to the idea, with Mrs Strickland in support. The husbands of these two ladies merely nodded their agreement, clearly believing this should be enough to decide the issue. And so it was. The captain decreed that there would be a service in the cuddy for the cabin passengers and another on the main deck that anyone might attend.

Elisabeth hoped they would not find out she was born a French Catholic, as no doubt that would create further fuss. She had admitted it to their clergyman, but he had only smiled and, with a wink, told her that if Jesus could work with lepers, he could include a Catholic in his flock.

Reverend Robertshaw faced the assembly in a rather faded black frock-coat and gave a rousing sermon based on the parable of the Good Samaritan. From the nodding heads in the small congregation, Elisabeth gathered that the general message met with approval, whether or not some of the cabin passengers felt the personal need to apply it to their own actions.

Mrs Robertshaw's plans for a school were, as expected, strongly opposed by a vocal minority. The captain again interceded. He agreed it was the proper role of the clergyman's wife to organise schooling, but she must not deputise ladies from first class to assist. Lady Maynard magnanimously conceded that Elisabeth might read to her children, if she wished, as the maid cum nanny was illiterate. Elisabeth was tempted to refuse on principle, but the spark of joy in little Victoria's eyes was too hard to resist.

After the service, Elisabeth sat down with the Maynard children at the edge of the poop deck. Victoria Maynard, who was only six years old, was a sweet little girl who clearly adored her nanny. Francis Maynard, in contrast, was a nine-year-old boy with a nose for trouble. Lady Maynard had provided two books: *Lessons for Children* and *Little Goody Two Shoes*. Victoria seemed to find them enjoyable enough, but Francis listened for less than a minute before making a rude noise and scampering away.

The nanny rolled her eyes and sped after him. She was a tiny, waif-like girl who looked like she would blow away in a breeze, but she had a surprising turn of speed. Perhaps that was why Lady Maynard employed her, along with her willingness to do three jobs – nanny, maid and general servant – for the meagre price of one.

Elisabeth noticed a few of the little children from steerage were staring up at them from the quarterdeck, so she raised her voice. By the time she had finished, there was quite a crowd on the deck, with a few of the braver faces peeping over the ladder. Thankfully, Lady Maynard had used the free time to rest in her cabin, as she was finding it difficult to sleep at night because of the ship's bells and the constant roaring of the sea.

Mrs Robertshaw was beaming. She came over to Elisabeth after she had finished reading and pressed another book into her hands, with a smile. 'Jolly good reading, Mrs G. Perhaps you could try this book next. More exciting than *Little Goody Two Shoes*, if you are willing to take a wee risk.'

Elisabeth looked at the title: *Oliver Twist: The Parish Boy's Progress* by Charles Dickens. 'This is recently published, is it not? I've not read it, but it has to be better than the other options.'

Anne and Mr Penrose were also waiting for her, their heads together in whispered discussion. She thought they looked well together. In the first few days, Anne's gaze had often rested on Mr Amberley. Since then, Elisabeth had noticed that Anne's attention had increasingly switched to the doctor. Perhaps it was just that they spent a great deal of time together helping the many seasick passengers. Not that she minded in the least. He seemed an excellent doctor, and she suspected there was a good man under the reserved exterior. Time would tell. She trusted Anne's judgement and wished only that she be happy.

She wandered over. 'What are you two plotting?'

Anne leaned forward and whispered, 'Mr Penrose thinks Charlotte is in pain with her illness, but Mrs Strickland refuses to let her see him. He suggests you and I might act as chaperones to help to question her. Symptoms, what has been attempted, diet and so forth.' She paused to give the doctor a stern glare. 'He also says I cannot help him in steerage at present, as two children have come down with an unknown fever.'

The doctor seemed undaunted by her annoyance. 'Not just for your own safety, Miss Godwin, for the wellbeing of all the cabin passengers. Illness can spread extremely fast in confined quarters. I'm sure you wouldn't want your sister to become ill.'

Elisabeth looked between their stubborn expressions, thinking them well-matched in temperament, as well as looks. 'Mr Penrose is the expert, Anne. I'm sure he will welcome you back once the crisis has passed. And I agree Charlotte needs our help. Shall we look for her now?'

As luck would have it, Charlotte was alone in the cuddy, Mrs Strickland having retired with a headache. Charlotte was plucking at a small harp, looking ethereal with her pale blonde hair and porcelain skin.

Elisabeth was intrigued by the harp, which was small enough to sit in Charlotte's lap. 'Good morning, Charlotte. What a lovely instrument. I have never seen one like it. Would you be kind enough to come closer to the skylight, so I can look at it?'

'Of course, I would love to.' Charlotte showed Elisabeth the features of the harp, holding it with as much care and pride as a mother with a new baby.

'Beautiful. I would love to hear you play. But before you do, would you be willing to talk about how you are feeling? I'm worried that you appear to be in such pain. Mr Penrose and Anne would like to talk to you too, if that is acceptable.'

The sparkle with which Charlotte had talked about her harp now vanished and her shoulders sagged. 'Mother's doctor says I should improve now that he has bled me. He said to eat plain bread soaked in thin soup until my stomach pains are gone, but honestly, I think it has made me worse. I sometimes feel like I won't make it as far as New Zealand.'

Elisabeth saw the doctor and Anne exchange horrified glances. Even with her own limited medical knowledge, she could see that the girl's doctor must be a charlatan to be bleeding her when she was so weak and pale. 'How long have you had this condition?'

'It seems like forever,' the girl replied miserably.

Elisabeth glanced up at Mr Penrose, who asked a few more questions, before standing quietly, rubbing his thickly bristled chin as he thought.

'Miss Strickland,' he said, 'I can't say for sure what the problem is, as there are many causes of stomach pain, but I can give you a restorative tonic to help with your anaemia. May I suggest you return to a normal diet, but with no bread. I know it seems strange, but some people feel ill when they eat it. If your condition doesn't improve after a few days, I have some other ideas to try.'

Charlotte darted a quick glance at him, perhaps unsure of any doctor who wasn't clean-shaven, pomaded, and sitting across a fancy desk from her.

Elisabeth put a hand on her arm. 'A simple change of diet can do no harm, and surely it's worth a try, isn't it?' Elisabeth took her silence as tacit agreement. 'Anne, would you like to go with Mr Penrose and get the tonic while I listen to Charlotte playing? Any tune you like.'

'I'm not very good. I only began to play this instrument recently, as Father said I could not bring my piano on the voyage.'

But she ran adroit fingers across the strings and proceeded to play with a level of accomplishment that amazed Elisabeth, especially for someone so young and new to the instrument.

When she finished, a vigorous clapping erupted from the doorway, where Mr Templeton stood entranced. He forgot his shyness in his enthusiasm. 'Bravo, Miss Strickland, you play beautifully. Do you sing as well?'

Charlotte blushed the brightest shade of red Elisabeth had ever seen outside of a tomato patch. She gave the smallest of nods in his direction. Mr Templeton promptly launched into a popular song, '*Home Sweet Home*', with gusto. As he started the second verse, Charlotte's sweet soprano unexpectedly came in alongside his pure baritone. They finished the song with a resounding '*There's no place like home, oh, there's no place like home*', looked at each other, and burst into giggles.

Elisabeth looked on in fascination at this instantaneous meeting of kindred souls. She clapped loudly. 'Bravo, you two. We now know who to ask when we want some entertainment.'

She turned sideways, to give them a little privacy for their animated discussion of favourite music, without completely abandoning her unintended role as chaperone. The joy on Charlotte's face might just prove to be a better tonic than whatever medicine the doctor could prescribe.

Elisabeth opened *Oliver Twist* and was instantly captivated by Mr Dickens' witty prose, although a little shocked at the gritty storyline. She wondered how young Victoria might cope and saw why Mrs

Robertshaw had mentioned taking a risk. Oh yes, Lady M was going to have a fit over this. She was deep into Oliver's dismal stay with the undertaker when she noticed Anne standing in front of her, grinning. The room was otherwise empty. So much for being a chaperone.

'You're even worse than John when you get your nose into a book, Elisabeth.'

'Charlotte?'

'Has just left with a bottle of tonic in her reticule and Mr Templeton supporting her arm. I'm off to join them on deck, although I hardly think Charlotte needs a chaperone when it's near impossible to get a moment alone on the ship.'

Elisabeth thought she might as well read a few more pages…

When Anne came back to check she was all right, the book was half-finished and her eyes were aching. Elisabeth and Anne retreated to their cabin to freshen up. Next door, they could hear occasional words from a heated exchange between Mrs Strickland and Charlotte. Or rather, a stream of heated words in Mrs Strickland's imperious tone ('unqualified quack', 'peasant', 'foolish nonsense', 'don't touch that poison') and gaps where Charlotte's soft voice was presumably responding.

Anne rolled her eyes. 'Honestly, did she even think to check Mr Penrose's credentials before casting him as a quack?'

'I have an idea. Back in a minute.' Elisabeth went off to find Mr Thomas. She returned as Mrs Strickland and Charlotte were leaving their cabin.

'You'll do as I say, my girl. Our doctor has fifty years' experience and only treats the cream of society.'

Elisabeth wondered how much experience a doctor could truly have if he only dealt with the wealthy, especially if he was trained fifty years ago. Practically the dark ages of medicine, which probably explained his use of leeches.

The door to Mr Strickland's cabin opened, releasing a cloud of nauseating cigar smoke. 'What's all the fuss?' Mr Strickland demanded. 'We are trying to work in here.'

Charlotte shot Elisabeth a look that was half-pleading, half-apology. 'Mrs Godwin and the doctor have been kind enough to offer some advice to improve my health, Father. Mother does not approve.'

'Come in, come in. I don't wish to talk about it out in the corridor.'

Elisabeth would rather have left them to it, but Charlotte clutched her arm and pulled her into the office. Both women coughed from the cigar smoke.

'For heaven's sake, Edmund, open the deadlight,' said Mrs Strickland. 'How many times do I have to tell you not to smoke those foul cigars in the cabin? Poor Mr Gilbert is quite green from it.'

Elisabeth could see the top half of the clerk's head over a tottering pile of documents. He did look rather sickly. Mr Gilbert got up to let in fresh air, then excused himself from the fray, pushing past Elisabeth as if she wasn't there, although he nodded politely at the Strickland ladies. She was surprised at how tall he was, as he was mainly to be seen hunched over either the desk or dinner table. A waft of strongly scented pomade followed him out the door from his neatly slicked-down hair.

Mrs Strickland waited until the door closed behind him. 'We had no wish to disturb you, my dear. I was simply telling Charlotte not to take whatever it was the so-called ship's surgeon gave her. He had no right to go behind my back and countermand our own doctor's instructions.'

'Mr Penrose was trying to help, Mother,' Charlotte said. 'He said he had seen other cases like mine. It's only a strengthening tonic made up by a respectable chemist shop.'

'My dear girl, we have no idea what qualifications the man has, if any. He looks more like a common labourer than a doctor. Certainly not a gentleman.'

Elisabeth was attempting to blend into the wall by the door, but Charlotte's need for help won out over her reluctance to invade a family argument. 'Please forgive me, Mrs Strickland. It was I who asked Charlotte about her health, as I was worried that she appeared to be in such pain. My sister and the doctor happened to be with me, so I took the liberty of asking his professional advice.'

She leaned in towards Mrs Strickland, as if imparting a secret. 'I do understand your concern, but I am in the happy position of being able to reassure you that Mr Penrose was employed on the highest recommendation of Sir Wallace Ingram-Somerfield. My sister-in-law, who has some medical experience herself, has assured me she has seldom worked with a more competent doctor. His appearance is, I grant, rather dishevelled at the moment, but that is only because he has been working so hard. A broken arm, twisted ankles, seasickness, children with fever – the list of maladies is never-ending.'

'Sir Wallace Ingram-Somerfield, eh,' said Mr Strickland. 'Well, if he recommended our ship's surgeon personally, that's good enough for me. I see no harm in a reputable brand of medicine either. As long as you agree, of course, my dear.'

'It is only a tonic, Mother,' Charlotte added, 'and, of course, I shall stop taking it if it does no good.'

'Oh, very well. Try it if you must. It would certainly be a blessing if it worked.'

Mrs Strickland sounded resigned rather than cross, to Elisabeth's relief. The dinner bell went right at that moment, giving Elisabeth an excuse to politely excuse herself and escape. Prior to this, she had been intimidated by the Strickland parents, but now they seemed more human.

Thomas – who was an infallible source of all knowledge – had told her that Mr Strickland had been appointed to an influential position as a government official in Wellington, in charge of resolving land disputes and ensuring the ongoing land acquisition from the native peoples. It seemed as if he wasn't letting the grass grow under his feet on the voyage, judging from the long hours he worked.

He was a perfect match for his wife – upright, self-assured, and no doubt an indomitable protector of Queen and Empire. Elisabeth had yet to see him appear outside without a top hat and perfectly tied cravat. Even his hair and sideburns were trimmed and pomaded into regimental symmetry, although the overall effect was rendered less precise by his bulbous, skewed nose. She thought this small imperfection made him look far more approachable, although she would never dare say so aloud. And this encounter had shown her that he was a man who listened calmly and made decisions based on facts. She found to her surprise that she rather liked him.

Mr Strickland's clerk, Joseph Gilbert, was a very different character. He was a nondescript man of indeterminate age, who dressed like a gentleman undertaker and had a face to match. The only splash of colour about the man was the ever-present ink stain on his right hand, although it was of such a dark blue as to hardly warrant the word colour. She had scarcely exchanged half a dozen words with him and yet she had the distinct impression he despised her. Perhaps he was simply shy around women, as she had seen him talking to Mr Forrester, with whom he shared an interest in commercial law. But Anne had talked to him and said he looked quite charming when he smiled.

Elisabeth updated Anne over dinner. She was relieved to see the Strickland family happily chatting together over their soup and fish and pleased to note that Charlotte ate a modest serving of everything except the bread – without her mother noticing.

After dinner, the younger passengers, whom Elisabeth was beginning to think of as 'our group' – herself, Anne, Charlotte, Templeton, Amberley and Knight – went up to the deck to play quoits. They were all fiercely competitive, while trying to maintain the facade of gentlemanly and ladylike behaviour. Charlotte and Templeton won the first game, to their surprise and delight. Mr Amberley was very gracious in defeat, which had been entirely due to Elisabeth's inability to get the rope circles anywhere near the pin. One had even been headed overboard, saved only by a dramatic lunge from her partner.

Mr Templeton joined Elisabeth at the rail to watch Anne begin the next game. 'Miss Strickland tells me that you were in magnificent form today, convincing her parents to trust the doctor and try a new treatment. I'm thankful that someone has taken the initiative, as it pained me to see her in such distress.'

'Oh, it was nothing, really. I simply pointed out what an excellent and highly recommended doctor he is. It's Mr Penrose we'll have to thank if she improves. I do hope she does, because she is a lovely young lady.'

'Indeed she is.' His eyes hadn't left Charlotte for more than a few blinks since they had been talking.

'Excellent and highly recommended, eh? That was kind of you, Mrs Godwin.'

Elisabeth almost followed her wayward quoit overboard at seeing the doctor pop up out of nowhere. He must have been sitting behind the ship's boat. 'Sir Wallace Ingram-Somerfield's name seemed to do the trick.'

'How on earth did you know I was recommended by Sir Wallace?'

Anne came up to join them. 'Elisabeth made an ally of the chief steward within five minutes of boarding the ship, and he knows absolutely everything. Who is this Sir Wallace who thinks so highly of you?'

'I never met him and he does not know I exist, but he owns the mining company I worked for. Not sure how the mine superintendent got him to sign the letter of recommendation. Probably said it was an acceptance letter for an award.'

'You might be surprised,' Elisabeth said. 'Wise business owners always know who their best people are.'

'I shouldn't think he ever came within a hundred miles of where I worked. He owns so many mines and factories, I doubt he could name half of them, let alone the people who work in them.'

'You weren't at dinner again, Mr Penrose. Shall we ever see you eat on this voyage, do you think?'

'I don't feel comfortable with so many grand folk, Miss Godwin. There are those who have made it clear I don't meet their standards.'

'Nonsense,' said Mr Templeton. 'Most of us would be delighted to have you there to add some fresh conversation. Just brush your hair, put on a decent set of clothes and join the fun with us.'

'Thank you. When I get time, perhaps I will.' Mr Penrose bowed, then abruptly turned and strode away.

'Mr Penrose,' called Anne. 'How are the children with the fever?'

The doctor's shoulders slumped still further. 'I'm sorry to say that we will have our first funeral tomorrow. Fever is very cruel to infants. At least the older child is recovering. Thankfully, it does not appear to be anything particularly contagious.'

On that sobering note, they passed a minute of silence before quietly dispersing to their cabins.

24 August 1841

There was not a whisper of wind. All hands were on deck, heads bowed before the tiny body stitched into sailcloth and covered with a Union Jack flag. Reverend Robertshaw must have said a few words, but Elisabeth was unaware of what they were. She did not know the infant or the parents, but she felt overwhelmed with sorrow for a life not lived. Charlotte Strickland and Mr Templeton sang a hymn, followed by another from the steerage singers. And then the body was sent to rest. The waves had died down to an inky swell, which seemed to wrap around her tiny body like a blanket as it disappeared.

Everyone was subdued for the rest of the day. Elisabeth and Anne attended to minor tasks like washing and mending, and caught up on their diaries.

When the silence became unbearable, Anne said, 'What a transformation in Mr Penrose today. He must have had a haircut and put on his best suit out of respect for the infant. I hardly recognised him.'

'Did you notice how embarrassed he looked last night when Mr Templeton mentioned decent clothes? And how today's trousers had been taken up a few inches? I wonder if Mr Templeton has loaned him a set of clothes because he had nothing decent to wear. I heard the two of them talking in the corridor last night.'

Anne was intrigued and went off to find Charlotte, who confirmed Elisabeth's deduction. 'What's more, he felt he couldn't join us for dinner without proper clothes. Apparently, the correct standard of dress is an essential part of ship etiquette. To think that might have continued for the entire trip if Mr Templeton hadn't worked out the problem and had a spare frock coat and trousers with him. I wonder how many other good people in the world are held back by something as simple as the right garments.' She sighed. 'Fancy clothes or not, he's an attractive man, don't you think?'

'He did look rather dashing, I agree. I should think even Lady Maynard and Mrs Strickland might accept his presence in the cuddy now, if he can stop working long enough to join us.'

Dinner and supper were quiet affairs. The only jarring departure from the solemnity was Sir Julius's suggestion to resume the poker game that evening, which was rejected by all but Mr Knight. The two of them left the cuddy straight after supper, with a muttered resolution to seek more lively entertainment elsewhere.

The rest of the cabin passengers enjoyed another song from Charlotte and Mr Templeton, followed by a poetry reading. All the ladies and some of the men retired early, including Mr Penrose, who had joined their group to eat, but left early to get a much-needed night's sleep.

Echoes from the Past

25 August 1841

Elisabeth stood alone at the stern rail, half-dozing as she watched the mesmerizing churn of curling white water retreating behind the ship. There appeared to be a faint thread of land to the east, which the helmsman confirmed was the tip of Brittany.

France. A thin line of brown haze on the horizon seemed an inadequate last view of such a beautiful and tumultuous country. Sadness overwhelmed her, and she felt tears welling at the corners of her eyes at the sight of her homeland disappearing.

Elisabeth had never considered herself overly emotional, having had more than her share of tragedy to cope with in the past, but now she could not seem to control her emotions at all. Perhaps it was simply that she had not had the time and solitude to mourn her husband until now.

She noticed another figure looking out to France from the bow, as still as the carved figurehead. She went back to her own thoughts, but a strong sense of being watched made her turn again. The man was moving down the deck in her direction, partially obscured behind the main mast. But something in that fleeting glimpse set her nerves on edge. The way he stood, so erect, like a soldier. Without warning, a wave of nausea welled up inside and forced her to lean over the railings to empty an already-empty stomach, leaving her with the metallic taste of bile in her mouth.

When she lifted her head again, she saw the man heading towards Sir Julius Maynard, who had been standing by the companionway. The two met by the main mast for not more than a couple of seconds, a small item passing from hand to hand. She saw the man inspect it and nod. Sir Julius slipped away, his hat pulled firmly down on his head, his whole manner the very definition of furtive. As the man stepped out from behind the mast, she glimpsed his profile, just enough to trigger a long-suppressed memory. The world went black.

She woke to the sharp jolt of smelling salts and a soothing voice. Worried grey eyes, pitch-black hair. Not John. Then who?

'Mrs Godwin. You fainted. May I check you for injury?'

Her mind slid back to reality. 'Thank you, Mr Penrose. I am fine. Maybe a bump on the head and a little nausea.'

'Have you ever fainted like that before?'

'Never. I had a shock. My imagination playing tricks on me.'

She lay back and closed her eyes again, but the memory of the man came back to haunt her. She had been so sure that she had escaped her past. Even unresolved doubts about Frederick seemed trivial now, as if she had been distracted by swatting annoying flies at a picnic, only to look up and see that a wolf was watching.

Surely it could not be the same man, still tracking her down after so long. How on earth could he have found her, and how could he be on the ship? She hadn't seen his face properly and couldn't be sure she had seen a scar rather than a shadow. She prayed it was not him. Her memory filled with a vision of her mother slashing at him in an attempt to save their lives, carving a gash from his mouth to the corner of his eye. And the soldier, with his sword raised, ready to plunge it into her mother.

She drifted back to the comforting sound of Anne's voice, talking rapidly. Something about strong tea with a dash of brandy. Anne disappeared, and the doctor leaned over her again, concern written in the lines on his forehead. She felt gentle hands on her head and a stab of pain as he found a lump. She forced her brain to focus.

'There was a man on deck…a big man with the bearing of a soldier.'

'Was he bothering you? He has caused problems in steerage already, so he'll be feeding the sharks if he has distressed you too.'

'What problems?'

'He sneaked aboard without proper papers. Says his name is Victor Smith and claims he bought his berth from a man at the docks. The man's friends and relatives are angry about it, as the fellow was simple in the head and easy prey. They're a group of fruit-pickers from Kent who had planned this voyage together.'

'You've talked to the man? Is there any chance he is French?'

'Odd you should ask. He was overheard mumbling in French in his sleep. Now some of the women in steerage seem to think he's one of Napoleon's men come to slit their throats as they sleep.'

'Not all of my fellow countrymen are evil monsters, whatever people in England think.'

'You're French? Forgive me, I didn't know. You speak English perfectly. But you are not a hard-drinking, hard-gambling, belligerent Frenchman who tricked their friend.'

'Nevertheless, if it's the same man – and it seems almost impossible to me that it could be – I may be the reason he is here. I would need to see his face more closely, but he resembles the man who tried to murder my parents.'

'Good heavens. No wonder you fainted. I do hope you are wrong.' Penrose was silent for a long moment, his lips pursed. 'I could alert the officers and crew. Perhaps the more trustworthy of the colonists as well. I'm not sure what we can do without evidence of wrongdoing, unless you are sure it is the same man. But be assured that I will take all possible steps to ensure your protection.'

'Thank you, that's a relief. Perhaps we should wait until I can positively identify him. I hope that my mind was just playing tricks on me. I still have nightmares about him, even though the incident was more than ten years ago.'

The doctor rose to leave, but must have had second thoughts, for he sat back down. He drummed his fingers for a few seconds, before clearing his throat. 'There is one more thing I have been wanting to ask you, but it's a little delicate and the timing is not good, as you have had a nasty shock. But it has been difficult to find a private moment to ask you.'

'Please, go ahead, it can't be any worse.'

'Well, I've noticed you are often sick in the morning, though you have never been seasick before, and improve throughout the day. And there are other signs too. I wonder if it's possible that you are with child?'

'Oh no, I can't be.' Elisabeth's hands slid down her bodice, which had become unaccountably tight in recent weeks, and stopped over her belly. Was it a little rounder than normal? She tried to remember how long had it been since her last monthly visitation. Not since before John's death, certainly.

Her life had been turned upside down, so she hadn't given it a thought. Was it possible, after all these years of hoping? Suddenly, it seemed obvious. She burst into tears and a face-splitting smile simultaneously, and flung her arms around the doctor's neck.

Over his shoulder, she saw Anne standing in the doorway, tea in one hand, mouth forming an 'O' and bright spots of colour high on her cheekbones. Elisabeth let go of the startled doctor and turned to her sister-in-law.

'Oh Anne, I'm going to have a baby!'

Anne took a step back, almost toppling the cup. 'How is that possible? John has been dead for nearly three months.'

The doctor rescued the cup. 'Sickness in the morning is a common symptom at three months, often disappearing soon after. My condolences, Mrs Godwin, I was not aware that you were a widow. I can see that my timing has indeed been poor.'

The last words of the doctor were almost drowned out by a delighted shriek from Anne as she launched herself into Elisabeth's arms. 'Wonderful' was the only word she could manage amidst her sobs. The doctor let himself out, easing the door closed behind him.

26 August 1841

Elisabeth had slept little the previous night. She lay in bed, running her hand over her belly, trying to detect a hint of a curve. The irony was so painful, she hardly knew whether to laugh or cry, and had done a great deal of both. She and John had been praying for a child and now he would never have the joy of holding his son or daughter. On the other hand, it was a great comfort that a part of him would live on and her dream of being a mother would finally be fulfilled.

She and Anne spent most of the day in their cabin, as Elisabeth did not wish to have the news generally known as yet, and felt unable to contain her emotions. At least, that is what she told Anne. In truth, the sight of the Frenchman had rocked her to the core. The ship, which has once seemed an island of safety, might now be prison harbouring a murderous inmate.

The doctor visited briefly late in the day. 'We searched the man's kit and found two sets of identity papers. An English set in the name "Victor Smith" and a French set for "Victor Cloutier". Do those names mean anything to you?'

'Cloutier? Yes, my aunt thought that was the man. I'll certainly never forget his arrogant face.'

'I hate to ask, but would you be able to have a look at him and confirm his identity?'

Her heart lurched at the thought of facing him, but she nodded. 'Perhaps tomorrow?'

Today, she didn't want to burst the little bubble of happiness at the thought of the baby growing inside her. How was it possible to feel so many emotions at once – ecstasy, sadness, terror?

27 August 1841

It was mid-morning before Elisabeth went up to the deck for fresh air. The *Lady Rosalind* was forging ahead at speed, with a favourable wind at last. She had resolved to face the threat head-on. She certainly couldn't stay cooped up in the cabin for the whole voyage.

The chief mate was at the helm, his broad hands on the salt-scarred wood of a wheel as tall as her. His eyes flicked between the compass, sails, horizon and her, as he made constant minor adjustments to their heading. 'All right there, Mrs Godwin? Seen our row of beauties this morning?'

He gestured towards the quarterdeck, where a dozen men were shackled in a row, huddled against the wind and looking very sorry for themselves. 'Doc tells me you've had trouble with the Frenchman. A vicious brute and roaring drunk last night. Started a fight, but didn't reckon on our doc throwing a right hook as fast and mean as a jibing boom. And here's me thinking him such a quiet, respectable lad. We've half a mind to keep that demon shackled for the entire trip, darn troublemaker. If you can positively identify him, that will be the nail in his coffin.'

Elisabeth was loath to look upon him but steeled herself to the task. Her mother had named her after a woman of outstanding bravery and loyalty, who had lost her life to the likes of the man in shackles. She owed it to her – to all of them – to do her duty.

She went to the edge of the poop deck and looked over the rail. Most of the shackled men had minor cuts and bruises, but the Frenchman looked very much the worse for wear, with his head and arm bandaged. He was on the end of the line, the other men having shuffled as far away from him as they could.

She couldn't identify him for certain at first, as he had his head down. He must have felt the poisonous intensity of her stare, because he raised his head, revealing a black eye and a broken nose. A tremor passed through her at the sight of that distinctive scar down his face, but hatred and pride kept her feet firm on the deck.

A sneer crossed his thick lips and his bandaged hand cut across his throat in a slow, deliberate slashing gesture. She spun away, stopping only to give a brisk affirming nod to the chief mate, before stumbling below to her cabin.

Elisabeth was still shaking when a sharp knock on the door made her jump. 'Who is it?'

'Penrose.'

She unlocked the door and gestured for him to take a chair. His left eye was puffy and livid from breaking up the fight.

'Are you all right, Mrs Godwin? Enys said you looked like you'd seen a ghost.'

'I'm fine.' It came out as a squeak. She took a breath, told herself to calm down, and tried again. 'To be honest, seeing him did give me a fright.'

'I take it that it's the same man?'

She nodded.

'I can see you are upset, but it would be helpful to have a bit more information about him, so I understand the nature of the threat. Perhaps I should come back later?'

He rose to leave, but Elisabeth put a hand on his arm to stop him. She closed the door and sat on the bed. 'You're right, of course. I'm sorry you have been dragged so painfully into this,' she said, gesturing at his eye. 'Could I ask that this conversation go no further than those who absolutely have to know?'

'I give you my word.' He drew the chair closer, as if to confirm his discretion.

She couldn't explain why she trusted this man, but she did. And, given his injury, it was only fair that he should be in no doubt of the threat Cloutier posed. 'Eleven years ago, my mother was entrusted with a valuable pearl necklace, to hold until it could be returned to the owner, who had fled France. Its existence became known to a relative of this woman, who wanted the necklace and would go to any lengths to obtain it.'

'And this relative sent Cloutier to get it?'

'Exactly. He would have killed my parents if my nephew and I hadn't intervened. My mother gave him that scar and I gave him a headache he wouldn't forget or forgive in a hurry. I escaped with the necklace, intending to return it to the rightful owner, who was in exile in England. She asked me to keep it, as she felt it was safer if I had it rather than her.'

A flash of anger crossed his face. 'Safer for whom? Not for you, certainly.'

'The circumstances were unusual. She was constantly at risk, while I was a nobody, and her enemies were given the impression the necklace had been thrown into a lake and lost forever. I cannot imagine how they found out that I still had it.'

'Someone must have told him.'

'Cloutier and his master knew almost nothing about me, as far as I know. I do not know how he found me in England, especially since I had married and changed my name.'

'You didn't see him at all in England?'

'There was a big man who followed us to the docks, probably the same one who was in the Godwin and Sons Shipping office looking for me. But it makes no sense, as that man knew my brother-in-law and spoke fluent English.'

'Cloutier speaks fluent English, according to his bunk-mates. They only knew he was French because he talks in his sleep. I must say that I admire your bravery, but you took a dreadful risk.'

'It was a matter of family loyalty. I made a promise to my mother.'

His eyes softened and he leaned forward, placing a warm hand on hers for a moment. 'Then I admire you all the more. May I ask what happened to your parents?'

Elisabeth struggled to keep her composure. How much easier it was to be resolute when angry, rather than faced with a sympathetic gaze and genuine concern. 'They told me not to contact them when I got to England, but I couldn't bear not to know. My mother sent a note to say they were safe, but we heard nothing more. John Godwin sent a man to find them, discreetly, but they had all vanished and the soldiers had burned down our farmhouse. A neighbour, who was looking after the farm, said he had seen none of my family, but he had heard that my brother had been arrested. Three times we sent someone back to find them, but … nothing. By then I was married to John and with child, so I couldn't go back myself. When I lost the baby, John wouldn't risk any more stress on me.'

She was openly weeping now, unable to stop the flood of pain from pouring down her cheeks. He moved to sit beside her, his hand gently on her arm, allowing her to cry without interruption, until the racking sobs died away.

'I'm so sorry to burden you with this. I've never told a soul besides John before now.'

The doctor stood up and stepped away, his face showing nothing but concern for her. 'Sometimes it is better to talk about an ordeal, rather than bottle up the pain.'

Elisabeth realised she did feel a little lighter after sharing the story, as if the memories had been lying hidden, poisoning her, for far too long. 'Thank you. I believe you are right.'

He hesitated. 'Shall I get you a cup of tea?'

She mustered a weak grin at that. 'You English. A cup of tea is the solution to all problems.'

He smiled back. 'I have a rather nice bottle of French brandy, if you'd prefer that?'

'Tempting, but a little early in the day for me. Again, thank you for being so kind.'

He paused with one hand on the door. 'On a more practical note, perhaps your valuables could be put in the ship's safe.'

'A good thought, but I would rather have them with me. My trunk is more secure than it looks, and I will keep the door locked. There's no way anyone from steerage can get near the cabins anyway and Cloutier will be safely locked away. I hope this will be the end of it.'

'So do I,' he said, as he turned to go out.

'Mr Penrose,' she called after him. 'Will you promise me one thing?'

He came back to her bedside. 'Whatever you wish.'

'Please, promise me you'll be careful around him. He is a trained soldier and utterly ruthless. Do not trust him and never, ever, turn your back on him.'

He looked at her, his expression unreadable. 'I'll do my best. Get some rest now.'

Anne arrived soon after, sent by the doctor to keep her company. After Elisabeth told her what had happened, they chewed over the possible ways Cloutier could have found her, before giving it up as another unsolvable mystery. Elisabeth was shaken much more than she cared to admit by this unexpected turn of fortune, but there was little she could do to improve the situation. She was grateful to have Anne beside her, ever understanding and ready to help.

'So much for leaving our troubles behind us,' Anne said. 'Do you think it was Cloutier who assaulted Mr Rivers in the office?'

'He certainly fits the description. Mr Penrose says he speaks fluent English and it would explain why I had such a strong feeling of déjà vu when I saw the bulk of the man at the dock, even if I dismissed it as impossible at the time.' Elisabeth didn't mention the thought uppermost in her mind – why had Mr Rivers said the man knew Frederick? The only sensible conclusion was that he was mistaken or there had been two separate men seeking her.

By unspoken mutual consent, they spent the rest of the day chatting about trivial matters and reading, nestled into the cosy cocoon of their cabin.

A Fresh Start

28 August 1841

The cuddy was cleared after breakfast for a rehearsal. The young ladies and gentlemen had been looking for an amusing diversion and Charlotte had come up with the idea of a play. Mr Templeton was an enthusiastic supporter and had cajoled Mr Amberley, Anne, and Mr Knight to join the fun. Anne had refused to divulge the plot, except to say that it was loosely based on a Shakespearean play and she and Mr Knight were to play the lead roles.

Everyone had pressed for Elisabeth to take a role, but she wasn't feeling up to it. Thus, she found herself separated from Anne's reassuring presence for the morning. Part of her wanted to hide behind a locked door, but she squared her shoulders and went onto the deck. She tried to strike up a conversation with Mr Gilbert, but he gave her a sharp look and a curt 'good day' before walking off.

To her surprise, Mrs Strickland approached her.

'Mrs Godwin, what a lovely day.'

'Good morning, Mrs Strickland. The sea air is so refreshing, is it not?'

'And so charming that the young folk have found themselves a suitable diversion. Man's desire for culture reigns supreme even in the most unlikely of places.'

'Yes indeed. We have all been most impressed by your daughter's beautiful singing. The duets she sang last night with Mr Templeton brought tears to my eyes.'

'I am much obliged to you for introducing my Charlotte to Mr Templeton. She is such a reticent girl and was in such poor health that I had quite despaired of her prospects.'

'She is a charming young lady. I am delighted that she is looking so much better.'

'Once again, I am in your debt. We tried all the best doctors in London to no avail. I was in despair, as she was slipping away before my eyes. Now, the dreadful pains are fading and she has colour in her cheeks again. I want to apologise for the way I treated you when you were trying to help.'

'Thank you. I know you only wanted the best for your daughter. I am truly delighted to see her looking so well, although it is the ship's surgeon you should thank. He may be a humble village doctor, but he is also a miracle worker.'

A faint blush tinged Mrs Strickland's cheeks at the reference to her friend's scathing dismissal of the doctor, but she was undaunted. 'I would be most grateful if you could pass on our thanks. You and your sister seem well-acquainted with the doctor.'

'Of course, it would be my pleasure.'

'You have also made the acquaintance of Mr Templeton, I believe? May I ask what opinion you have you formed of him?'

Elisabeth knew exactly what Mrs Strickland was asking. Would this man be a suitable prospect for her daughter? Well, in that she had no need to prevaricate, nor any desire to stand between two young people in love. 'An exceptional young man, I would say. He and Mr Amberley are well-prepared to make a success of their New Zealand estates. Mr Templeton, in particular, has an expert knowledge of farming methods and many clever ideas. And of course, the funds to bring his ideas to fruition.'

'Oh? He is from a wealthy family?'

'I cannot claim an acquaintance with them, but I understand Mr Templeton's family has a large estate and they are backing him handsomely in his New Zealand venture. I believe the exact words Mr Amberley used were "they own half of Somerset", although no doubt that is an exaggeration.'

'I am very much obliged, Mrs Godwin.' Mrs Strickland made a gracious exit, with a smile lighting up her usually austere features.

At dinner, Mr Templeton was invited to sit with the Strickland family. A trivial shift of no more than two yards up the table, but a momentous move nevertheless. He was soon in deep discussion with Mr Strickland about the prospects for the development of the new colony, with each man sharing his views equally and nodding in agreement with the other's opinion. Elisabeth took great pleasure in the evident delight of all parties and, later, in watching Charlotte and Mr Templeton dancing in the moonlight.

As the nights were getting warmer, the evening entertainment had been shifted outside. The poop deck, at around forty feet in length, provided enough space to dance if one took care to avoid the mizzen mast, helm, binnacle, stairs, skylight, coils of rope, and other obstacles.

Mr Amberley favoured all the ladies with a dance under the stars. He was a fine dancer and an amusing conversationalist, and no doubt would fill up the dance-cards of adoring young women wherever he went. After twirling an effervescent Charlotte and a composed Anne, he approached Elisabeth with a dashing bow.

'Mrs Godwin, at last I get to dance with the most beautiful woman here.'

'Save your flattery for the young ladies, Mr Amberley. As a widow, I am immune to it.'

''Tis but the truth. *She walks in beauty, like the night, of cloudless climes and starry skies.*'

'Lord Byron does seem appropriate to the night. Away from the haze of London, the stars shine a hundred times brighter.'

'You know your romantic poets, then? Byron would counsel that a lovely young woman need not be a widow forever, I think.'

'Perhaps, in time, although my present view is that my beloved husband is irreplaceable.' Elisabeth was keen to turn the conversation to safer topics, as he waltzed her expertly around the deck, dodging hazards with nimble footwork. 'Do you know what caused the fight amongst the steerage men?'

'Not just them. Sir Julius Maynard and Mr Knight were caught up in the fray. Quite the scandal, especially as the captain had already warned them off from fraternising with steerage. Apparently, Sir Julius had a rotten run of bad luck at cards and far too much brandy to boot. He claimed that one of the players was cheating. Of course, the man demanded payment, which led to a dispute and then an all-out brawl. Mr Knight ducked out as soon as he smelled trouble, but Sir Julius was only saved by the intervention of the crew.'

'Sounds as if Sir Julius and Mr Knight should have been shackled to the deck with the others.'

'Heresy. A gentleman is never at fault. Though I hear the captain gave them a stern talking to and

Maynard will have to front up to Lady M, which might be the greater punishment.'

She suppressed a laugh at the thought. 'Do you know with whom they were playing cards?'

'Knight did say that there was only one man in steerage with the funds to get up a decent stake. A bear of a man by the sound of it. French, I hear.'

'That man seems to attract trouble like flies to a dung heap.'

'Mr Knight? A lively fellow and good company, though I fear he is not a man to be trusted around women or money.'

'Actually, I meant the Frenchman.'

'Oh. Well, he won't be causing any more trouble. The chief mate told me this afternoon that has had more than enough of his troublemaking and has resolved to shackle him to his bunk for the rest of the voyage.'

'I am very relieved to hear it. Will he not be allowed out at all?'

'I expect he will be allowed out for supervised time scrubbing the deck and emptying the toilet buckets. Good thing too. These French radicals cannot be trusted. Just look at how they destroyed their own country. Even killing their king – appalling. Thank heavens we were born in England.'

Elisabeth agreed it was appalling but held herself back from mentioning that regicide was not exactly unknown for the English as well, with

Charles the First merely the last in a line of executed or assassinated monarchs.

She retired early, checking twice that the door was securely locked. The Frenchman may have the look of an ordinary, over-muscled bully-boy, but she was well aware that he was a great deal wilier and more persistent than the average street fighter. He had been an experienced soldier ten years ago and who knew what skills he had added to his ruthless armoury since then. Worse still, he must harbour a deep hatred of her family for thwarting his mission. His master dealt very harshly with those who failed them. She thought of her family and the loyalty and fortitude they had shown all their lives and was determined to follow their example.

And yet, even the assurance that Cloutier was securely shackled was not enough to give her a peaceful night's sleep. The rising wind did not help.

29 August 1841

The wind had risen to a gale by morning, bringing brooding clouds, squalls of intense rain and occasional periods of lightning. Elisabeth watched the sailors scurrying to reef the sails, wondering how they managed it so high above deck with the three masts swaying dizzyingly back and forth. The second mate spotted her and hurried her back below. No one was to be allowed on deck because of the high waves and sudden lurches that could send a person overboard. The helmsman was roped up to stop him from being swept away.

The day was punctuated by the sounds of crashing from below, as poorly secured items were flung about, and an eerie whistling from above, as the wind roared through the rigging. The livestock were thrashing about in their pens and coops in terror. The boom of thunder frightened Victoria, so Anne and Elisabeth distracted her with games in the cuddy, until the rolling of the ship was too severe to continue. Dinner was a simple and quiet affair due to a resurgence of seasickness and the need to concentrate on keeping the plates anchored.

By late afternoon, the wind dropped to a stiff breeze for a short time. Everyone flocked to the deck to escape the claustrophobic conditions and mess below. Passengers wandered around in a daze, worn out by the unpleasant mix of fright at the ferocity of the storm and growing boredom, now that the initial excitement of the voyage had worn off.

The boys were especially troublesome, getting under the sailor's feet and trying to kill birds with their slingshots. Without surprise, Elisabeth noted that Francis Maynard was the ringleader. She wished they would turn their weapons on the rats and cockroaches that plagued the ship, instead of the graceful birds gliding past it.

Elisabeth decided it was a perfect moment to start reading the story by Mr Dickens. A crowd of children soon gathered. Judging from their squeals of laughter and horror, the novel was a winner. They were an enthusiastic audience, sometimes cheering and laughing, sometimes shrieking, as Oliver Twist lurched between comfort and peril. But mostly they sat still with heads jutting forward, captivated by the story. Even the constant scratching of lice-infested heads ceased for a while.

At the end of each chapter, they begged her to continue, until her voice gave out. She was amused to see many of the parents loitering on the deck within hearing distance, pretending to be engaged upon some task or other. Little Victoria, to Elisabeth's surprise and relief, was more excited than terrified by Fagin's evil gang. No doubt, she would have a visit from Lady Maynard as soon as Victoria told her what the story was about. She resolved to be calm and unrepentant.

When she could read no longer, she handed over to Mrs Robertshaw, who taught them writing.

Mr Knight looked up from his surveying instruments as she walked back across the deck. 'Bravo, Mrs Godwin, marvellous entertainment. You really should be in the play.'

He smiled at her with such an engaging show of dimples and white teeth that she nearly agreed on the spot. Instead, she asked if he would show her the theodolite, which he said was for measuring angles. A beautiful piece of engineering, with a brass barrel adjusted by a series of wheels and knobs. It was polished to a gleam and looked brand new, leaving her to wonder, perhaps unjustly, whether he had secured his position based on brash confidence rather than experience.

She went to sleep that night well satisfied with her new role and dreaming of the pleasures to come in reading to her own child. To Anne's evident amusement, Elisabeth had taken to having whispered conversations with the growing child inside her. Elisabeth had the last laugh when Anne sleepily wished them both a good night's sleep.

30 August 1841

The previous day's storm had stirred up massive rolling waves, sending the *Lady Rosalind* on an exhilarating, high-speed ride, racing up mountains of water before plummeting down the other side. Their ship had never looked smaller or more fragile against the ocean's power.

The deck was off-limits, but the crew was far too busy to stop passengers from sneaking up to take a much-needed bath in the rain. Mr Penrose clung to the stays in sodden clothes, directing the collection of fresh water. The water on board had become absolutely foul after being stored in barrels for weeks.

Elisabeth was given permission to visit the married and family section of steerage, to continue reading the Dickens story, as the children needed entertaining, and their parents needed a break. The second mate acted as an escort. He was not a talkative man, but he was an expert sailor, and she was grateful for this strong arm to keep her upright on the slippery, heaving deck.

Steerage was appalling – cramped beyond belief and reeking of unwashed bodies, wet clothes, over-cooked gruel and human waste. The bunks were squashed together in near darkness down both sides of the vessel, ventilated only by simple scuttle holes cut through the hull, as well as the main hatch, when it wasn't closed to keep out waves. The straw mattresses were damp where water dripped – and occasionally cascaded – down through loose areas of caulking between the planks of the deck. Her little cabin seemed like a stateroom by contrast.

The passengers told her they mostly survived on basic food such as salted meat, rice and ship's biscuits, with plum pudding twice a week, supplemented by any stores they had brought onboard themselves. The only vegetables were dried peas and pickled cabbage. No wonder Mr Penrose needed such large quantities of Epsom salts and castor oil. Despite these hardships, they seemed a cheerful group, well organised and determined to make the best of it. She had not realised there were so many children on the ship, including several infants. A couple of the mothers looked no more than children themselves.

Elisabeth sat at the long table running down the centre of the cabin, with the book propped up against the wall of its central cavity, which held assorted tins, pots, jugs and plates. Oliver Twist's experiences in the workhouse were surely no grimmer than this. The lurching of the vessel and the wildly swinging lamp, which gave off only a feeble and jaundiced light, made it impossible to focus on the words. Instead, she amused the children by teaching them a song in French. They thought it hilariously improbable that there were places in the world where people did not speak English.

Before she left, she was approached by a painfully thin woman dressed in a much-mended smock. She realised it was the mother of Ned Bell, the monkey-boy who had reminded her of her own nephew.

Strong, calloused fingers reached out to pat her hand. 'We've heard talk that the devil of a Frenchman is an enemy of yours. I want you to know that my oldest sons, Tom and Jack, are keeping a close eye on him in the single men's quarters. An' young Ned, my youngest, who has a nose like a bloodhound for sniffin' out trouble.' On hearing his name, little Ned flipped off the top bunk and landed on his feet beside her. Elisabeth started, but his mother carried on as if nothing had happened. 'One more peep outta' Frenchie and my lads'll feed him to the fishes.'

The crowd gathered around her murmured their support, including one girl who looked no more than seventeen and appeared ready to give birth at any minute. A boy who looked about the same age had his arm around her shoulders.

'Thank you for your concern. But, please, do tell your lads to keep well away from him, for he will be armed. He's a trained soldier and as ruthless as they come.'

'Tom and Jack know what they're about. They made sure the Frenchie were searched.'

Elisabeth was pretty sure that Cloutier would have a weapon hidden somewhere, but she let it go. 'Are you the family of the missing fruit-picker from Kent?'

'Yes, ma'am. Harriet Bell is my name, and these folks are the families of myself, my sister Agnes Trimble and my brother-in-law John Bell. And we don't believe a word of his lies 'bout buying our Jim's ticket. He's come to harm, I've no doubt of it.'

'I'm very sorry for it. I do hope your boy is all right. Perhaps he will come out on a later ship and join you in Wellington? What are your plans when you arrive?'

'Working on an orchard, if we're lucky, but we can turn our hand to any type of farming or labouring or learn a new trade if we have to. Our Tom is a dab hand at carpentry and he's been teaching the others. When we were put out of work back home, we'd have done anything, but there were no work to be had. The landowner simply tossed us out of our cottages, ploughed over our gardens and left us to starve. We had no choice but to take the emigration offer.'

'It's scandalous that such ruthless behaviour is allowed. I pray you have a better situation in New Zealand. I can certainly understand your desire to work the land, as I grew up in an orchard too. Can there be anything better in the world than to bite into the first apple of the season on a late summer's day?'

'No, ma'am. My mouth is watering just thinkin' about it. I haven't had a taste of fruit since we left Kent.'

'Then I will try to smuggle you some apples, because I could not bear to be without.'

'Don't you go getting into trouble for our sake. It's our Tess that is the most desperate for an apple. You know how it is when you're with child – always craving something. All I wanted when I had Tess was peaches – it fair killed me that it wasn't the right season.'

'Then I will be certain to bring some. Tess, you look like you're due very soon. I hope you have seen the doctor?'

Tess looked at her as if she had suggested having all her teeth pulled out by a blacksmith. 'Don't be trusting no doctor, it's a waste of hard-earned money. Me mam can see to the birth.'

'Mr Penrose is a good doctor and his service is free. He'd be able to see you right.'

Tess shook her head vigorously, and her young husband moved forward protectively.

'Well, only if you need him, then. Goodbye for now.' Elisabeth climbed up the steep stairs and into the wonderful freshness of the open air. She purged the fetid air from her lungs with relief, until the second mate spotted her and escorted her back down the deck.

The visit had given her a lot to think about, not least the twinge of envy she felt at seeing the Bell's tight-knit extended family with their simple dream of a better life in the New Zealand countryside. Memories of her own childhood flooded back. A sea of blossoms in the springtime, her nephew swinging like a monkey from the apple tree, her mother's succulent *tarte tatin* hot from the oven, the joy in her father's eyes when he unveiled the first strawberries of the season and popped one in his wife's mouth. And the sweet, sticky juice of a ripe peach dripping down her chin. She got quite a start when she was jolted out of her daydream and found herself being tossed about on a bucking ship.

The rest of the day passed as usual, except for the stir caused by young Francis Maynard, when he was overheard telling another boy that he had seen Mr Knight behind the cooking shelter with a young woman, making a funny grunting sound. The single women were supposed to be kept under tight control by the matron, but several had taken to parading the quarterdeck in low-cut dresses, 'flaunting themselves like street-walkers', as Lady Maynard had put it irately to the captain. Elisabeth had heard that some of the girls had found a way to sneak out at night to meet men in the darker corners of the deck, which tallied with what Francis reported.

Mr Knight was taken before the captain and reprimanded again. Mr Strickland vowed to end his employment if there were any more incidents. The girl was found and whipped by the matron. And so, the social order prevailed.

31 August 1841

Elisabeth rose before dawn and went up to observe her ritual viewing of the sunrise. Mr Enys was at the helm. He seemed to share her enjoyment of early mornings, unlike the captain, who barked at anyone who disturbed him before breakfast. She raised her hand in salute and received a gap-toothed grin in reply.

As they moved south, it was becoming noticeably warmer. The woollen cloak she had shivered in for the first few days was now loosely resting around her shoulders, despite the brisk wind. Other things were changing too – the sunsets were ever more glorious, but passed more quickly, and many of the seabirds were new to her.

This morning, she watched in delight as a group of porpoises cavorted in the wake. The sight of their playfulness crowded out any grim thoughts. That's the way to live, she thought, leaping for the sheer joy of it.

'Magnificent, aren't they?'

The voice was close, but there was no one to be seen, besides Enys, who had his back to her. She looked down and saw a hand wave from inside the light skiff, which was tied vertically to the side rail. She had seen them use it only twice so far – once to take the pilot back to his boat and once to row between ships to exchange news during a calm spell. The skiff looked as if was hard against the rail, but by leaning over the side, she could see that there was a small gap and a space inside.

Mr Penrose sat with his back to the floor of the boat and his legs dangling over the side of the ship. A perfectly sheltered and private refuge. The skin around his eye was still puffy, but he seemed cheerful.

She leaned on the rail next to the skiff. 'Looks like a grand spot to escape from the madmen on this vessel.'

He crawled out, cradling a book in one hand. 'I need a quiet spot to sketch or I'd go mad too.'

'I've been hoping to see you. Mrs Strickland asked me to thank you for the miracle cure of her daughter, Charlotte. She compared your skills favourably with London's best surgeons.'

'Not bad for an ill-trained village quack, eh?'

'Exactly what I said to her.'

'Brave of you.'

'I hate the hypocrisy of them. Lady Maynard slighting you when her own husband is so obviously a drunken fool. You are a thousand times more worthy than he will ever be.'

'That's kind of you to say, Mrs Godwin. I try not to concern myself with what they think. Especially not on a lovely day like this.'

She scanned the sea for more fins curving through the waves, wishing that she had his ability to shrug off spiteful comments. 'A shame the porpoises have gone. They seem so playful and carefree.'

'Perhaps you would like to see the sketch I made of them?'

'I would love to see it, if you wouldn't mind.' She took the offered sketchbook, open to a half-finished sketch of porpoises. 'Wonderful. You've captured their exuberance perfectly. May I look at the rest?'

She sat down in the shelter of the boat and leafed through the sketchbook, taking her time to look closely at each of the pencil drawings. They were so realistic, they seemed to pop off the page. His sketch of the scene at the docks took her back to that day instantly, reliving the sounds and smells as well as the sights. The rest of the journey was laid out in sequence – the seasickness, the dancing, the funeral, the wildlife and the sea itself in all its guises.

She was startled to see a sketch of herself, reading to the children, with Mrs Robertshaw beaming like a proud mother behind her. The only pictures of herself she had ever seen were a couple of formal portraits, so it seemed odd to see the scene as it happened, as if she was a bystander looking on. She smiled to see the little children hopping about with excitement.

Elisabeth flipped another page and gasped. This was the only picture he had done using pastels, or rather, mainly pencil enhanced with swirls of colour. She was standing at the rails, the sunrise making her hair glow gold. She was looking up, surrounded by rays of light, like an angel ready to ascend to heaven.

'You are not only an incredible artist, but also a poet. I am sure I never looked quite so angelic in real life.'

'On the contrary. I draw only what I see.'

'You flatter me, Mr Penrose. But truly, all of your drawings are wonderful. Have you never considered making a living as an artist?'

'No. I only ever wanted to be a doctor. My brothers worked down the tin mines. I did too as a young lad, but I hated being trapped in the dark so deep underground, reliant on pumps to keep the water level down.'

'Terrifying.' She shuddered at the very thought of it. She'd been trapped in the cellar once as a child and still had nightmares about it. 'How did you become a ship's surgeon?'

'Mining's a hard business. The lucky ones survive long enough to die of clogged lungs in middle-age.' He paused, subconsciously rubbing the scars on his hands. 'My father and brothers were not so lucky. They died in a cave-in.'

'You were there.'

'I tried to dig them out, but it was no use. My mother died of a broken heart. The mine closed, and I had no family left to hold me there, so I decided to see a bit of the world beyond the valley I was born in.'

'I'm so sorry, Mr Penrose. What a terrible tragedy to lose your whole family at once.' That too was something she could empathise with, although she could only imagine how awful it must have been to be at the site of the disaster and not be able to do anything apart from dig through rubble.

'I rarely tell people, but I knew you would understand.'

Elisabeth reached out a gloved hand to touch his scarred hand. 'Someone once told me it is better to talk about an ordeal, rather than bottle up the pain. Good advice, I think.'

He smiled. 'I find it a lot easier to give advice than to take it. I think myself lucky in one way. If it hadn't been for my mother teaching me about herbs and healing, and the clergyman's wife setting up a local school, I'd have been down that mine shaft too. Learned most of what I needed from books thanks to a kindly teacher who shared his library. The mine owners weren't too fussy about formal qualifications if they could get any sort of doctor on the cheap.'

'Which explains your support of Mrs Robertshaw's plan?'

'Indeed. When I see you reading to those children, I know it's their best chance to move ahead in the world, out of poverty.'

'I don't have healing skills like you and Anne. Reading is a small thing by comparison.'

He looked off into the distance, scanning the empty seascape with an artist's eye. 'It seems as if everyone on board this ship has made a brave choice to sail away from everything they know, so they can have a chance for a fresh start with better opportunities. It's good to know we can help each other, each in their own way.'

She raised an eyebrow. 'And you think *Oliver Twist* might help them?'

With a laugh, he said, 'You may not realise it, but it is all the children talk about. I had to patch up two lads yesterday after a fight over whose turn it was to be the Artful Dodger.'

'I sincerely hope they will not turn into a gang of fighters and pickpockets. Not quite the moral of the story I was hoping to instil.'

'Or that they should hope for a rich relative to save them?'

'Which is about as likely as a beanstalk taking them to a magical land filled with gold.'

His laughter had a rich deep tone, which reminded her of the mate's rolling Rs. 'May I ask where you come from? You and the chief mate occasionally speak together in a language I've never heard before.'

'We're both from Cornwall. The Cornish language has all but died out, but some of the small fishing villages in the west still keep up the tradition. My wife's family is one of them, so I've picked up enough to get by. Mr Enys, who is my wife's cousin, knows far more than me. It was Enys who got me the ship surgeon's position in truth, not that letter.'

'What does your wife think about you going to the far side of the world for months at a time?'

'I expect she'd have been astounded. She died in childbirth four years and seven months ago.'

'I'm so sorry, Mr Penrose. A dreadful tragedy.' Elisabeth watched him turn away from her and knew that feeling of looking silently inward. 'What was she like? If you don't mind talking about her.'

He looked up again, with a faint smile on his lips. 'Kind, clever, cheerful, hard-working, a wonderful person in so many ways. I miss evenings the most, relaxing together by the fire after a busy day. And the flowers. She always had our little garden overflowing with flowers.'

Elisabeth sighed. When she thought of John, it was often a vision of the two of them cuddled up together in front of a fire. She hoped that John would have used similar words to describe her, rather than the more usual flatteries about beauty and accomplishments. 'My husband was just the same, except that he didn't know a daffodil from a violet. Why is it always the good ones who are taken too soon?'

'Few people are lucky enough to experience such happiness. Perhaps it is too much to ask to be so happy forever?'

As a philosophy, it did not reflect well on the all-embracing benevolence of the Almighty, but it gave her some comfort, nevertheless. It was certainly true that she would rather have had eleven wonderful years with John Godwin than a lifetime with a lesser man.

'Mrs Godwin, could I ask you to keep it to yourself? I may have given the impression to some passengers that I am still married. There are some fearsome mothers on board who seem to think their daughter would make a perfect doctor's wife. And those single girls! I have to be married in self-defence, although even that scarcely keeps them at bay.'

She couldn't help but laugh at the thought of him being chased around the deck by a pack of girls. 'Don't worry, I'll keep your secret.' Elisabeth reluctantly closed the sketchbook and handed it back. 'Thank you for sharing this with me. And now I really must go, as I am keeping you from your only leisure of the day with my chatter.'

The doctor got to his feet. 'Not at all. It was delightful to talk to you, as always. Do let me know if you have any further issues.'

'Medical or madmen?'

He grinned. 'I am equipped with both medicines and fists. They are at your disposal.'

Slander

1 September 1841

The weather was much warmer now, and the sea seemed a brighter blue. Elisabeth had been honoured with a glimpse of Madeira through the captain's prized telescope – their first sighting of land for many days. The captain was in a good mood and delighted with their rapid progress. He had shed his gruffness and was even cajoled into taking a minor role in the play.

The crew had rigged an awning over the poop deck for shade, while the main deck was covered in drying mattresses, adding the smell of damp straw to the humid air. Above the mattresses, rows of washing hung from every available line, taking advantage of the sun. The sailors had given up shouting at passengers for taking over their ropes and frustrating their work. After unceremoniously yanking the washing off the essential rigging, the two sides reached a truce.

Elisabeth and Anne stood at the stern, making the most of the breeze and chatting about the play. Anne seemed very taken by the acting abilities of Mr Knight, the romantic hero of the piece.

Victoria Maynard skipped over to them, wearing a pretty dress stained with tar and trailing a red ribbon, which ought to have been restraining her hair. Without pausing for breath, she resumed her precocious torrent of questions – how does a telescope work, why could they not stop at the island, why is it hotter here than at home, how does the captain know which way to go, why can birds fly when people cannot?

They were more than happy to answer her questions as best they could, if only to give the Maynard's nanny a little time to herself. Anne tried to explain how birds fly, which involved much flapping of arms and drifting of lightweight handkerchiefs on the breeze, accompanied by giggling from Victoria and chuckles from the onlookers.

Meanwhile, Elisabeth attempted to stop Victoria's brother, Francis, from tormenting the hens in their coops with the end of his slingshot. She had already told him off twice for pinging stones at the steerage boys. Each time, he had simply stared at her with surprise and indignation.

She noticed the nanny was sitting in the shade with one of Victoria's picture books, her finger slowly moving along the line of words as she mouthed the few she knew. 'You would be welcome to join Mrs Robertshaw's classes, Janie.'

'Oh no, ma'am, 'er ladyship would not want that. I has my duties to attend to.'

Francis poked his head over the row of crates they were leaning on. 'Mother says she's too stupid to learn anything.'

Elisabeth turned to tell him off, but he had already dashed away to join a boisterous game with the other lads. 'That boy must be a handful. Don't you take any notice of him, anyone can learn to read.'

'Not the likes o' me.' She got to her feet, with a furtive look around to see who else had noticed her loitering. 'Pardon me, ma'am, or I'll be late to do her ladyship's hair.'

Dinner that day was soup, roast mutton, plum pudding, cheese and fruit, accompanied by wine and port. Most of the passengers drank little, if any, but Sir Julius and Mr Knight indulged in several glasses despite the early hour. Elisabeth was pleased to see Mr Penrose engrossed in conversation with Mr Templeton. The two of them had become firm friends since the funeral, as had Anne and Charlotte.

Lady Maynard leaned across the table, her voice a piercing whisper, 'Mrs Godwin, I do ask that you not put ideas into the maid's head about bettering herself. She is not a clever girl, so encouraging her to read is as futile as it is inappropriate.'

Elisabeth reached for an apple, controlling her annoyance by focussing on the tight coils of apple-skin twisting off her knife. Her face was expressionless as she turned to Lady Maynard. 'My apologies, Lady Maynard. I assure you I only had your best interests at heart. The girl seems adept as a nanny and might be of even more value to you if she could read, as you do not have a governess.'

Sir Julius swung his arm in a wild arc, knocking over his glass of wine, before remarking in an unnecessarily loud voice, 'The damned governess refused to come, disloyal little wench.'

Lady Maynard gave him a look that would have felled a battle-horse. 'Mrs Godwin, you appear to have few prospects. Perhaps you would like to be employed as a governess.'

A ripple of shock went around the table. Everyone was used to Lady Maynard's wasp-sting tongue by now, but this was beyond the pale.

Mrs Robertshaw was the first to react. 'Really, Lady M, Mrs Godwin is a remarkably intelligent woman, but far too much of a lady to take employment as a governess.'

Lady Maynard raised her eyebrows. 'Is that so? I heard she is the daughter of a French gardener and a servant girl, and lately the widow of a London merchant.'

Anne could take it no longer. She rose from the table, throwing her napkin down, turning a steely glare on Lady Maynard. 'How dare you call my brother a merchant as if he was a barrow-boy? The Godwin family business is a successful enterprise with many ships transporting goods around the world. Indeed, my father received a commendation for service to king and country during the Napoleonic Wars. As for Elisabeth, she is most certainly a lady, as you can see, whose parents owned an estate in France, with an extensive orchard, dairy, and much besides.'

Elisabeth put a restraining hand on Anne's arm, smiling around the tableful of mortified faces. 'I thank you, Lady Maynard, for your compliment on my educational accomplishments, but I do not wish to be a governess. And now I think it is time to take some air.'

Mrs Robertshaw had the last word on the matter. 'One might equally call you a farmer's wife, Lady Maynard, since your family owns land.'

Anne was rigid with anger, but Elisabeth smothered a laugh as they hurried out the door. She did not hear Lady Maynard's reply, but she did hear a round of chuckles and a loud snort of laughter from the captain. Mrs Robertshaw caught up, a little out of breath and scarlet of face, as they made their first turn of the poop deck.

'Really, that woman is impossible. I hope you are not too aggrieved, my dear.'

Elisabeth laughed. 'Goodness no. There was a grain of truth in what she said. There was a time when I would have been grateful for a position as a governess.'

'Your restraint does you credit. Everyone is appalled and entirely on your side.'

'If Lady Maynard was the worst problem in my life, I should think myself lucky indeed. Although I do feel she needs a subtle reminder that we may not be quite as lowly as pond scum. Not that it matters what she thinks.'

'Well, I shall look forward to that with bells on.'

'Then be sure to attend the dance tonight. And thank you, Mrs Robertshaw, for your support.'

'Please call me Grace, as I rather think we shall become firm friends on this voyage.'

'I would be delighted. Thank you, Grace. You must call us Anne and Elisabeth.'

'You mustn't be upset by baseless gossip. Honestly, I can't imagine where it all comes from. I had to reprimand a girl who was telling the others a grand tale about how you were a French princess with a whole chest full of gold and jewels. She was probably trying to salvage her reputation after being caught with Mr Knight. Outrageous hussy.'

Elisabeth rolled her eyes and let out a sigh. 'Well, perhaps better to be thought a rich princess than a thieving peasant girl, if one had to choose between equally ridiculous fantasies. I hope your husband will not be upset that you have ruffled the feathers of the wealthy colonists.'

Grace Robertshaw drew herself up to her full height of five feet, shoulders squaring off above her ample bosom. 'I should think not. My Matthew is proud to be on the side of justice.' With a small sigh, she added, 'Although, of course, we are reliant on benefactors to support his good work. It may be un-Christian of me, but I suspect that charity is not one of the virtues espoused by Lady Maynard. I hope she does not undermine our efforts in the new colony.'

Elisabeth agreed but felt obliged to say a word in mitigation. 'Mr Thomas told me that Sir Julius is a baronet with no estate, after his father drank and gambled the family inheritance away. Despite the debts, he managed to find enough money to settle a modest pension on the remaining brother and sister, as well as to fund their New Zealand Company land purchase. If it's true, then Lady Maynard probably has good cause to be sparing with her charity and ill-tempered on occasion.'

'Can't say it surprises me. I will pray for them and seek atonement for my own uncharitable words to her,' Grace said, with a twinkle in her eye that rather offset the piety of her words. 'Your Mr Thomas seems well informed.'

'Please don't tell anyone, but I gather he has a contact in the New Zealand Company. It seems they do a little discreet checking of emigrants before departure to ensure no undesirables make it on board.'

Anne had been gazing out to sea, a tight frown bunching under her bonnet. 'I wonder how Lady Maynard knew about your background, Elisabeth?'

'Indeed,' said Grace Robertshaw, 'your English is so perfect that I had not realised you were born in France.'

'I learned English as a child and lived in London for over ten years after I left France. But the real question must be, as Anne said, who else knew that.' Elisabeth was fairly sure that only one person on this vessel, besides Anne and the doctor, was aware of her family history. 'I need to find out if Sir Julius has been talking to that Frenchman in steerage. But now, Anne and I must begin preparations for our little surprise.'

Anne and Elisabeth did not appear for supper, causing some consternation amongst the assembly. Mr Amberley, Mr Knight, the Reverend Robertshaw, and Mr Thomas each came to their door to check on them. The first three were told all was well and to make sure to be at the dance. Only Thomas was let in and he came out some five minutes later with a grin that transformed his normally neutral facade.

The air crackled with a sense of anticipation later that evening as the music started for a formal dance. The 'orchestra' was no more than a couple of fiddles and a flute, but the waxing moon and myriad stars lent a sense of ethereal drama. The first waltz had just finished when Elisabeth and Anne appeared. Men, women and children stopped as one and turned to gape, as they glided arm-in-arm onto the poop. Grace Robertshaw clapped her hands together in delight.

Elisabeth was wearing her favourite midnight-blue silk gown, cut across the shoulder, with a fitted bodice nipped into a V at the waist, widening to a bell-shaped skirt. John had insisted on having it made for her, despite the extravagance, as it was a perfect match to the sapphire and diamond necklace he had given her as a wedding gift, which she was wearing tonight. Her hair was swept back into an elaborate knot, except for a few loose curls at the side. Anne was similarly resplendent in emerald silk, with her mother's emerald and diamond necklace framing her slender neck. None gaped quite so wide as Lady Maynard, who had dressed modestly that evening in contrition.

All the gentlemen crowded forward to offer their hand for the next dance, apart from Mr Penrose, who slipped away into the shadows soon after their arrival, and Mr Gilbert, who did not care for frivolous entertainment. The quickest was Mr Amberley, who swooped in to claim Elisabeth, and Mr Knight, who seized Anne's hand.

'I rather think you have scored a knockout punch, Mrs Godwin,' Amberley whispered, as he swept Elisabeth around the deck. 'Any man would count himself fortunate to have you by his side.' He smiled down at her as he twirled her, before drawing her in again with a firm hand on her back.

2 September, 1841

Elisabeth was so worn out from the late night that she scarcely felt like rising from her bed, although the sun was well off the horizon. Anne was still sound asleep. She had looked so lovely last night, especially when her dark hair came unpinned and curled down over her emerald gown as she twirled in the moonlight.

What fun they had had. Both danced with all the gentlemen at least twice and Elisabeth danced four times with the persistent Mr Amberley. It was an inappropriate display from a widow still in mourning, but she felt sure that her husband would have been looking down from heaven with a smile on his face at seeing her wearing the blue gown and sapphires again. He had never been a man to wallow in misery.

Nor had he been a man to hold grudges, which reminded her that she needed to talk to Lady Maynard. Having made her point, it was time to mend fences. In the quiet period before dinner, Elisabeth found Lady Maynard alone in the saloon cabin. Her eyes were red-rimmed, although she was dressed as impeccably as always, with not a spaniel-curl out of place. Elisabeth settled herself into a chair close to hand.

'Lady Maynard, I must apologise for my behaviour.'

Her ladyship held up a gloved hand. 'No, Mrs Godwin, it is I who must apologise. My outburst at dinner was unpardonable and I see now that my information was completely in error. I was vexed by the loss of my diamond earrings, which are a family heirloom, but that is a poor excuse for acting like a shrew.'

'I do hope the earrings have only been misplaced. Your loss makes me feel all the worse for so vainly flaunting my own jewels last night. May we call a truce and be friends? It is too long a journey to hold resentments.' She paused until she saw a tentative nod of assent. 'If I might ask, who told you of my past?'

Lady Maynard had the grace to blush. 'I'm afraid my husband was talking to one of the steerage passengers. He claims to be a French gentleman with wealthy connections and indicated that you were a subversive and a thief. I see now that it was foolish to believe such a man. No doubt he had drunk a great deal and was making up tall tales. After all, why would a gentleman lower himself to steerage class?'

'It's true that there is a history between him and my family, but I assure you that my family was completely loyal to the legitimate king and suffered terribly for it.'

'Then I am truly sorry, my dear. I know a little of how the loyal French suffered.' She dabbed at her eyes with a silk handkerchief. 'Forgive me for my emotion. My mother knew the Princesse de Lamballe when she was in London and was much taken with her refinement and sweetness. Her slaughter by the rabble in so vile a manner during the peasant's revolt upset us all greatly. I cannot abide any talk of bettering the lower classes, after what happened in France.'

'England has taken a much better path. I hope that education and reform will achieve improved conditions for the poor without resorting to the appalling bloodshed we endured in France. From what I hear, the country we are going to espouses the ideals of greater equality, so perhaps we must get used to it.'

'I certainly hope that is not so. England has always been the most successful nation in the world because of the superiority of the aristocracy and the honourable service of the military. The common man is much better off working under a benevolent landlord without being given expectations of unnecessary education or advancement.'

It took all of Elisabeth's considerable willpower not to comment or roll her eyes, which would have undone her truce-making. 'Perhaps we can agree to disagree on that, Lady Maynard.'

'Perhaps. I only hope that Sir Julius can find a way to better himself, for there is no option to return home.'

'He may find some value in talking to the other colonists. Mr Templeton and Mr Amberley seem like fine young men, with grand plans and experience of estate management.'

'I fear Sir Julius is more one for the city than the country. Now, I believe I will retire for a nap. This heat is most aggravating.'

3 September, 1841

The Reverend Robertshaw emphasised the evils of drink and gambling in his daily service and encouraged everyone to look within themselves for ways to improve the lot of their fellow man. He finished with a reminder that the devil finds work for idle hands.

Despite the rousing sermon, Elisabeth found her mind wandering back to what Lady Maynard had said, although she could not pin down what was troubling her. Halfway through the second hymn, she finally had it. Lady Maynard had mentioned she was missing her diamond earrings. Elisabeth realised she had not seen her own necklace since she had left it on the small shelf above her bed, having been too tired to put it away after the dance. She had locked the door when they went to breakfast the following morning and she had been delayed in getting back to the cabin. She had assumed that Anne had put the necklace away in the jewellery box but had forgotten to check. As they returned to their cabin, she asked Anne when she had last seen it.

'Before breakfast, I think,' Anne replied. 'No, wait, I think it was there when I got back from breakfast before you, because I was thinking it needed to be secured. But Charlotte Strickland had just cut her hand and needed a bandage. Why?'

'Unfortunately, it's missing. It was foolish of me to leave it out.'

Anne's her hand went to her mouth. 'Oh, Elisabeth, I'm so sorry. I might have left the door open when I rushed off to help Charlotte. I didn't think – it was only next door, and I was only gone a few minutes, as the cut was a minor.'

'Don't worry, I'm sure I'll find it.' But she had to work hard to stay cheerful. The necklace wasn't just a piece of jewellery, it was a reminder of John's love.

She searched down the side of her bed, through her bedding, and in the drawers below, but could not find it, while Anne did the same on her side of the cabin.

'I would hate to think somebody stole it,' Anne said.

'Did you happen to see anyone pass the door while you were with Charlotte?'

'Mr Strickland was having an argument with someone and I remember a door slamming, but I was focussed on seeing to the cut and I don't really recall who went past. At least two people, I think, but several more after word went around that Charlotte was hurt. You know how it is on the ship – rumour swirls like a ripple building up to wave, gathering power as it goes.'

'The problem is, almost anyone could have taken it, although I suppose the most likely suspects are those in the cabins around us.'

The cabins in their area were laid out in a loop around the central cuddy, from the captain's and surgeon's cabins on the starboard side, to the Maynards' cabin and Mr Strickland's office at the stern, then Charlotte and her mother, and finally their own, next to the pantry, on the port side.

'We know that Sir Julius and Mr Knight are in need of money and have a reckless streak, but I cannot believe that any of the gentleman would stoop to theft. Mr Strickland is certainly above suspicion and Mr Gilbert can scarcely muster the courage to look one in the eye, so hardly seemed a likely jewel thief.'

'Elisabeth, are you, of all people, underestimating the fairer sex by assuming it was a man?'

'Oh! You're so right. And we needn't look far to find a woman who dislikes me and needs money.'

'Lady Maynard?'

'Well, I can't see Mrs Strickland lowering herself to theft, unless she is a secret kleptomaniac. But, of course, we cannot really rule anyone out unless they were elsewhere at the time. Any of the cabin passengers could have come past. Or that little devil, Francis Maynard, might have taken it as a prank.'

'I expect if you report the necklace missing, the first to be suspected will be the steward and cabin boys, or some other crew member with an eye to embellishing his meagre wages.'

Elisabeth had little doubt that Anne was right that the crew would be blamed. 'I would hate to get anyone into trouble. Let's make a thorough search. I won't report it until we are sure the necklace has disappeared. Maybe not even then, as there is little chance of finding the culprit or the necklace on a ship with so many hiding places.'

They expanded their search to every nook and cranny in their cabin, but with no success. Thankfully, all her other treasures were safely hidden and lay undisturbed. She put a fragment of fine silk thread under the latch of her mahogany trunk, so she would know if anyone had returned to search the cabin for more valuables. She fervently wished she hadn't given in to pride by wearing the necklace, but it was too late now for regrets.

Despite the mate's assurance that the Frenchman was safely secured, Elisabeth felt the hairs of the back of her neck rising every time she left the cabin. The theft of the necklace could only mean that there was a second person on board with ill intentions. Perhaps Cloutier had an accomplice?

Heating Up

4 September 1841

The vessel was in a state of chaos. The persistent hot weather meant that the steerage passengers had hauled up their trunks from the hold to swap their wool clothes and bonnets for pale muslin and straw hats. Anne and Elisabeth looked on enviously, with fans at full flap, as they had brought no clothing suitable for hot weather.

Mr Forrester must have overheard them. 'Pardon me, ladies. Perhaps I could be of assistance? I have many fine fabrics in the hold, destined for my shop. Haberdashery too. If we can find a seamstress, you could have as many new clothes as you wished. I also have a wide range of other items – everything a colonist might need, from the best quality tools, to lovely crockery, to…'

The Maynard's nanny popped up at Elisabeth's elbow, interrupting what promised to be a long list of desirable merchandise, delivered with the panache of a showman. 'Beg pardon, ma'am. I know a seamstress.'

She darted off and reappeared shortly afterwards with a strapping young woman in a tartan dress, who held her head high and looked them in the eye. 'Miss Mary Jamieson at yer service, ma'am. Top seamstress with one o' the best dressmakers in London.'

'Mrs Elisabeth Godwin. Pleased to meet you. I'd have picked Scotland over London as your home.'

'Aye, yer right. From as far north as a lass can go. No more work up there, nor place to live, with the land being cleared of crofters. If it doesna' stop, there'll be none left.'

Elisabeth shook her head. 'Seems most of the people on this ship have been forced off the land or out of work in one way or another.'

'Aye, and they call that progress.'

'Well, I hope you might make a dress or two for me, as I'm roasting in this wool.'

'Aye, I'd be happy to have the work. I expect fair pay for good work, mind. I've my whole family on board, so we can work together to have it done quick as you like.'

Elisabeth and Anne were whisked off to their cabin, measured up, and a price negotiated. Mary promised the first dress by the next evening, as long as Mr Forrester could supply suitable fabric. By the time they came up to the deck again, that gentleman had crates arrayed on the deck and customers lining up for his muslins and fans. A born merchant. Mary Jamieson set herself up beside him and was soon doing a brisk business too.

Elisabeth chose a dove-grey cotton for her first dress, as a compromise between the coolness of white and the necessity of maintaining decorum during the mourning period. She was feeling exhausted after the heat and disorder of the decks, so she left Anne to make the rest of the decisions.

She was glad to find the Strickland ladies alone in the cuddy, fanning their faces and sipping tea. After a decade in England, Elisabeth had grown used to the constant cups of tea and had come to enjoy the ceremony of it. But, oh, what would she give for a good cup of thick French coffee?

She sat down next to Charlotte, who was vastly improved on her new diet. 'Charlotte, how lovely to see you looking so well. How is the cut on your hand?'

'Fine, thank you. Mother was only concerned because she had heard about tropical infections.'

'Wisely so. Anne says Mr Penrose is meticulous about keeping any cut clean and bandaged.' Elisabeth racked her brain for a way to mention Mr Strickland's argument, but Charlotte came to her rescue.

'Father was so cross, but it was hardly their fault that I stepped into the office as Mr Knight was moving his equipment.'

'Oh dear, did he hit you with that heavy tripod?'

'No, but he did bump into poor Mr Gilbert, who stumbled into me with a small knife he'd been using to sharpen pencils. Really, it must have been quite amusing to watch, like those bumbling clowns at the circus. It was only a minor scratch, which Anne kindly fixed it up in no time in my cabin. Not at all worth all the fuss it caused.'

'I expect your father was upset to see you hurt.'

Mrs Strickland chimed in. 'Edmund was furious. He reprimanded Mr Knight for his clumsiness and reminded him he was on a final warning for his behaviour. Instead of apologising, that wild young man stormed out and slammed the door. What a temper he has. He will find himself without a position if he does not mend his ways.'

'And Mr Gilbert?'

Mrs Strickland waved her hand dismissively. 'Edmund sent him to see if Charlotte was all right. He claims to have a weak heart, which cannot stand any excitement, but I rather think it is a spine he lacks, if you'll forgive my forthrightness. Edmund's own clerk refused to travel to New Zealand, so Gilbert was reassigned to the role by the government offices. I know little about him, but Edmund is very pleased with his work and says he is a meticulous record-keeper.'

Charlotte added, 'When I came back out with Anne, I found Mr Gilbert in the corridor, shaking like a man chilled to the bone, even though Father had not said a word against him. I suppose that stabbing your employer's daughter would be rather terrifying, poor thing. Whereas Mr Knight was up on deck, happily chatting about navigational instruments with the second mate, as if nothing had happened. What a nerve! He laughed and said he would apologise as soon as father had calmed down. Knight appears to think that his surveying skills will be in such demand that he will find other employment if necessary. He said straight out that he cared not at all if he was let go.'

'Did you see anyone else or hear anyone in our cabin?'

'Not that I can remember. Mr Templeton rushed down as soon as he heard I was hurt. He is such a kind man. He insisted I sit down and take some tea, which was very thoughtful.'

Elisabeth could see from the dreamy look in Charlotte's eye that she would get no more useful information, especially as the cast from the play was drifting in to continue their rehearsals. Elisabeth stayed to watch for a while, with a growing disquiet at the apparent intimacy between Anne and Mr Knight. She hoped it was merely that they were doing a remarkably fine job of acting the romantic pairing of the roles they were playing.

5 September 1841

Despite Elisabeth's attempts to keep the loss of the necklace a secret, rumour had spread of its disappearance just days after the loss of Lady Maynard's diamond earrings.

A torrent of angry voices interrupted their breakfast. Lady Maynard stalked into the cuddy, holding the cabin boy by one ear. 'Steward, I want this boy flogged until he tells us where he has hidden everything he has stolen.'

Thomas maintained his bland expression, apart from a slight flaring of his nostrils. 'What crime has he committed, your ladyship?'

She towered over the boy like a bird of prey clutching a small rodent. 'He is a thief. I found him in my cabin, with this hanging out from under his shirt.' She held up a white silk handkerchief, which was knotted around a cluster of objects.

'Where did you get this handkerchief, lad?' Thomas undid the knot, revealing a few ha'penny coins, a small locket, a thimble, and a few round stones.

'Please, sir, it were given me. I didn't steal nothing. The locket were from me mam before she died.'

Lady Maynard yanked his ear higher. 'Liar. Who would give you a lady's handkerchief?'

Charlotte stepped forward. 'I did, Lady Maynard. I used it to mop the blood when I cut my hand. The handkerchief was ruined, so I told Johnny he could keep it if he cleaned it. The coins are from me too, as I've tipped him a copper or two for his services. He's a good lad.'

Lady Maynard was not to be defeated. She glared at Grace and Elisabeth. 'I blame you. You are corrupting the children's morals with that outrageous story about pickpockets and God knows what other sinners.' With that, she swept from the room.

Elisabeth thought it just as well her ladyship hadn't seen the guilty look that flashed across Johnny's face. She had caught him only yesterday practicing pickpocketing with a group of laughing lads. Just for a lark, they swore. He caught her eye and looked down again. Hopefully, a lesson learnt – for all of them.

They kept to their cabin in the heat of the day, with the porthole open wide to catch the light breeze. Shouts of laughter brought them back on deck to witness the spectacle of flying fish. These marvellous little creatures really did seem to fly like birds, but with fins, not wings. Most of the little silver fish flashed by out to sea, but a score or more landed on the deck or in the washing. One landed right inside freshly hung drawers, creating mayhem as the owner attempted to bat the poor thing out, accompanied by a great deal of shrieking. The children, predictably, were rolling on the decks with laughter or chasing after the strange creatures as they flapped about. The boys gathered them up to examine them before taking them to the cook. Much easier than fishing with a line.

Elisabeth noticed the doctor furiously sketching and went to stand behind him to watch the scene unfold as if by magic. The expression on the woman's face was so comical she let out an unladylike snort of laughter, causing him to glance sharply at her.

'Sorry, doc. I didn't mean to disturb you.'

'Not at all. It's a pleasure to hear you laugh.'

'My mother always despaired of me. Acting like a lady does not come easy.'

'I must admit, I am struggling to reconcile the fashionably dressed lady who wears exquisite jewellery with the clever linguist and teacher, who grew up in the country milking cows.'

Elisabeth sighed. 'I don't know that you'd believe me if I explained it. Nothing about my life has been normal. Sometimes I feel like my family has been tossed about between two worlds – the wealthy and the mundane – never able to settle in either. That's the reason my mother insisted on teaching us to speak perfect English and German, so we could blend in anywhere. Just as well as it turned out.'

'Your mother did an excellent job. Nobody would think you out of place, no matter how grand the occasion. Whereas my parents would be astonished to see me dining at the same table as lords and ladies, being not at all in the same class. I forgot that distinction when I agreed Anne could assist me, for which I apologise.'

Elisabeth weighed her words, as she did not want to embarrass him by saying outright that she would approve if he and Anne courted, if that was what they wished. Indeed, she would be relieved if Anne was removed from the influence of Mr Knight. 'The Godwins were a fine family who prospered through hard work, exactly as you have. They would have been happy to see Anne assisting you and indeed would be honoured to count you in their acquaintance, as do I.'

'Your sister-in-law is such a strong character that I fear she is unlikely to heed my orders, whatever I say. I hope she marries a man with political aspirations, for she would stand beside him and change the world very much for the better. Mr Amberley might do – he is wealthy, charming and amenable. Anne would be the making of him.'

At that, Elisabeth admitted defeat in her campaign to bring Anne and the doctor together. Really, she was no better than Anne's brother at matchmaking, albeit with far more concern for Anne's happiness. She shook her head at her foolishness and tried to ignore the spark of relief she felt. The doctor must have seen her gesture and misinterpreted it.

'Mrs Godwin, I realise I have been terribly indiscreet. I do apologise. I quite forget myself when I am talking to you.'

'There is nothing to apologise for. Honestly, I am very grateful to have someone I can talk to so openly. I'll leave you to finish your drawing, before all the fish have flown away.'

After supper, they sat down to cards. Anne had become an enthusiastic bridge player, partnering Mr Amberley or Mr Knight against Mr Templeton and Charlotte Strickland. Elisabeth played with the Robertshaws and Mr Forrester until they retired early for the night. Mr Strickland was smoking one of his cigars again and the cuddy had become unbearable, so Elisabeth left the other players to their game and went up for fresh air.

The only lights on deck were a dim safety lantern in the main hatchway and another over the compass by the helm. The moon glowed high in the sky, transforming the ocean into a shimmering blanket of silver, with the huge wooden pulleys and web of ropes attached to the sides of the ship casting eerie shadows in the dim light.

An odd glow drew her to the stern. She was so entranced by the unusual twinkling green streamers of light in the ship's wake that she did not hear the man approach until he was right beside her.

'Mrs Godwin.'

'Mr Penrose, you gave me a such as start. You must have padding on the soles of your boots. Look at these odd lights, like clouds of stars in our wake.'

'That must be phosphorescence. Enys told me to look out for it, but he never said how extraordinarily beautiful it was.' After a couple of minutes of silent contemplation, he added, 'I thought we had agreed you would not be out alone, Mrs Godwin.'

'I had thought myself safe since the Frenchman was put in chains. Although it seems we have more than one scoundrel aboard.'

'How so?'

'Lady Maynard has lost a pair of diamond earrings and my sapphire necklace has disappeared too.'

His head snapped around – his angular face made ghostly by the phosphorescent glow. 'I am disturbed to hear it. Is it quite certain they were stolen and not lost?'

'I fear so, though I cannot speak for Lady Maynard. I realise nothing can be done, as searching a vessel this size would be impossible. But I thought I had better warn you that there is a thief amongst us.'

'Was the necklace valuable?'

'Yes, but the value to me was more sentimental, as it was a wedding gift from my husband. I cannot believe I was foolish enough to leave it insecure. My brain seems to have turned into porridge since I found out about the baby.'

'I'm afraid I must take some of the blame for your loss.'

'How can that be so?'

'I made enquiries after Lady Maynard's outburst at dinner. I figured that Victor Smith, or Victor Cloutier, or whoever he really is, must have been the source of her slander, but I wondered how Lady Maynard came to know.'

'I can answer that. Amberley said Sir Julius Maynard had been gambling with Cloutier. His slanted version of events thus reached Lady Maynard, just when she was cross with me. A not uncommon state of affairs.'

'You're right, but there is more to tell. I found out more details from a couple of steerage passengers who have been keeping an eye on Cloutier for me.'

'Spies! What a clever idea. Tom and Jack Bell perhaps?'

'You're very well informed. It seems both Maynard and Knight had been in the habit of visiting the foredeck for late-night gambling with the Frenchman and another steerage passenger. Several groups of men gamble on the decks at night, but none with such high stakes as their group.'

'They must be mad. Anyone with eyes can see that Cloutier is a dangerous man.'

'And an expert cheat, by the sound of it. Maynard had a bad run at cards several nights ago and ran up a large debt. He was able to pay part of it, but claimed the rest of his money was missing.'

'I'm sure that went down well with Cloutier.'

'Our informant said he was quite calm about it and gave Maynard a day to come up with the funds. And here's the important part. Cloutier offered to wipe the debt completely if Maynard agreed to search your cabin and bring him your jewellery box. Or to pay a large reward to anyone else who would steal it. I assume he was meaning Mr Knight.'

'Oh.' This was most unnerving. She had never considered the possibility that Cloutier might recruit an accomplice from amongst the cabin passengers. 'I suppose he could not get near me himself with your precautions in place.'

'I'm truly sorry, Mrs Godwin. This must be a shock for you. I should have warned you, but I didn't want to alarm you and I felt sure – wrongly, as it turns out – that you were safe from harm. I feel terrible.'

'You shouldn't. It was my own fault for wearing the necklace and failing to secure it.' She steadied herself against the rails and closed her eyes. 'It seems that no sooner is one enemy disabled than another two spring up in his place. What was their reaction to the offer of a reward for stealing my jewellery box?'

'Mr Knight made no reply. I gather he was rather distracted by the appearance of a young woman he had, er… become attached to, and he left soon after. Sir Julius was outraged and said he would do nothing of the kind. He said he would pay the debt the next day. So perhaps he is more of a gentleman than he appears.'

'I saw him on the deck, passing something to Cloutier after the funeral. Lady Maynard's earrings, perhaps?'

'Possibly. It would have to have been a colossal debt to repay with diamond earrings.'

'Well, I hope he learned his lesson.'

'I'm afraid not. On the night of the fight, Sir Julius was gambling again. Thought his luck would change no doubt, as his sort always does. By the end of the evening, he was desperate. He was stupid enough to accuse Cloutier of stealing from him and cheating at cards, which started the fight. The whole lot of them had had so much to drink, it just took that one spark to set off a major brawl. Maynard was lucky to escape with no harm done to himself, thanks to the intervention of the crew.'

'Thank you for telling me. I will take extra care. Do you think I should warn Anne? I would hate to alarm her unnecessarily.'

'Perhaps a reminder about locking doors and not being alone at night. But really, I can't believe Sir Julius or Mr Knight would stoop to outright theft, even if they are not perfect gentlemen. As for the rest of the passengers and crew, they hold you in such high regard that any act against you would be unthinkable.'

'I hope you're right. This voyage is certainly not dull. I pray we have seen the end of these incidents.'

'I fear not. There's been another theft as well, although it must have occurred as we loaded the vessel in London. Some rogue swapped the stores of lime juice for bottles of rum.'

'Lime juice? Is it necessary?'

'It is essential to prevent disease on long voyages without fresh fruit. We will have to make an unscheduled stop in Cape Verde in a few days to obtain some more. The captain is most put out at both the delay and the risk. He says he has no money for extra supplies, but I'm sure I can barter using the ridiculously large supply of spirits issued for medical use. I cannot belief they intended me to cure all ills with gin and brandy.'

They stood in the moonlight for some time, enjoying the relative silence of a sleeping ship running with the wind into the unknown. Despite the mayhem that seemed to swirl around her life, right at that moment, Elisabeth felt strangely at peace.

Trade Winds

6 September 1841

With a sigh of relief, Elisabeth slipped on her new gown over one light petticoat and a loosened corset. She packed away the heavy wool layers, feeling like an old skin had been shed in favour of a fresh new one. Thank goodness for Mary Jamieson, who had done an expert job in a short time. One of her younger brothers had even crafted a straw hat, which was just the thing for the intense sun of the tropics.

Elisabeth was not the only one feeling refreshed by lighter clothes. Everyone was taking pleasure in parading their new and retrieved clothes, pleased to have even a small change to routine. Some of the young men had become quite daring, shedding their jackets, and even their waistcoats and ties, and rolling up their sleeves. Not to be outdone, some of the young women were wearing light dresses with no petticoats at all and one girl even shed her shoes. The guardians of standards would no doubt take the matter up with the captain before the sun was over the yardarm.

The entire atmosphere on board had changed. There was so much merriment and so little sickness of late that Mr Penrose had no need of Anne's assistance. The favourable wind kept seasickness at bay, while the fresh air and sun did wonders for the passengers' health. Even the much-reviled steerage food was an improvement for many of the impoverished families, who had been close to starvation in England. It seemed to Elisabeth that Mr Dickens' tale was closer to reality than she had realised. The city children in particular had come on board looking sickly and pale, but were now robust and energetic. The doctor was still busy with organising rosters, ensuring hygiene, and seeing to minor ailments and accidents, but with enough free time to enjoy chatting over a relaxed meal and a decent sleep at night.

A group of steerage passengers had set up a trades school to pass the time. Each man or woman would teach some basic skills of their own trade to anyone who wished to learn. There was much experience to draw upon, as the passengers included seamstresses, carpenters, cooks, a blacksmith, weavers, bricklayers and many more trades, as well as agricultural labourers by the dozen. By afternoon, the deck was covered with an astonishing variety of tools. The children were eager to learn new skills, though some were rather too excitable with the saws and hammers, to the detriment of ship fittings and fingers.

Mr Knight had his surveying instruments out, causing great interest amongst several of the boys and men. Surprisingly, the usually troublesome Francis Maynard showed particular interest and aptitude. Knight waved at Elisabeth, flashing one of the cheeky grins that couldn't fail to make the recipient smile back. He certainly seemed to bounce back quickly from adversity. She suddenly felt old and jaded, compared to his youthful exuberance and obvious certainty that all would be well if he kept laying on the charm.

The ship had also become something of a floating employment service. Mary Jamieson and Mr Forrester combined forces to set up a dressmaking business, while Messrs Amberley and Templeton were quick to see the potential of the trades school for amassing a skilled workforce for their estates. Mr Strickland, following their example, was busy recruiting builders and bricklayers for the planned government works in the township of Wellington. Soon, there would not be a person on the vessel in want of employment.

Reverend Robertshaw circled the negotiations with an eagle eye, ensuring fair wages and conditions. He had not much need of his gentle persuasive skills, with Mr Templeton at least. He had already agreed to twice the wage of farm workers in England and a plot of land for a home and garden as well.

'My father used to say: "Starvation wages might buy a worker for the day, but a decent living buys a lifetime of loyalty." Just good business sense.'

Mr Amberley cheerfully went along with his friend's advice, while Mr Strickland was more concerned with maintaining efficiencies, given that he was tasked with spending on behalf of the Crown. But he conceded the sense in having a contented workforce, especially in a new colony, where the supply of workers was less than the demand.

All this activity left Elisabeth with the desire to make firmer plans for their future. She left the cuddy for her usual late-evening walk on deck, knowing the fresh air would help her think.

For no particular reason, she felt uneasy, as if someone was watching her, though the only people she saw were busy with sailing duties or casually strolling in the cool night air. She jumped at every shadow and choked back a scream when a hen flapped about in a cage beside her. Time to return to the safety of the cabin. Mr Penrose was right, being out alone was not a good idea.

Anne was still playing cards, so the cabin was empty and, of course, locked. She found herself stopping in the doorway, feeling that something was wrong, but unable to decide what. Mr Thomas passed by with a tray of whisky and water. He must have seen her hesitation and asked if she was well. Glad to have someone with her, she asked if he would top up her water carafe from his jug. Besides themselves, the cabin was empty, with no possible hiding place. She thanked Mr Thomas and locked the door behind him, chiding herself for her over-active imagination.

She sat on the bed, eyes closed, breathing in and out to calm her nerves. The air seemed to hold an unexpected scent. Had someone been in their cabin again? Her first thought was for her mother's portrait, but it was still hidden beneath the pillow. She pressed it to her heart for a moment, wishing that her parents could be with her again.

She put the picture aside and bent down to the mahogany trunk. The almost-invisible strand of silk that she had left under the latch was now on the floor. Somehow, the thief had broken into the locked cabin and rifled through her trunk. Her chest felt tight as she checked the contents, only releasing her breath with a hiss when she saw that the secret compartment was intact. The loss of her beloved sapphire necklace was nothing compared to the other items she was entrusted with.

Her heart was still beating in quick-time as she intercepted Mr Thomas coming out of the Strickland's cabin with an empty tray. Mr Strickland sat at the table in his makeshift office with Mr Gilbert, the table covered in documents. One whiff of their cigar smoke explained the smell in her own cabin. The air in the Strickland's cabin was so dense with smoke, it could easily have drifted down to her cabin two doors away. She couldn't imagine how the men could stand it. Perhaps that was why the clerk always looked so sour.

She was just about to ask Thomas how many spare keys there were to the cabins when Anne came up behind them.

'Elisabeth, I'm glad I found you. I cannot find my key anywhere. I'm sure I took it with me to supper.'

Elisabeth knew that Anne usually took a shawl and small reticule with her to the cuddy, but usually set them aside while playing cards. 'Who else was in the cuddy this evening?'

'Everyone, I suppose, at some point or another. Is something wrong?'

'Someone has been in our cabin again. Please, don't be alarmed. But we will need to be doubly cautious. My foolish little prank showing off our jewellery has put us both at risk. I am sorry, Anne.'

While Anne and Thomas discussed getting a spare key from the ship's safe, Elisabeth pondered the implication that the thief now had access to their cabin at any time. Tonight, they would put a chair against the door. Tomorrow, she would check with the mate to ensure that the Frenchman had remained shackled. Surely the single men in the adjacent bunks would have seen him leave, even if he had got loose? Unless he had an accomplice aboard or someone's greed had been ignited by his offer of a reward. That thought robbed her of another night's sleep.

As she tossed in the narrow bunk, she turned over the possibilities for a safer hiding place. Perhaps the ship safe? But who knew how many people could access that? Penrose's cabin? He was one of the few people on board whom she trusted completely, but was his cabin any more secure than theirs? The only other options were to take the risk that her trunk's hidden compartment was secure, or to stand guard for the remaining months of the voyage.

If she hadn't made a solemn promise to her mother, she would have taken the precious jewellery box and tossed it over the side for all to see.

7 September 1841

At breakfast, the chief mate had reassured her that Cloutier had been shackled to his bunk the previous evening, with a bevy of distrustful men keeping a watch on him. Neither Mr Thomas nor the cabin boy had seen anything untoward as they cleared supper from the cuddy, although the boy had left about nine, while the steward was busy until after ten o'clock. He could not remember who was present, except for the card-players.

Meanwhile, *Lady Rosalind* sailed steadily south, making good time and crossing another major waypoint, the Tropic of Cancer. Midday temperatures were now too hot to do anything, but at least with the high temperature and humidity came regular downpours of rain. Elisabeth would never have believed that rain could fall so intensely in short squalls, as if a giant bucket had been upended on them all at once, before clearing away to blue skies as if nothing had happened. Every available container was used to catch fresh water, which was a relief after the disgusting ship's water.

She watched with amusement and envy as every downpour brought a rush of men to the deck with soap, cleaning themselves and their clothes at the same time. She would have to speak to Mr Penrose about setting up an enclosed area for the women, perhaps using spare sails. The only other option was washing with sea water, which was not at all pleasant, even with so-called marine soap, because fresh water was too precious to waste.

Elisabeth spent much of the day in the cabin, with the porthole open wide and a wet cloth on her forehead. She dozed off and on, starting awake at any unexpected noise. The ship was alive with sounds, but she was so used to these that they were like a lullaby. Creaking timbers, the thud of feet on the deck, the regular clanging of the bell for changes of watch, shouted commands to the sailors aloft, and the ever-present whoosh of the waves on the hull. Twice she had to leap up and close the porthole as squalls of rain hit like a high-pressure hose.

Despite the mate's assurances, it was Cloutier she was worried about, not the thief. That he was clever and utterly ruthless was beyond doubt. He had tracked her down after all this time and risked his liberty by joining the ship, indicating a determination beyond all common sense. She assumed he was doing it for money, so the reward must be great indeed. Of course, he could be planning to take the pearls for himself. They were certainly worth a great deal of money, although only a fraction of the true value they held for the rightful owner.

The logical time for him to strike, if he was able, was in the next couple of days, so that he could make his escape during their stop at the Cape Verde islands. Either that, or wait until they reached New Zealand. Neither thought comforted her. Perhaps she should leave everything on the desk with the door wide open, and be done with the worry forever. Tempting. But her sense of loyalty to her family was too strong.

Elisabeth threw down her book ten minutes after the dinner bell sounded. The cramped cabin was getting to her. She locked the cabin, determined not to spend the rest of the voyage in a state of anxiety.

Anne was already at the table, deep in conversation with Mr Penrose and Mrs Robertshaw. The Maynards and Stricklands formed another huddle, while the single men were telling tall stories at the other end of the table, to raucous laughter.

Elisabeth sat down next to Mr Enys, who was intent on shovelling his food down before something else needed his attention.

'Good day, Mr Enys, or should I say *dydh da*?'

'You speak some Cornish, Mrs Godwin?'

'Only a couple of phrases picked up from the doctor.'

He glanced down the table. 'A good lad, the doc. I been on dozens of vessels in my time. You learn to be grateful for a surgeon who's not drunk all the time on the brandy, let alone one who can actually mend a broken bone or cure a fever.'

'I gather he's planning to trade some of the brandy for lime juice at Cape Verde. When are we likely to make landfall?'

'Not more than a day or two.'

So soon. Best not to think of it. 'You've been to New Zealand before, haven't you? How did you find it?'

Mr Enys pushed his plate aside with a satisfied belch. 'Beg pardon, ma'am. New Zealand is a sight to see. Three large islands and a load of little ones, with rocky shores and tricky currents enough to make any sensible navigator run screaming. More than a few shipwrecks already. And the land is just as fearsome. Mountains taller than any back home, with jagged snow-covered peaks no one would dare climb. And green as far as the eye can see, with endless forests and swamps, but no fields like at home. A wild place and no mistake.'

'And towns?'

'A few rough and ready clusters of shacks mainly. I trust you'd not be believing the rubbish spouted by the New Zealand Company about how it's some sort of paradise.'

By now, he had the attention of everyone at the table. A lively discussion ensued amongst the menfolk, with most of the young colonists remaining confident that their fortunes would be made. Mr Knight was positively bouncing with excitement at the description of mountains and untracked wilderness. Most of the women remained silent, unwilling to make light of the hardships the new country would bring into their previously well-ordered lives.

Deadly Games

8 September 1841

Elisabeth had been unsettled all day, feeling physically crushed by the headache-inducing tropical humidity and mentally sapped by a powerful sense of unease. The cabin had become an oven, despite the open porthole, while the deck was so hot that the tar between the planks was glue under her boots. Moving between the two gave no respite – each time she moved it felt as if she had shifted from the skillet to the fire.

The only bright spots in the day were the hints of nearby land – patches of seaweed, the occasional stray land-bird and even a few wind-blown butterflies of dazzling iridescent blue with red spots. While they could not yet see the islands, the air smelt faintly organic for the first time in almost a month.

The captain had increased the watch. Despite the secrecy, the news of their visit had reached all ears. The captain had to gather the crew and passengers together to announce that no one but the ship's surgeon and chief mate, with an armed escort, would be allowed off or on the *Lady Rosalind*. Women would be required to stay below decks and the men were to guard the ship from thieves. Later, the chief mate told her the guards would also be on the lookout for their own sailors trying to jump ship.

She was glad when evening finally came and the air cooled a little. Anne had brought out her chess set, a present from John, who had taught them both to play. It had small, beautifully carved pieces in ivory and ebony, nestled into a hinged wooden box. Elisabeth could not muster the energy to play, but she was pleased to see that Anne was now confident enough of herself to demonstrate her intelligence. John and Elisabeth were the only people she had played with before – Frederick preferred women to stick to needlework.

Mr Amberley looked up from his glass of port. 'Never seen a woman play chess before. I didn't think ladies' minds were inclined to such games.'

Anne placed the board on the table, the merest hint of a crinkle in the corners of her eyes. 'Perhaps you could show me how it's played then?'

Elisabeth settled down on her seat with a suppressed grin, confident that he would be choking on his words before too long. Sure enough, in less than twenty minutes, he was shaking his head as his army was swept from the board, while his king was quickly running out of places to hide. Mr Templeton, who fancied his chances, was next up, but fared no better in the end. By now there was a crowd around the board and exclamations at Anne's prowess, as if surprised that a woman could master the complexities of chess.

'Come on, Penrose,' Mr Templeton urged. 'It's up to you to reclaim the honour of men.'

'Oh no, not me. You forget that I have worked with Miss Godwin. I have great respect for her intellect.'

Anne leaned towards him. Elisabeth couldn't decide whether Anne's smile was that of a girl gazing at her sweetheart or a fox sizing up a chicken.

Anne raised one eyebrow. 'Not brave enough, Mr Penrose?'

Definitely the fox, Elisabeth decided, as the doctor sat down to play. The game went on for so long that most people had drifted away with glasses of port or cups of tea. Mr Strickland lit one of his pungent cigars, which brought Elisabeth's headache back. She could see that Anne was closing in for the win, so she wished everyone goodnight. Then she saw a tiny flicker of a smile at the edge of her opponent's lips. She settled back down to watch a rapid set of moves that almost wiped the board clean and left them at a stalemate.

Anne and the doctor grinned at each other, while Elisabeth laughed out loud. She was looking forward to their rematch already. The salon cleared as everyone either went to bed or headed up to the deck to refresh themselves in the cool night air. The buzz of excitement kept the laughter and conversation flowing.

Elisabeth left Anne and the doctor to stroll together and dissect the game, while she joined up with Charlotte. A dark shadow flitted across the quarterdeck below them. Elisabeth stood at the rail of the poop deck, heart thumping, trying to convince herself she was conjuring phantoms. A cloud flitted across the moon, creating another darting silhouette. The deck was always alive with dancing shadows, she told her herself. And no wonder, with three tall masts, a dozen or more sails, and a tangled web of stays and ratlines above, and boats, boxes and equipment cluttering up the deck. She really mustn't let her imagination get the better of her. Time for bed.

She had walked through the door before she realised it wasn't locked. In the hazy light of a lamp, she saw her diary open on the edge of the bunk and her mother's picture on the floor, along with the entire contents of her trunks. The side of her mahogany trunk had been slashed with a knife, but the base was still intact.

She smelled him a split second before he grabbed her from behind, pulling her into the cabin and kicking the door closed. His hand was over her mouth, right up against her nose, so tight that she struggled to breathe. His body odour was overpowering. Rough bristles rubbed against her cheek. She shivered as she felt the hard ridge of the scar down his face.

'You look just like your treacherous mother.'

It took a second to register that he was speaking French. He held up his other hand, which clasped a vicious dagger. The razor-sharp edge slid down her neck, leaving a warm trickle of blood. She felt the knife pressing under her rib cage, pointed up to her heart.

He eased his hand off her mouth slightly. 'Scream and you die.'

Elisabeth gasped for breath and desperately tried to come up with a plan. Pointless denial was all she could come up with, but at least it might be a delaying tactic. She stammered in English, her words muffled by his filthy fingers. 'I don't know what you're talking about. I am just the wife of an English merchant. Let me go.'

'Should I switch to English for you? I grew up in England, you know, before order was restored to France.'

'You have the wrong person.'

'Oh, I know exactly who and what you are. The daughter of a traitor and a thief. You and your family ruined my life the day you escaped. I might have only seen you for a second, but I will never forget your face. I lost my commission as captain of the guards, had to scrape a living nurse-maiding minor diplomatic missions. And now I'm trapped on this god-forsaken, fetid prison ship, not bound for Canada, but for some squalid hell-hole on the other side of the world. Your family owes me.' His fingers squeezed her lips. 'You owe me.'

The stench of his breath made her gag. The knife dug in harder, ripping her dress and pressing her corset into her flesh. There was nothing she could say – she knew she would die here, in this tiny cabin in the middle of the ocean. And her baby – John's baby – would die with her.

'Funny thing, life. I gave up trying to track you down years ago. Fate delivered me a meeting with one Frederick Godwin at a diplomatic event, to our mutual benefit. You can imagine my surprise when, weeks later, I walked into the Godwin Shipping office to arrange passage for a diplomatic mission back to France and saw a picture of you on the desk.'

The shock made her forget her denials. 'You met John?'

'Not then. But Frederick Godwin was most interested in hearing the truth about you, while I was stunned to hear that the pearl necklace was still in your possession. In fact, we struck a deal. Your loving brother-in-law agreed to steal the jewellery box for me – a promise he failed to honour – and I would arrange a little accident for your husband to shut him up. Such a shame he slipped and fell overboard.'

The shock of this revelation wiped all sanity from her mind. With the fierce hiss of a cornered feline, she bit into his fingers, wrestled her arms free and scratched at his face, clawing at his eyes, unconsciously scoring a track down the scar-line.

He grabbed her wrists, forcing them into one of his enormous hands, the dagger dropping to the floor. His other hand whipped out, slapping her so hard on the cheek that her eyes lost focus. He reached down for the dagger, then clamped her tight against his chest within the iron grip of his muscular arms. 'Enough. You will tell me where it is, right now, or you will die. And the money from selling all those books you stole from your fellow countrymen. Your stupid brother-in-law was seething with rage when he found out you had tricked him.'

She could feel a sharp pain where the blade pushed deeper. 'You will kill me anyway, so why should I give you anything?

The tension eased a little as he drew the dagger back. 'I think you might be right. Perhaps I would have more success if I wait for your precious sister-in-law. How would you like to watch me cut off her fingers? One by one?' He lifted one filthy finger at a time, cleaning each nail in turn with the point of the dagger.

Her body shook as the long-remembered threat hit home. He had threatened her mother in exactly the same way. There was nothing she could do to stop the reaction, and he would be sure to see her weakness.

'So, it seems you are not the innocent little English madam after all. Time to give me what I want.'

'Help!' her voice box screamed, but the sound that emerged wasn't loud enough to reach beyond the cabin door.

A knock startled them both.

'Mrs Godwin, are you well?'

George Penrose, thank God. Cloutier shifted his weight to the side so he could jam his heavy boot against the door, giving Elisabeth just enough space to twist away from the dagger. Instead of trying to get away from him in the cramped cabin, she shifted her whole weight backwards, driving her elbow into his groin as hard as she could.

'*Merde*!' He folded over in pain, instinctively clutching at his crotch with both hands.

The narrow heel of her booted foot slammed down his shin, then swivelled to kick at the door. 'Help!'

She heard the doctor yell for help a split-second before he smashed open the door, using his shoulder as a battering ram. Cloutier was spun around, half facing her. Hatred blazed in his eyes. He lunged forward, striking out at her with the dagger as the doctor threw himself on the man's massive back. The blade nicked the edge of her gown as she lurched backwards, tripping over the trunk in the narrow confines of the cabin. She kicked out at his hand as she went down, knocking the dagger out of his grasp.

Penrose was still hanging on from behind, trying to choke her attacker. Cloutier twisted around and turned on him, punching, shoving, kicking, using his superior weight to force her rescuer onto the floor. In seconds, he had his thick hands around the doctor's neck from behind, throttling him.

Elisabeth scrambled up and lunged at Cloutier, but her flailing fists and boots made no impact on his muscled bulk. She jumped onto the bed, giving her the advantage of height, and grabbed at his face, yanking an ear, stabbing at his eyes with her fingers.

With the roar of a wounded bull, he dropped the doctor and lurched backwards. When he came upright again, he was holding the knife. With wild eyes glinting in the dim light, he surged forwards and plunged the blade up under her ribs. Elisabeth fell back onto the bunk, her gown turning red as the dagger dropped to the floor.

Cloutier whipped back around and had his hands around the doctor's neck before he had even made it back to his knees. He wrenched his head up so the doctor's blotched face and bulging eyes were only a hands-breadth from Elisabeth's face. Time seemed to slow as she stared into his eyes, mesmerised with horror, although it took only a fraction of a second to snap out of the trance and act.

Her fingers frantically tried to pry loose the deadly grip, but it was like an iron manacle. As she watched the doctor's eyes roll back, her foot kicked against the dagger. She dropped to the floor, picked up the knife and stabbed it into Cloutier's thigh.

Without warning, his death-grip released and Cloutier collapsed with a grunt. Anne stood behind him, face white, eyes wide, bloodied chess set grasped in her hands. George Penrose was on the floor underneath him, lying still.

Anne screamed when she caught sight of Elisabeth's bloody gown – a scream that would have woken the dead.

Cloutier pulled himself up slowly, swaying groggily against the edge of the door, his eyes unfocussed and blood dripping from a head wound. He struck out at Anne, but she brought the chess set down again, catching his fist and splitting the skin of his knuckles.

George Penrose gave a deep, rattling gasp. He looked up in time to see a boot descending. His forehead caught a glancing blow as he tried to throw himself out of the way. Elisabeth swayed and collapsed to the floor beside him. The diary slipped off the bunk behind her, falling open across the seeping red stain on her motionless body.

There were voices in the corridor, feet running, women screaming. Mr Enys and the second mate appeared in the doorway, stout clubs in their hands.

The Frenchman yanked the knife out of his thigh, with little more than a fierce grimace to show the pain that must have caused, and barged past them, slashing wildly. The crowd peeled out of the path of this mad bull as he bellowed and charged his way onto the deck, with the mates in pursuit. He surged across the deck in an erratic zig-zag, limping and swaying, unsure which way to turn as pursuers converged, until he spotted the skiff at the edge of the poop deck.

He lunged towards the skiff and sawed frantically at the ropes securing it, slashing the blade in a wild arc when anyone tried to get close. With a burst of adrenalin-fuelled strength, he heaved the skiff over the side and threw himself after it.

The skiff landed upside down. Cloutier clung to one of the severed ropes and tried to right the boat, but only succeeded in pushing it further under the water.

As the ship forged on under the relentless pull of wind and sail, the onlookers saw a triangular dorsal fin appear, following the silver path lit by the full moon to the floundering body. By the time the *Lady Rosalind* went about and located the upturned skiff, the sound of thrashing and screaming had long since subsided into deathly silence.

Life and Death

Elisabeth forced her eyelids open long enough to see Charlotte Strickland standing in the doorway, white-faced at the carnage. Grace Robertshaw pushed past Charlotte with a determined shove.

'Oh Lord, are they alive?' Grace reached out to Anne's inert body on the bed. 'Anne is fine. Looks like she fainted.' She turned to the bodies on the floor. 'Doc, can you hear me?'

Elisabeth heard a groan and felt a body wriggling out from underneath hers, rolling her onto her side and shooting an agony of pain through her chest. She closed her eyes tightly and clamped her teeth to stop herself crying out. Charlotte started sobbing hysterically at the sight of the crimson stain soaking through the bodice of her gown.

'Get them out of here,' George croaked.

While Grace and Charlotte lifted Anne out of the cabin, Elisabeth felt her hand being gripped and fingers searching for a pulse. 'George…' Her voice was less than a whisper, but his hand moved from her wrist to touch her cheek softly. Her eyes closed again, a faint smile on her bruised lips.

'Elisabeth. Thank God. I thought I'd lost you.'

She forced her eyelids open, blinking back tears at his battered face. 'George, you're hurt.'

One of his eyes was glued shut by blood, but the other looked down at her with relief. 'Not too badly. You were stabbed – I saw him do it. I cannot believe you're alive.'

'Mother's secret,' she murmured.

He leaned close to catch her words, gently brushing her hair out of her eyes. 'I need to check your injuries. Lie still.' He took several deep breaths, forcing himself back to his doctor role. 'Blood, but only seeping, not pulsing. Good. Another bump on the head, superficial scratch on the neck.' His eyes came back to meet hers. 'It's a miracle. I saw the force of that blade going upward to your heart – you should be dead.'

'Mother's secret. She told me to keep the pearls safe by sewing them into my corset.'

His eyes went wide, and she felt his fingers carefully investigating the wound. 'Well, I never saw anything like this before. Looks like these pearls saved your life.'

'Ironic, that the very thing he was after saved me.'

He levered himself off the floor with a grimace and went to the door to ask Thomas to bring hot water and cloths, and for Grace Robertshaw to get his medical bag. Both lifted their eyes to heaven for the briefest instant before hurrying about their tasks.

'We'll have to get the corset off to see the wound properly, but it looks to be no more than a shallow cut. Presumably, the knife was deflected by the necklace and missed all your vital organs. A miracle indeed.'

Grace burst in, her eyes widening when she saw Elisabeth smiling weakly at her. She passed on the good news to the cluster of people outside before shooing them away and closing the door again. She carefully eased Elisabeth out of her clothes and into a shift, while the doctor hovered discreetly with a cloth pad in case of bleeding. 'What do you think, doc?'

'A stitch or two should take care of it.'

'My baby?' Elisabeth whispered.

'Well out of the way.'

Tears streamed down her cheeks. She reached for his hand. 'You saved my life. Our lives. How can I ever thank you?'

'Stay alive. Thank Charlotte for being worried that you looked unwell on the deck earlier. And Anne, for her excellent skills with a chess set.'

Thomas and the cabin boy came in with a jug of warm water and two basins. Thomas hustled the goggle-eyed lad out, then saw to the cut above the doctor's eye, wiping away the blood so he could see well enough to stitch.

Grace cleaned Elisabeth's wound, then pressed a clean cloth against it to staunch the trickle of blood.

She had to thread the needle, but the doctor managed to stitch Elisabeth's wound with one eye half-closed. Elisabeth gritted her teeth – a little pain was a lot better than the expected death. She could still smell her assailant's fetid odour in her nostrils.

Elisabeth was propped up in bed, with Grace bathing her neck and head injuries, and George slumped in a chair, when Anne came back in. She didn't say anything, just sat down beside Elisabeth and squeezed her hand until it hurt. Then she got up and saw to the rest of the doctor's injuries with quiet efficiency.

A clatter of voices and boots came to a stop outside the door. They could hear Mr Enys telling everyone to go back to their cabins, followed by a sharp rap on the door. All four of them looked up expectantly as the chief mate entered.

'Gone overboard. And good riddance. A right bad 'un.'

'You're sure?' Elisabeth was shivering, though the cabin was hot.

'Absolutely sure. A shark saw to that. How bad are your injuries?'

'We'll be fine with a few days' rest.'

'Maybe for Mrs Godwin, but no resting on the job for you, doc. We've got an island to visit.'

'You're a hard taskmaster, Enys.'

'Just as well you're tough as old boots then, eh, doc. Even if you play chess like a girl.'

'Pity I wasn't tougher than the old boot I got in the head. Feels about ready to explode. But I suppose you're right, Enys. Time to get back to work. I think we need to have a closer look at the Frenchman's kit. He's no petty thief.'

Mr Enys waved him back into his chair. 'I expect we can let you have tonight off. I'll take care of tearing apart his kit and bunk. Get some rest.'

Thomas and Grace left with the mate. Anne tucked her own blanket around Elisabeth, then tidied the mess. First, she gathered up the two pictures – one of John, the other of Elisabeth's mother – pressing them into grateful hands. The contents of the trunks were packed away, while the bloody dress was set aside for washing and mending.

Anne lifted up the corset and raised an eyebrow. 'I see now why you always wore this one. Better than a safe and handy armour against daggers. Every lady should have one.'

'Don't joke, Anne. I put you in harm's way. And you, Mr Penrose. I'm so sorry. I promised my mother I would look after the pearls, no matter what, but I wish now I had convinced her to get rid of them years ago.'

Anne sat beside her, wrapping her arms around Elisabeth gently. 'You brought immeasurable joy to John and I, and laughter into our staid household. A little excitement now and then is a trivial price to pay.'

Elisabeth was on the verge of telling Anne that John's death may not have been an accident. Tears flooded into her eyes. Anne had suffered enough trauma for one day, and Elisabeth wanted to reflect on what she had learned before troubling Anne. She would be so devastated that it might be best to keep it from her entirely.

It made no sense. Why on earth would Frederick want to have John killed? John had been more tolerant than most brothers would have been at the discovery of his theft of business funds. He must have uncovered something worse and threatened to expose Frederick. John had certainly been troubled in the weeks before his death. How she wished he had confided in her at the time.

And what of Cloutier? Could it really be just an awful coincidence that he had met Frederick and seen her picture in John's office? Surely, it was more likely that Cloutier had lied to her about Frederick ordering John's death. He was, after all, a ruthless and violent man, who hated her enough to kill John for his own revenge.

A thought scorched through her mind – a possibility she hadn't considered before. Could Cloutier and Kingston be the same man? After all, he had grown up in England and spoke fluent English. But could he pass as a gentleman? A charming, charismatic gentleman who could sell a railroad scheme? It seemed unlikely, but perhaps the tough, brutish man she knew him to be might look very different dressed up with charming manners and expensive clothes. This man Kingston had visited Frederick at the house. And a large, tough English man had visited the office the following day. The latter was surely Cloutier. She cursed herself for failing to ask her housekeeper to give a detailed description of the man who came to the house.

A knock at the door interrupted her train of thought. Mr Enys asked for the doctor to come with him, his voice grim. Anne's grip tightened. The two women looked at each other, fearing further trouble. Penrose levered himself off the chair like a geriatric and headed to the door with sagging shoulders and a stiff gait.

It felt like hours before there was a light tap at the door. Anne unlocked the door at the sound of the doctor's voice. He dropped like a sack of bones into a chair, his face grey, apart from a massive black bruise on his forehead and red welts on his neck. Anne sat next to Elisabeth, gripping her hands.

'No need to be alarmed. Cloutier drugged the meal in the single men's quarters. Enys thought they were all dead, but they're just sleeping heavily. He must have had lock-picks, though we searched his kitbag before locking him up. The lads gave his kit a thorough search again and only came up with this.' He showed them a crudely made instrument, like a stout wooden pipe.

Elisabeth reached for it. She twisted it in her hands and held it up to the light, then snapped it open along a near-invisible seam. Inside was a tight roll of banknotes and the lock-picks. 'French people have become rather adept at concealing things. The revolution was a hard lesson.' She handed the items back to George Penrose.

'His stash of gambling money, I presume. Quite a bit less that I would have expected, given his ability to cheat. Nevertheless, enough to fund a few extra supplies for the steerage passengers.'

'An excellent idea. I rather thought you might find the lost jewellery, but perhaps he had it on him.'

'If so, it's gone forever.' He levered himself up with a stifled groan. 'Enough excitement for one night. Try to get some sleep.'

Elisabeth thought there was little chance of that, but found her eyelids drooping even as she heard the click of the lock.

9 September 1841

Elisabeth was roused by the sun streaming through the porthole. With Anne's help, she sat up in bed, grimacing at the sharp stab of pain under her ribs with every breath she took. Her body felt pummelled and bruised from her toes to her pounding head. Anne said that the first islands of Cape Verde were visible, so she shuffled stiffly across the cabin to look.

The view was one of the most beautiful she had ever seen. Jagged peaks rose sharply from a riot of green vegetation, surrounded by beaches of eye-achingly white sand and sea of the most exquisite aquamarine. Anne said she had been on deck and seen shoals of darting fish in a rainbow of colours. After weeks of steely blue ocean, the colours were a treat beyond imagination. And the smell! She had all but forgotten the rich scent of trees and fertile soil.

They stood by the porthole, entranced, until Elisabeth felt her legs shake. Anne helped her back to bed and left her to rest.

She had dozed off again when Anne returned with a tray of breakfast. Although she longed for more sleep, she felt better for a little food, lots of tea, and the news Anne had to share. The grim details of the Frenchman's demise were swiftly dealt with. At least they could be sure he was gone from their lives.

'The good news is that he dropped his hipflask before he went overboard. The second mate retrieved it and turned it in to Mr Enys at breakfast. Apparently, he had it on him at all times and was always drinking from it as he gambled. Mr Knight was sure he was faking being drunk, so he could cheat at cards. Mr Penrose remembered about hidden compartments and managed to open the flask. What do you think dropped out?'

'Lady Maynard's diamond earrings?'

'Yes! And a few other small pieces. You'd think Lady M would be pleased to have them back, but her face looked like thunder and poor Sir Julius was quivering in his boots. It was exactly as you thought. He had taken his wife's jewellery to pay his gambling debt.'

'I trust she apologised to the cabin boy?'

'Huh. She'd be more likely to throw the earrings overboard than admit to that mistake.'

'Was there anything else inside?'

'A great deal of money, which was taken to the captain's cabin. No necklace.'

There was a light tap at the door. Anne let the doctor in, excusing herself to return the tray.

He pulled a chair up to her bedside. 'How are you feeling this morning, Mrs Godwin?'

'Alive, thanks to you, though a little dizzy and sore. I was wondering … do you think, after all we've been through, that we might be permitted to use first names? Only in private, of course. I would not wish to undermine your authority.'

He reached out to take her hand, turning it over to feel her pulse. 'I would be honoured, Elisabeth. May I check your wound? Or should I wait for Anne to come back?'

Elisabeth pulled up the shift enough to expose the bandage. She tried not to wince as the covering came away and his gentle fingers probed the wound.

'It's looking fine, all things considered. Just a little seepage, but no blood. Pretty ragged stitching though. You might want to find yourself a better doctor.'

'I'll take valour over neat stitches any day. Even if you do look like a back-alley fighter after a rough night.'

He tucked the dressings back into place with a grin. 'Get Anne to clean it regularly in boiled water and report to me if there is any sign of redness, swelling or bleeding. Any sign at all. The tropics are a terrible place for infections. Promise?'

'Yes, George, I promise. How are you feeling this morning? Honestly?'

'Like I've been trampled by a herd of wild horses. It'll pass soon enough. I expect you feel much the same.' He paused to check her eyes. 'Pupils good. Any vision problems? Headache?'

She shook her head, but her denial was undone by the wince of pain the movement caused. 'Maybe a little, but getting better.'

George tucked the bedclothes back around her. 'Did you hear about the flask?' She nodded, so he continued. 'The captain, chief mate and I have discussed what to do with the money. He had a huge stash – far more than could be explained by gambling on the ship. By rights, it should be all yours, as your sapphire necklace is still unaccounted for.'

'By no means. We cannot even be certain that Cloutier took the necklace, and others have suffered worse. The family of the missing man whose bunk he took. All the single men sharing space with that foul creature. Even Sir Julius, I suppose, if he really did have money stolen. Not to mention the extra work and bruises he caused for the crew.'

'Indeed, I knew you would say so. Our proposal is that each crew member will receive a bonus on arrival in New Zealand, with the captain taking a cut, of course. The single men and families in steerage who have suffered at Cloutier's hands will also receive a share. The rest will go to you, Elisabeth.'

'I agree on two conditions. One, that my share is used to purchase extra supplies. Books and pencils for the school if you can find them. Extra rations of tea, fruit, medicine and whatever else is needed for the steerage passengers.'

George looked as if he was about to protest, but she returned his gaze with steely calm. He blinked first. A quick nod. 'And the second condition?'

'That you receive a fair reward as well.' She waved away his refusal before he could speak. 'We will need a well-equipped doctor in New Zealand. All the passengers hope that can be you, if you are willing to stay on in Wellington.' He still looked uncertain. 'George, surely you would not refuse my child the best of care?'

The activity on deck intensified – the rattling of the heavy anchor chain adding to the clamour of heavy boots and shouting.

He gave in with a shake of his head. 'I dare not refuse anything to the Godwin sisters. I have never met their match. And now, I'd better be quick or Enys will have me flogged.'

Elisabeth watched him leave with a smile on her face. How nice it was to have a kindred spirit to talk to – someone who shared the same values and understood without explanation. She very much hoped he would set up practice in Wellington and not sail off back to England. She would need all the friends she could get in this strange new world.

Cape Verde Respite

The ship dropped anchor offshore from the bustling township of Mindelo. Here, the earthy smell and peace of the outer islands were over-powered by the odours and cacophony of a throng of people and animals. Elisabeth watched with trepidation as the shore party rowed away in one of the longboats.

The town was used as a coal depot for steam ships, so one might hope there would be a firm British hand upon the place. However, the captain had warned that the islands were frequented by rum-swilling whalers and ruthless slavers, who were not well-disposed to the British following their decision to abolish slavery. Officers and a few trusted sailors had been issued with firearms, as were the guards for the shore-party.

Before their feet had even touched solid ground, the shore-party was mobbed by street-sellers of many exotic types, from lithe men with sharp noses and dusky skin, almost completely covered in white robes, to near-naked children with skin the colour of ebony. Merchants and their bully-boys beat a path through the rabble with heavy sticks and began their negotiations. She soon lost sight of the party as the crowd surged up the beach to the town.

The *Lady Rosalind* was besieged by another mob – a flotilla of crudely carved canoes, paddled by boys who waved and yelled at them, holding aloft all manner of items: a bunch of bananas, a dented tin without a label, a basket woven from palm fronds and filled with pretty seashells. The dugouts were soon followed by longer boats with curved prows and triangular sails set on a steeply angled mast. While the canoes had been pushed away with laughter and boathooks, these new arrivals were met with stern commands and a visible show of arms.

The only vessel allowed alongside was a tub-shaped steamboat, which the captain seemed to be expecting. He conducted a brief negotiation, with much waving of arms from the visiting captain and stoic arm-crossing from theirs. Money changed hands and, soon after, a hose was snaking across the bulwarks and the barrels were being refilled with fresh water.

To everyone's relief, the shore party returned in relatively short order with a small train of donkeys and carts, piled with barrels, ceramic jugs and baskets of fresh food, and followed by a swarm of chanting children. As soon as the returning men were aboard, the sails were unfurled.

The ladies were allowed back on deck when they cleared the harbour entrance. Out of the lee of the land, they picked up a fair wind and soon the islands receded like a particularly vivid dream that fades rapidly on waking.

The captain was at the helm and in an expansive mood after the tension of the island visit. 'Enjoy the view while you can, Mrs Godwin. It might be the last land you see before we reach New Zealand.'

Elisabeth inhaled the fresh sea air and was content to focus on the ocean ahead with cautious optimism. 'Did they purchase some lime juice?'

'Aye, lass. Lime juice, tea, fruit, medicine and who knows what else.' He gestured at the crowd of steerage passengers on the main deck. 'This lot don't know how lucky they are to get more than Company rations.'

'No doubt the New Zealand Company will be pleased when you land a bunch of healthy passengers, ready for hard work.' And, no doubt, the captain would be happy to get a hefty bonus for that, she thought.

Elisabeth retreated to the cabin for a rest and must have fallen asleep. A tap at her door roused her, but the aroma that edged its way into the cabin was what brought her back to full attention.

'Come in.'

George Penrose appeared with a package in one hand and a steaming cup in the other. 'I gather you've been missing coffee. I'm reliably assured that coffee doesn't come better or stronger than this.'

The scent was tantalising, and she reached for the cup eagerly, closing her eyes as she sipped the thick brew. 'Mm, heaven. What a wonderful treat, George, thank you. Are you not having a cup?'

'It's a pleasure to see you enjoying it, but, personally, I'd rather drink tar than that stuff.' He passed her the package. 'I hope I bought enough.'

'That'll be plenty, if I don't have to share it. Though I might have to ask the captain to turn back, so I can spend the rest of my life in paradise.'

'Life on the *Lady Rosalind* wouldn't be half as exciting without you on board. Besides, you really wouldn't want to live on that island. It may look beautiful from a distance, but it had far too many cutthroats and mosquitos for my liking.'

The ship's bell interrupted with a long peal, calling everyone on deck. George helped Elisabeth to rise and walk up to the deck.

As the sun sank towards the horizon, it became a giant glowing orb, painting the sky and sea a fiery red. The cook and stewards laid out a banquet of fresh foods, and every man, woman, and child crowded the deck for a picnic feast. The buzz of excited chatter died away as everyone savoured the simple pleasures of eating fresh food and drinking clean water again after weeks at sea.

Elisabeth's previous life surrounded by a bounty of grapes, apples and peaches had not prepared her for the sweetly perfumed richness of these strange fruits.

Mrs Robertshaw came to sit with her. 'I can see by your expression that it's your first taste of tropical fruit. Amazing, aren't they?'

'Hello, Grace. The taste is so intense, it's almost too much for the senses to cope with.'

'I expect there will be a few people whose stomachs can't cope with the change of diet. Pity the poor souls rostered on slop-duty tomorrow morning.' She gestured to the doctor and mate, who were exchanging banter over mugs of ale amongst a group of young men puffing on pipes. 'The lads did well. The single men were well pleased with their box of tobacco and they even found some preserved milk for the infants. I gather I have you to thank for the pencils and paper, although goodness knows how they found those items on an island in the middle of an ocean.'

By twilight, the decks were cleared, and the ship became a floating party, with singing and dancing well into the night. Elisabeth couldn't join in the gaiety, as her knife wound was still painful, but she was happy to sit in a comfortable chair on the deck and enjoy watching the fun. She felt a weight off her shoulders and a lightness of spirit, now that the past would truly be behind her. Hopefully, forever.

The next morning, Mr Penrose spoke to the cabin passengers about the events of the past days, putting the Frenchman's attack on Elisabeth down to the obsession of a common rogue who was acting on an entirely unfounded rumour. The captain added a few strong words regarding his conviction that this would be the end of any troubles, unless anyone else wanted to be fed to the sharks.

Life on board settled into a familiar routine – school for the children after chores, breakfast and the morning service, rest in the heat of the day, practical learning such as sewing and woodcraft in the late afternoon, singing and other entertainments in the evening.

Anne spent much of her day rehearsing the play and often played chess in the evening, seemingly indifferent to the faint dark stain remaining on the edge of the box. Elisabeth's knife wound was closing over nicely, although it still caused her pain for many days. She spent hours sitting on deck in the awning's shade, dreaming of the future, with her hand resting on her rounded belly. The thought of a child brought her such pure joy, she scarcely worried about how they would cope alone. She longed to feel the baby move, but George said it was still too early.

The occasional ship passed by. One homeward-bound British ship hove to and everyone rushed to send letters across with the second mate in the skiff. There was quite a pile for him to take, as many ships had passed, but few with a British flag, and even fewer willing to stop.

A fine run of weather helped the mood, and they made excellent time on days with a fair breeze. On other days, they lay becalmed in searing heat, for they were now in the doldrums. Tempers frayed over the smallest incidents, while the *Lady Rosalind* wallowed in the swell like a dead whale. On those days, the only things that moved fast were rats, cockroaches and petty accusations. Relief came in the form of daily downpours of rain in pelting bursts, soothing frayed nerves and allowing fresh water to be collected and washing to be done.

Elisabeth asked a few more questions about the railroad scheme, more to occupy her time while she healed, rather than in expectation of any new information. One morning, she was chatting to Mr Knight about surveying, so she asked him for his opinion on the feasibility of a rail route across Canada.

He brushed back a wave of hair as he considered her question. 'I've never been to Canada, but I've heard it has endless tracts of wilderness and rugged mountains. My guess is that a railroad would be an enormously expensive undertaking, which might take decades to complete, if indeed it is feasible at all. But it may be that the surveyors have found a viable route already. Sometimes, even a short section of rail in the right place can generate enough income to fund later expansion, although I really couldn't say without knowing more about the land and the experience of the scheme's promoters.'

That evening, she joined Mr Templeton for a stroll, to ask for more detail about his father's knowledge of Mr Kingston's scheme.

'I really don't recall much about it. He had visited a friend in London and joined the man at his club. All he mentioned to me was that there had been much talk of a railroad company, which sounds like the one you are interested in, but he never met the men promoting it or showed any further interest in it.'

'Do you recall the name of the club?'

'It wasn't his usual club, which is frequented by country gentlemen with business in the city. I think this one was near to Kensington Palace. In fact, I think it might have been called the Palace Club. From what I gathered, it was an exclusive place for extremely wealthy men with too much money and time on their hands, not to my father's taste at all.'

Later, she told Anne what she had found out about Kingston and his railroad company. 'It's little enough to go on, but it seems to me that it fits with Frederick's interest in Canada and the implication he invested a lot of money in a speculative scheme with this man called Kingston.'

'Did you know Frederick is a member of the Palace Club?' Anne said.

'No, I did not. I rather gathered it was exclusive to the obscenely wealthy.'

'Clarissa's father is a long-standing member, more as a hereditary right than any great current wealth. I suspect he accepted Frederick as son-in-law in the hope of shoring up the flagging family fortunes. But he did arrange a membership to the club, which Frederick crowed about for weeks.'

'Not to me he didn't, but then he never confided in me. I'm not sure he ever really accepted me as a proper wife for John. Too French, too rustic, and too little advantage to the Godwin family fortunes.'

'Too little common sense to see how happy you made John and how smart you are. He was a good brother to me until he married Clarissa. She always wanted more – more status, more possessions, more wealth. I fear she pushed Frederick to make foolish choices to satisfy her demands. Frederick was convinced Canada would be the making of him. He used to talk about the vast resources of timber, minerals and gold, just waiting for clever men to exploit.'

'Well, I can only hope it all works out for him. The general view of the gentlemen is that these railroads have great potential if they are well run and the investors are rich and extremely patient. It worries me that John was so concerned about it, but we'll never know what he thought for sure, without those missing documents.'

'I have been thinking about that,' Anne said. 'My instinct tells me Frederick was right in thinking that John would have entrusted them to you or hidden them where you would find them. He valued your advice above all others. Was there nothing he said or gave you that might give us a clue?'

'I've searched everywhere. I'm sure I don't have them.' Elisabeth thought for a moment. 'The one thing he impressed on me was that you should have his bible. It's where he put the letter warning us about Frederick and Kingston. Probably the one place he could be sure Frederick would not look.'

Anne got down the bible and flicked carefully through the pages. She turned it over in her hands, making a close examination of the book. 'The back cover is thicker than the front. Why on earth didn't I think of it before?' She eased up the thick cover from the book, revealing a hollowed-out gap filled with papers.

'Wait. I think we should open this in the presence of witnesses. Perhaps the captain or Mr Strickland?'

'Excellent idea. Shall we go find them now?'

Quarter of an hour later, they were seated in the cuddy with both the captain and Mr Strickland.

Elisabeth explained the background. 'I think my husband may have hidden the evidence in the cover of his bible, perhaps knowing that his investigation had put his life at risk. We asked you here as witnesses and because I believe Mr Strickland, as a senior government official, will be best placed to take the appropriate actions.'

She levered up the cover and withdrew the papers, passing them along to the captain. He slit the seal and removed the contents. The first item was a slim prospectus soliciting funds for the United British Canadian Railroad Company, which was painted in glowing terms as an investment which would reap rewards beyond the investor's wildest dreams. The document implied that the railroad development was well advanced, with a planned route, land purchases, and government permissions in place.

The second set of documents showing that no such company or railroad existed – the scheme was not even a high-risk speculative investment – it was an outright fraud. The person named as the instigator was Mr Kingston. Two letters were enclosed in the package. The captain read it all, glanced up at them, and wordlessly passed the letters back to Elisabeth and Anne.

The first, dated a week before John's death, was a copy of a letter to Frederick outlining evidence that the scheme, which he had stolen family money to invest in, was a fraud, and giving him two weeks to do the right thing. The second letter, original and unsent, was to advise the authorities of the results of John's investigation, presumably to be sent if Frederick failed to act.

The captain passed the documents to Mr Strickland, who read them with growing anger. 'I have heard of this venture and know people who put a great deal of money into it. I can assure you ladies that I will raise this matter as soon as we land in New Zealand. Sooner, if we meet another vessel heading home. Your husband appears to have done a thorough job of exposing this fraud, so I expect the authorities will be able to move quickly to shut it down and deal with the scoundrels behind it.' He added, belatedly, and without strong conviction, 'Naturally, I hope that your brother Frederick is an innocent party.'

Anne allowed no emotion to show. 'If he has done wrong, he must accept the consequences.'

A Play Within A Play

18 September 1841

Excitement had been building all week as they neared the equator. A dedicated group was standing in the bows, watching to see who could spot 'The Line' first. The second mate, who had told them the equator would be a visible line in the waves, thought it a marvellous joke.

On the night before they were due to cross over, they held a celebratory dance on the deck, in tropical night air so warm and humid it almost felt like a bath. Halfway through the first waltz, William Templeton dropped to his knee in the moonlight.

'My darling Charlotte, I do not wish to enter the Southern Hemisphere without knowing that you will be by my side forever.' He never made it to 'will you marry me', as Charlotte flung herself into his arms and shouted 'yes'.

The applause and cheering were enough to wake King Neptune from the depths. Templeton staggered back to his feet, with Charlotte clinging to his waist, just in time to be knocked backward again by an enthusiastic hug from Mrs Strickland. Mr Strickland ordered the steward to bring out champagne, before turning to clap his prospective son-in-law on the back and offer him one of his best cigars.

A slow waltz was called for, so that the happy pair could enjoy their first dance as an engaged couple. Mr and Mrs Strickland looked like a pair of lovebirds themselves, as they smiled at their daughter, and joined the waltz, holding each other close and moving as one.

The *Lady Rosalind* crossed 'The Line' the next morning, with a combined cry of 'We are Southerners now!', followed by the traditional parade and ceremony. 'King Neptune' and his attendants wore long beards made of frayed rope and a variety of outlandish garments. Sailors crossing for the first time were put to the test, ending with all their hair being shaved off and a dunking in the tank. They took pity on Mr Penrose, who still had a lump on his head, cutting off all but the last inch of hair. Another feast was held in the evening, followed by a show and dancing into the night.

Everyone was encouraged to perform in the 'Grand Line-Crossing Show'. After the joy of last night's engagement and the raucous fun of the crossing ceremony, a carnival atmosphere prevailed and almost all agreed to contribute.

The second mate continued his Neptune role with a fiery, but slurred, soliloquy, which trailed off towards the end when he staggered off to find a fresh cask of rum. Anne and Mr Knight performed an excerpt from the play with great feeling and rather more sobriety. Charlotte and her beau sang a beautiful love serenade, while Amberley insisted on singing a bawdy ballad full of wenches and innuendo to 'even up the balance of sentiment'.

Enys and Penrose sang a Cornish folksong, although only after being plied with several extra tots of rum each, which enhanced the volume more than the tunefulness. The Robertshaws surprised many, and delighted all, with a hilarious skit of slapstick comedy, which relied on swirling objects, perfect timing and their contrasting heights. The steerage choir, fiddlers and harmonica players, a juggler and other acts added to the festivities, while the children acted out a scene from Oliver Twist, with varying degrees of talent but a great deal of hilarity.

Elisabeth was exempt from performing because of her injury. The laughter may not have helped her healing wound, but it did wonders for her spirits. As the evening drew on, the revelries grew more boisterous. Apparently, allowing the crew and passengers to drink as much as they wanted was part of the tradition of crossing the equator. Mr Knight, who had imbibed more than most, demanded that Elisabeth perform. The call was taken up by others until Elisabeth found herself at the centre of an expectant audience.

Her mind went blank. Nothing she had heard tonight – from romantic opera to wild ballad – suited her untrained voice. Her gaze drifted to Anne, who was holding a sleepy Victoria. She was reminded of Mrs Palmer, who used to sing an old lullaby to Anne at night when she was missing her mother. Elisabeth's voice was so soft as she sang that the rowdy audience fell silent and strained to hear the sweet melody.

Sleep my child and peace attend thee,
All through the night
Guardian angels God will send thee,
All through the night
Soft the drowsy hours are creeping
Hill and vale in slumber sleeping,
I my loving vigil keeping
All through the night.

By the time she reached the final verse, Charlotte was accompanying her on her harp, Anne had tears in her eyes, and Victoria's drooping eyelids had given up the fight to stay open. Elisabeth felt a weight lifting off her shoulders, as if the soothing words were carrying her outer layers of grief away into the velvet night air, leaving behind a core of peace.

Love, to thee my thoughts are turning
All through the night
All for thee my heart is yearning,
All through the night.
Though sad fate our lives may sever
Parting will not last forever,
There's a hope that leaves me never,
All through the night.

Silence reigned for long seconds when she finished, followed by soft applause, as if nobody wished to break the mood. Mothers took the opportunity to scoop up their children and whisk them to their beds, while the fiddlers began to play a slow waltz. Mr Amberley asked Elisabeth to join the dance. He said nothing, simply holding her as gently as a newborn and moving slowly to the music.

Gradually, the tempo rose, and the former mood returned. When the dancing switched to lively reels, Elisabeth was happy to sit to the side and watch on with pleasure as Anne laughed and whirled. Even George danced, his unevenly hacked hair standing upright like bristles on a broom.

The music got faster and louder as the tide line in the rum casks dropped lower. At the tipping point between merriment and anarchy, which comes to every rum-fuelled party, Matron rounded up the single women and sent them to their quarters despite loud protests. This disappointment did little to quell the high spirits of the men.

Mr Knight insisted on dancing with Anne, whom he drunkenly declared to be 'even more desirable than Helen of Troy'. Anne struggled to push him away, but he was so tipsy he tripped over, landing on top of her in a heap on the deck. He added insult to injury by pulling Anne into his arms and kissing her. The sober Mr Gilbert was deputised to remove him, while George restrained Amberley from throwing Knight overboard to the sharks.

Anne and Elisabeth retreated to their cabin. Drunken shouts, raucous laughter, and dancing feet continued long into the night. Elisabeth drifted in and out of sleep, dreams of wild dancing interwoven with nightmares of soldiers and daggers.

The next morning, the deck was littered with sleeping bodies. Knight was found tied to the bowsprit, a single white feather attached to his forehead with tar.

19 -24 September 1841

The days passed in intense heat, sometimes with no wind at all, so that it felt as if they were in an oven. Elisabeth found it hard to gather the energy to move, let alone to think. Passengers moved around the decks sluggishly or rested in what shade they could find, fanning their flushed faces with makeshift fans. Even the sailors worked slowly, as if wallowing through treacle.

In contrast, the nights were glorious. Whole new constellations of stars dotted the heavens, but the Great Bear had disappeared over the horizon for the first time in their lives. It was a small thing, but it made everyone realise nothing would be the same again.

The only excitement came late one evening, as they were tossing quoits with little enthusiasm in the relative cool of the night air. Harriet Bell tore across the deck and begged for the doctor's urgent help with her daughter's labour. From Harriet's hurried explanation and frightened expression, they gathered Tess had been pushing for hours and the baby wasn't moving.

George sprung up from where he was lounging on the deck.

'I'll get your bag and come to help,' Anne said.

'It could be distressing.' George hesitated and glanced at Elisabeth. 'But I suppose you could use the practice.' He raced after Harriet while Anne disappeared down to the cabin.

When they had gone, Elisabeth sank to her knees, hunching protectively over her belly, praying that mother and child would be all right. She had been trying not to think ahead to her own child's birth, which was a terrifying prospect. She had no idea what to do – no mother to hold her hand, no book for sage advice – she could only be grateful that she would not have to give birth on the ship.

25 September 1841

At the morning service, they gave thanks for the safe arrival of their newest passenger, a child born last night and named Georgianna Rosalind, after the doctor and ship. Despite the long labour and breech birth, both mother and child attended the service, supported by a dazed young man barely old enough to shave and a proud grandmother, surrounded by the extended Bell family. George Penrose took one look at the ashen face of his patient and hurried off to get her a chair, while Grace Robertshaw shaded mother and child with a gaudy pink parasol.

Elisabeth went to see Georgianna after the service. Tess and her child were propped up with pillows in the shade, wearing identical expressions of drowsy happiness.

'Adorable! Congratulations on your new granddaughter, Mrs Bell.'

'Please, call me Harriet. The doctor saved her life last night and I've you to thank for getting my Tess to see him.'

'I'm amazed to see Tess on her feet again already.' Elisabeth handed Harriet a package wrapped in the remnants of muslin from her new gown. 'A few things we got together for Tess and your family.'

'Goodness, thank you, ma'am,' Harriet said, as she unwrapped the parcel.

'Call me Elisabeth, please. The present is not much really.'

'It means a lot to us. These muslin squares will come in very useful for the baby. Oh, what pretty wool. Apples and fresh bread too. Heavens, I can't tell you how much I miss proper food. Thank you for your kindness.' Harriet turned to scan the deck but forgot to look up. Ned dropped neatly to the deck beside her and sniffed at the apples, his tongue already licking his wind-chafed lips. 'Take this for the young 'uns, Ned,' she said, handing him an apple and a cob loaf.

Ned got out a small knife and carved up the food meticulously into even slices, taking one slice for himself and racing off with the rest to find his siblings and cousins.

'He's a good lad, our Ned. Many children would have taken the biggest share for themselves.'

'He reminds me very much of my nephew. Both will be fine young men. Does he miss England?'

'He'll settle soon enough. He misses the orchard, but he hated the big city. Poor lad had quite a fright the night we boarded the ship, so he's glad to be away from London.'

'What happened?'

'We couldn't afford no place to stay, so we squatted in an empty building at the docks for a few days. Ned couldn't but help climbing all over it, bless 'im. The night we boarded, he were on the roof and saw two drunken gents walk by. He said he heard them talking about sailing on the *Lady Rosalind*, so he looked over the edge of the roof and saw one of them push the other down a flight of steps. Our poor Ned almost fell off the roof at the sight of all the blood coming out of his head.'

'Was he sure it wasn't an accident?'

'Even if it were, the pusher didn't stop to help, but stripped the poor wretch of his clothes before shoving his body through the basement door and closing it again. Then he took off like a hare with a fox on his tail. We checked the man, but he were dead, God rest his soul. We were rushing to get on the ship ourselves, so had to leave the poor wretch in the street for someone to find. 'Twas the best we could do.'

'I'm sure his family will be grateful that you left him where he would be found. Poor Ned, what a dreadful thing to see. Was he able to describe the men?'

'Ned only saw them from above, before he came to get us. We didn't stay more than a few seconds with the body to check if he were alive, but I'd say the dead man were in his twenties. Clean-shaven, tall and well-fed, but not fat like some of them. Just your regular gentry type.' Ned was back on deck, licking his fingers, so she called him over. 'Ned, Mrs Godwin wants to know about that man what killed the other at the docks. Did you get a look at him?'

Ned stared at her with wide eyes and shook his head vigorously.

She smiled at him. 'You were very brave, Ned, and smart not to let them see you. I only wondered how you knew they were gentleman?'

'They had them tall black hats and fancy clothes of well-to-do gents. I could smell they were gents too – all soapy and that smelly stuff they put in their hair – not like normal folk. Fair reeked of it.'

'Were they both drunk?'

'One more than the other. The bad man were holding up the drunk one to keep him from falling, before he pushed 'im.'

'Might he have just slipped?'

'No, it were a push an' no mistake. Soon as he dun it, he were down the steps pulling papers out of the man's pocket. It looked like he were going to leave, but he came back and took the dead man's clothes too. All but his drawers, I mean.'

Elisabeth shivered, but tried not to let her shock show. 'And what did they say about the *Lady Rosalind*?'

'The drunk one were worried they might not make it back in time to board, but the other said they had plenty of time to get on the ship and they may as well make the most of their last hours on dry land. I heard 'em clearly, 'cos the street were quiet and they weren't keeping their voices down.'

'What a strange thing. You did very well. You should try to forget about it if you can, Ned. Well, Harriet, time I left you to enjoy being a grandmother.'

George Penrose strode across the deck towards them. 'Good morning, ladies. How's our littlest passenger this morning?' He smiled down at mother and child, both of whom looked back with bright blue eyes. 'Morning, Tess. I am astounded to see you looking so well. Is your baby feeding all right?'

'Yes, sir, she's a wee angel, now that she's out, thanks be to you, sir.'

'Marvellous. Try to keep up your strength by eating well. I'll assign some extra rations and a tonic for you. Let me know if you or the baby feel unwell, otherwise I'll leave you to the excellent care of your family.'

'Thank you, sir.'

'Mr Penrose, might I have a word with you when you have a moment?' Elisabeth asked, as the doctor was turning to stride away to his next task.

'Certainly, Mrs Godwin. Now?'

They said their goodbyes and retreated to the poop deck. When they were alone, or as alone as one could be on a ship with over two hundred passengers,

Elisabeth said, 'George, can you tell me whether any of the gentlemen who were supposed to be on the ship failed to show up?'

'No, all the colonists boarded as expected, except your Major Carruthers and his wife. Why do you ask?'

Elisabeth told him what Ned had seen. 'I can't make sense of it. It sounded as if both were due to sail on the *Lady Rosalind*. They had no luggage, so it must have been loaded already, yet nobody is missing.'

'Strange indeed. If it was a robber disguised as a gentleman, then we would be one passenger short.'

'The only explanation I can think of is that he was out to steal the dead man's ticket. Ned did say he took some papers from the man's pocket…' She paused, unwilling to state the obvious conclusion.

'And that would mean we have an impostor on board who was willing to kill to take the dead man's place.' He gripped her arm and looked into her eyes. 'Elisabeth, once again, it seems you are not safe, assuming this man was working with Cloutier. He must have been the one who stole your necklace. Please promise me you will not leave your cabin without someone by your side. I wish I didn't have to work, so that I could protect you myself.'

Elisabeth leaned her elbows on the rail and sank her head into her hands, feeling shaken to the core by this latest revelation. 'But who can I trust? I cannot believe any of our gentleman would do such a thing. Perhaps Ned misheard the ship's name?'

'Let's assume not. Better safe than sorry. There are few men it could be. I cannot believe it was Templeton, who seems completely genuine, which means it can't be his friend, Amberley, as they came together. I'd be willing to believe it was Maynard, except that he boarded with his family, as did Mr Strickland. That only leaves Knight, Gilbert and Forrester. Or me, not that I own a top hat or fancy clothes.'

'George, you know I trust you completely. I cannot believe it of any of them – even Gilbert who so obviously dislikes me. Mr Forrester seems to be exactly what he says he is and I cannot help but like Mr Knight, despite his faults. I'll have to see what Thomas can tell us about their backgrounds. I know Mr Knight was appointed to his position at the last minute and was unknown to Mr Strickland. I really think it must have been someone dressed as a gentleman. Or a misunderstanding on Ned's part.'

Elisabeth spent the rest of the day in the cabin, helping Anne rehearse her lines for the play, which was to be performed the next day. Anne was a little nervous, even though she was a confident speaker and had an excellent memory for lines. Little Victoria Maynard had demanded a part as a fairy princess, as she could not bear to be left out. There was little doubt she would steal the show, as she was so sweet and funny.

They ventured out only for meals. Elisabeth sat silently at the end of the table, trying to see into the darker spaces in the hearts and minds of the men around her, with no success whatsoever.

26 September 1841

The play was loosely based on Shakespeare's '*As you like it*', with Anne as 'Rosalind of the *Lady Rosalind*'. The actors and actresses did a fine job, but Victoria provided the most laughter, as she bounced in and out like a jack-in-a-box from behind the wings (which were spare sails strung beside the 'stage') in eager anticipation of her part. The final scene had been rewritten to crown Victoria as the fairy princess, for which she had to change into her princess costume.

She skipped out in high spirits, her hair up and wearing a dress in a similar midnight-blue colour to Elisabeth's gown at the formal dance. The laughter from the audience stopped abruptly as she turned to face them, a sparkling loop of sapphires and diamonds around her neck.

Lady Maynard's applause stopped in mid-clap, her hands going to her mouth to smother a cry. Sir Julius went white as a sheet, dappled with a flush of flaming red on his cheeks. Victoria held her ground for a moment, waiting for the applause to resume, before bursting into tears at the stunned faces of her audience.

Anne was the first to react, crouching down by Victoria and whispering in her ear, 'It's all right, my sweet. We were all just a little surprised to see Mrs Godwin's necklace. Do tell me how you were clever enough to find it.'

Victoria whispered into her ear, too quietly for the eager audience to hear.

'Well now, I think we must swap it for a proper princess crown. Then you can perform a graceful curtsey for the audience.'

That done, Charlotte was deputised to take the two children off to see about a treat from Mr Thomas. The cabin passengers retreated to the privacy of the cuddy, sitting around the table with Elisabeth, Anne, George and the captain at one end and the Maynards huddled a little apart at the other. Mr Enys stood with crossed arms at the door, with Mr Knight lounging beside him, as if unsure of his welcome. His forehead still looked blotchy where he'd had to scrub off the tar.

The captain raised his hand for silence, gesturing for Anne to begin.

'Victoria says she found the necklace while playing hide and seek with her nanny. It was concealed behind a set of drawers in her parents' cabin. Naturally, one does not wish to jump to conclusions without examining all the evidence.'

'What need for evidence?' Mr Knight snorted. 'Surely, the culprit is obvious. Damned scoundrel admitted to stealing his wife's diamonds to pay his gambling debts.'

Sir Julius leapt to his feet. 'How could I steal what I already own? I was forced to hand them over as security on a debt to that cheating Frenchman because someone stole from my roll of banknotes. And I wonder who that could have been, Knight, since the Frenchman did not have them? Seems to me it wasn't just Cloutier who cheated.'

Knight was mid-stride toward the table, his fists at the ready, when Mr Enys halted him with an iron hand on his shoulder. A lifetime of hauling and climbing made the sailor's grip a formidable force.

The captain turned to Sir Julius. 'Did you or did you not take the necklace?'

'Most certainly not. I may be fond of gambling, but I am a gentleman, not a common thief. You'd do better by asking Knight, who has amply demonstrated he is no gentleman.'

'Mr Knight?'

'Of course not.'

Sir Julius was not done. 'Must we accept the word of a foreigner that it was even taken in the first place? I've heard it said that the necklace was stolen by her family in France, so how can we trust her?'

Anne, George, and Amberley all leapt to their feet. Enys again stepped in, while the captain pounded his meaty fist on the table.

Elisabeth sat in shocked stillness. On the other side of her, she overheard Mr Gilbert whispering to Mr Forrester that, in his view, Sir Julius had a good point.

'That Godwin woman has demonstrated poor morals by making eyes at all the rich men on the ship, and even consorting with the crew, while no doubt shamelessly kissing her husband's picture before bed every night. Women are all the same. Harlots, the lot of them.'

Unfortunately, the room had been silenced by the captain's fist just as Gilbert said these words, so everyone heard his whispered slander. A new uproar swelled. Elisabeth blinked back tears of shame, wondering if this was the general opinion of her.

'Enough!' bellowed the captain. 'Not a word from anyone, unless asked a direct question by me. And for goodness' sake, you men sit down and put your fists away.'

'May I say something, Captain?' Anne asked.

'By all means, Miss Godwin. I would heartily welcome a bit of common sense.'

'First, let me make it absolutely clear. My sister-in-law Elisabeth is entirely above reproach. These malicious slanders are absolutely untrue.' She looked at each accuser in turn until they looked down under the force of her glare. 'Second, we need to look at the evidence. The necklace went missing when I left the door open to tend to a minor cut suffered by Miss Charlotte Strickland. Two people were known to have passed the open door – Mr Knight and Mr Gilbert. Either could have slipped into our cabin, taken the necklace, and quickly hidden it in the nearest empty spot, which happened to be the Maynards' cabin. We all know that their cabin is never locked so the young children can come and go as they please.'

Knight and Gilbert both protested angrily, while the Maynards nodded eagerly.

Anne continued. 'Of course, they were not the only ones who could have passed the open cabin unseen, as we are, as you all know, close to the entrance to the stairs and cuddy. I was busy with Charlotte and may not have heard anyone moving quietly. However, Elisabeth smelled cigar smoke in the cabin soon after the thief left the second time, suggesting the thief had been in Mr Strickland's office. Again, Knight and Gilbert.'

George added, 'Knight and Sir Julius were the ones who knew the rumour about Mrs Godwin carrying something of great value to the Frenchman.'

Mr Knight was trembling and pale, but adamant. 'Nonsense. Everyone saw her wearing the necklace. And I was so appalled by the Frenchman's insinuations that I mentioned his outrageous offer of a reward to several people, including Gilbert.'

Mr Strickland could no longer be silent. 'Knight. I have warned you numerous times that any more incidents would lead to your dismissal without pay. Consider yourself banished from my employment.'

Elisabeth held up a hand. 'One moment, Mr Strickland. There are other points to consider. The evidence suggests that Mr Knight went straight past the cabin and up to the deck on the day the necklace was taken, while Mr Gilbert was known to have lingered.'

Gilbert responded angrily, 'I am a loyal employee. I was waiting to see if Miss Charlotte needed assistance. Knight was out the door well before me.'

Elisabeth continued in a calm voice, 'I ask you, Mr Gilbert, how did you know I keep a picture of my late husband above my bed?'

Gilbert went still, his usually surly face going completely blank. He stammered, 'I must have seen it from the door in passing. And anyway, what decent married woman would not have a picture of her husband?'

'But it is above my bed, just as you said, and therefore cannot be seen from the door. In fact, it is right by the small shelf where my necklace was sitting, also out of sight of the door.'

'I do recall glancing in briefly to see if Miss Godwin was there. But I assure you, I touched nothing.'

George Penrose interrupted the momentary silence. 'Might I suggest a search of Gilbert and Knight's cabin. There is still the matter of the missing key, taken from Miss Godwin, as well as Sir Julius's missing money to account for.' He turned to the captain. 'With your permission, sir, I will find Mr Thomas and conduct a search.'

Gilbert leapt to his feet, shouting, 'No, you are not an impartial observer. Anyone with eyes in his head can see you are lusting after the Godwin woman.'

A collective gasp of deeply drawn breath was the only sound for a split second before George Penrose lunged across the table with his fists clenched. He was intercepted by the captain, who had reached boiling point.

'Gilbert, any more of that foul language, and I'll set the mate onto you with the lash. Now, everyone, calm down. Mr Enys, find Thomas and search their cabin. Quick as you can, don't mind what you break.'

The captain forced the doctor down into his seat, where he perched with ill-disguised rage. The assembled passengers waited on tenterhooks for the searchers to reappear, not knowing which way to look. No one dared look at Elisabeth, except Anne, who wrapped a protective arm around her. Elisabeth wanted only to disappear into her cabin and not come out until they reached Wellington.

The chief mate stomped back into the cuddy quarter of an hour later, throwing a small wad of banknotes onto the table. 'No key. But that's a lot of money for a clerk to be carrying, Mr Gilbert.'

Gilbert slumped even lower in his seat. 'I will swear on the Bible that I did not touch the necklace or take the key.' His voice trembled, and one of his eyelids was twitching like a trapped fly.

Sir Julius glared at him. 'You will know if it's my stolen money, by the tiny pinpricks in the upper left corner. I always do that to ensure that no one tries to take my stake.'

Mr Enys flipped through the roll, holding the notes up to the skylight. 'None with pinholes. All these notes are brand new, with consecutive numbers. About twenty pounds' worth.'

'Brand new notes?' Mr Strickland sat bolt upright, outraged. 'You damned devil. Stealing from the government money entrusted to me.' He turned to the captain. 'Captain, I have a list of the numbers of the new banknotes issued to me, so we can easily check. Seems I might have dismissed the wrong man.'

'Lock Gilbert in the brig, Mr Enys.'

Mr Enys grabbed Gilbert's collar and shoved him towards the door. The clerk looked to be on the point of tears as he turned back to Mr Strickland. 'I only took the little that was rightfully mine. I slaved for a pittance for years, with never a word of thanks or a raise to recognise my good work. I was owed me that money as fair wages, by the government and you and all the other rich dandies who make beggars of the working man.'

The remaining passengers released a collective sigh of held breath as he exited. Elisabeth rushed out of the salon, away from the escalating babble of voices, with Anne at her heels.

Anne closed their cabin door behind her firmly, leaning her back against it as an added barrier to invasion. 'What an appalling scene. Dreadful man, although I simply cannot believe he might be a murderer as well as a thief.'

Elisabeth curled up on her bed, with the portrait of John held tight, trying unsuccessfully to hold back tears. 'How will I ever face everyone again?'

Anne sat down beside her, laying a warm hand on her shivering arm. 'You will face them with pride and a straight back. That odious man knows nothing. You have done nothing more than talk and dance with some cheerful young men with absolute propriety, the same as the rest of us. As for anyone believing the Frenchman's lies … well, I cannot believe we have so many imbeciles on board one ship.'

Elisabeth felt wretched. 'I have spoken to Mr Penrose several times at length, with only the helmsman and other sailors present. That is not the proper behaviour of a lady in mourning. I have exposed him to an accusation of impropriety, possibly put his position at risk. Oh, Anne, all I wanted was to do was to see you two together. How did it all go so wrong?'

'Elisabeth, listen to me. Not a single person on this ship thinks you or George have done anything improper. My darling sister, you are the most intelligent and loving woman I know. But in this case, your short-sightedness astounds me. Mr Gilbert is a foul viper, but there was a skerrick of truth behind the venom on one point. It is blindingly obvious George Penrose only has eyes for you, although he acts like a perfect gentleman and tries to hide it. He and I are firm friends, but it is you he has the connection with. Do you not feel it too? Unless it is Mr Amberley's attentions that you prefer?'

'Oh no, Mr Amberley is not my type at all. I confess that I enjoy George's company – much more than I ought. But I am a married woman in mourning and with child. It is ludicrous to think there could be any attachment given the circumstances.'

'So you say, but Cupid doesn't care a whit about circumstances. Elisabeth, I know you are still mourning John and, of course, it is important not to rush into a new attachment. But don't deny yourself the chance to love again, for the sake of society's silly conventions. Not least because living as a widow with a baby will not be easy in an unknown country.'

'I will think on it. And what about you? Mr Knight seems very keen.'

'He may be charming when he is sober, but he has a wild side not best suited to marriage. No, I shall resign myself to being the doting aunt to your adorable baby. Unless I can make the gorgeous Mr Amberley see that there is more to a woman than beauty. He could use a sensible woman to help make his estate a success. And there's always that fur-trapper.'

'I can see I have been wasting my energy on the wrong prospective brother-in-law. I might have saved a lot of trouble if I had kept right out of it and left it in your capable hands.'

'What, and deny me the fun of watching your efforts with George on my behalf?'

'I'm glad I amuse you, Anne. With John gone, I suppose I have been rather over-protective. You mean everything to me.'

The two sisters clung to each other for a long while, at first in silence and then quietly talking about the future they were determined to make together, once this interminable voyage was finally over.

Reconciliation

27 September – 10 October 1841

The following two weeks were a blur of days passing, with little to distinguish between them. South-east trade winds filled the sails, propelling the ship south at speed, parallel to the coast of South America. Routine duties were completed, indistinguishable meals were eaten, and always the dark ocean extended without relief to the horizon and far beyond. The occasional novelties – a morning watching a sail on the horizon or a momentary glimpse of a whale spout – served only to highlight the sameness of the intervening hours.

The weather became markedly cooler as they raced south, so the hauling of trunks from below, to exchange cool for warm clothes, made for a busy day or two. Otherwise, within the tight confines of the vessel, the sailors got on with their work and the passengers waited with trance-like patience for the journey to be over, numbed by the knowledge that they were still only halfway to New Zealand by distance.

The one bright spot was that the atmosphere was much improved since the capture of the thief and the disappearance of Cloutier. The general feeling on board was that of a good-natured community of neighbours, getting on with what needed to be done, knowing their fellow passengers would likely continue to be their neighbours in the small settlement of Wellington. Minor fights and petty grievances rose from time to time – over who finished all the preserved potatoes or failed to clean the toilet bucket or cheated at dominoes – but the disagreements never went beyond an angry word or a cursory shove.

Even Sir Julius and Mr Knight mended their ways. Sir Julius decided to sell his land on arrival, not being of the farming disposition, and set up a business in town. He was even heard to ask Mr Forrester's advice on the matter. And he received it, at length. Mr Knight set himself to training surveyors, in the hope of redeeming himself in Mr Strickland's eyes. Neither drank more than one or two glasses of wine with dinner, and both were polite and genial. Mr Gilbert was locked up in the brig and not missed.

George Penrose was rarely seen, so busy was he about his duties, despite the almost total lack of sickness aboard the ship.

Elisabeth gradually emerged from the shell of her cabin, but she was far from her usual joyful self, despite putting her troubles behind her. Teaching helped pass the time. With four teachers – Grace,

Anne, Charlotte and Elisabeth – the students were making good progress. Lady Maynard shocked them one day by arriving with a donation of books. A most welcome peace offering.

Anne struggled to cheer Elisabeth up, as did Mr Amberley, who was increasingly to be found at Anne's side.

Surprisingly, it was in the company of Mr Templeton and Charlotte that Elisabeth found the most relief. They were so wrapped up in their music and plans for their shared future that they treated her just as before – as a valued friend rather than someone to be pitied and jollied along. She enjoyed discussing wedding ideas with Charlotte, even if neither of them had any idea what would be feasible in Wellington. Would there be a suitable venue? Would there even be roses in this alien world? It didn't matter – the fun was in the vision, not the details.

A fortnight after the thief was unmasked, Elisabeth found herself alone in the cuddy with Mr Templeton late in the evening, while Charlotte was off retrieving a notebook.

'You've made Charlotte very happy, William.'

'I hope so. I know I am the happiest man in the world. Emigrating to New Zealand was the best decision I ever made, despite my parents' dire warnings.'

'Had you and Amberley been planning it for long?'

'I do not know about Edgar, but I put in many months of preparation to ensure I would have every necessary skill.'

'Oh, I thought you had planned to make the voyage together.'

'Not at all. I only met him at the docks. But he's a fine, cheerful fellow. We became friends on the spot. Cheese to my chalk, if you know what I mean.'

Elisabeth was unsettled by this unexpected revelation. The close friendship that she had assumed between the two men had made her warm to Mr Amberley, despite … despite what? Hard to put a finger on, but she had found his charm to be superficial and wondered about the true nature of the man below the surface. He told a lot of amusing stories and talked knowledgably about books and the theatre, hunting and balls. But he gave away very little of his background or deeper motivations. And if Amberley was unknown before he boarded the ship, that changed their assumptions completely.

'Do you know much about him? Family background and so forth? I don't mean to be indiscreet, but … shall I just say that trust is in short supply after recent events.'

'Of course, I appreciate your concern for your sister. It does you credit, Elisabeth. Edgar is wonderful company, as we all know, and has been a good friend to me.' Templeton paused for a few seconds, drumming a light beat on the table with his artistic fingers. 'Do you know, I really can't recall him talking about where he's from or who his people are. Somewhere to the north of London, I think – Derbyshire, perhaps? But he's obviously a gentleman and well educated. As to wealth and connection, I could not say.'

'All I'm concerned about is that he is a good man, underneath the charming manners.'

'I should say so. He has his New Zealand Company land deeds and cargo in the hold, so I feel his future is sound, even if he knows little of the intricacies of farming.'

Charlotte appeared in the doorway. 'What are you two plotting with your heads so close together?'

Elisabeth smiled back. 'I was just saying you will be the loveliest bride in the history of New Zealand. Your fiancé disagrees. He says you will be loveliest bride in the history of the world.'

Charlotte positively glowed, as did her fiancé. She left the two lovebirds alone and retired to her cabin.

Thomas was in the corridor. He could confirm that Mr Amberley was from a highly respectable family of landed gentry from Leicestershire. Assuming he really was who he said he was. Elisabeth knew she was tying herself in knots for nothing – the thief was caught and she could far more readily believe Gilbert a murderer than Amberley, who might be superficial but was also sweet-natured and caring. It was still her view that the killing on the docks had nothing to do with any of them, as surely Ned had misheard the name of the ship.

11 October 1841

Elisabeth flipped over another page of her book without seeing the words. She had read her few books, and those of her fellow passengers, so many times already that she could just about recite them. The cuddy was crowded, as a stiff breeze had whipped up the whitecaps, making the deck unpleasant. Everyone was chatting amiably or occupied with a task such as sewing or writing, leaving her alone in the corner.

No matter how she tried to distract herself, she still had a nagging doubt that all was not right within the limited confines of their maritime world. Reverend Robertshaw had talked about judging others fairly in his daily sermon and the words were echoing in her subconscious. She was worried that they had passed judgement too hastily, assuming that Mr Gilbert had stolen the necklace with scant evidence, just because he had taken the money. But she was unsure what to do and felt he would be unlikely to welcome any attempt on her part to get the full story. She had just decided to talk to their resident clergyman, who she had seen speaking to Mr Gilbert on many occasions, when the Reverend Robertshaw entered the room and headed for her corner.

'Mrs Godwin, the very person I was after. I trust you are well?'

'A little out of sorts, to be honest. I was about to seek you out to discuss Mr Gilbert's situation, which I cannot help but feel may have been misjudged.'

'That is very Christian of you, Mrs Godwin, after his outburst.'

'He was under stress at the time. His remarks seemed very out of character, even though he had made his dislike of me clear frequently. I may be naïve, but I felt inclined to believe him when he denied stealing my necklace. And to steal only a few notes from a large supply seems … I scarcely know how to put it…'

'Wrong, but not the act of a habitual thief?'

'Exactly.'

'I thought so too. I have talked to Mr Gilbert on several occasions and found him a devout man, but also a man struggling with inner turmoil. He would not open up to me, so I sent Mr Knight to see him this morning. I came to you, hoping you would hear what he has to say.'

'Of course.'

'Mr Knight is up on deck, waiting to talk to you. I suggest you take a warm wrap, my dear.'

Up on the deck, the wind whipped through her hair, flicking pale tendrils around her face. It was chilly but refreshing after the close atmosphere below deck. The chief mate and doctor were deep in conversation at the helm. Mr Enys gestured for her to come over and join them, but she had spotted Mr Knight huddled at the side rail.

'If you'll excuse me, I'll be back in a few minutes once I have talked to Mr Knight.'

George opened his mouth to say something but closed it again with a shake of his head. She could feel his eyes boring into her back as she walked over to the side of the vessel and gripped the top rail to safeguard against rogue waves.

'Mr Knight. I gather you have news of Mr Gilbert.'

'Thank you for seeing me, Mrs Godwin. It's a strange thing to have shared a cabin with a man for so many weeks, and yet to know so little about him.'

'I take it the Reverend Robertshaw was right in thinking there is more to the story?'

'Joseph Gilbert has had a tough life. It all started well – he married his childhood sweetheart and was studying law. His future seemed bright, but then his father was bankrupted in the Panic of 1825. Duped into investing in a fictional enterprise in central America, poor soul. The son had to give up his legal studies and take a clerk's job in the government offices. He and his wife had to move into a cheap room with no heating, which caused his heart problems. He was reluctant to give me all the details, but I gather they ran out of savings and his wife deserted him for a man with better prospects.'

'Perhaps explaining his dislike of women, and me in particular?'

'He did say he couldn't bear to look at you because you look like his wife and have the same ability to make men go weak at the knees. He is deeply ashamed of what he said about you in the heat of the moment. Anyway, he was grateful to get the government job and didn't even make a fuss when he was assigned to go to New Zealand with Mr Strickland, even though he wanted to stay in England. He has worked hard for the government for more than a decade, with little thanks and still on the same salary as when he started. Mr Strickland is a fine man, but he does tend to be rather focussed on getting the job done, rather than the welfare of employees. Not through meanness, you understand, just through his dedication to the work. And perhaps he did not know Gilbert's background.'

'Well, that certainly explains a great deal. Not that I condone theft, but desperation can lead to poor decisions even in the best of men. Does Gilbert still deny taking the necklace?'

'Absolutely and unequivocally. I have to say I believe him.'

Elisabeth considered the options and decided a direct and honest approach was the only antidote to distrust. 'Would you be willing to back me up if I talked to Mr Strickland? I realise that would put you in a delicate situation with your employer.'

'Mr Strickland has a very low opinion of me already. But, of course, I would be happy to help Gilbert if I can.'

She looked him straight in the eye. 'Forgive me for being frank, but I have been wondering if your own bad behaviour was also rather out of character. I think you are a much better man than you have shown to Mr Strickland on this voyage. Were it not ridiculous, I would suspect a deliberate attempt to be released from your position, so you could forge your own path?'

'My god, woman, you cut to the very heart of a man! I admit I am ashamed by what I have done. Most especially as it has diminished my standing in the eyes of you and your sister.' He seized her hand. 'Elisabeth, can you tell me if I still have any chance with Anne? Nothing would make me happier than to have her by my side. I've been such a fool.'

He slipped a chunky ring with a family crest off his little finger and thrust it at her, as if demonstrating his honest intentions. He fumbled it and dropped it to the deck, forcing him to kneel to retrieve it. She glanced over towards the helm, where the two men were watching on with open mouths. They looked away immediately. George abruptly turned and left via the quarterdeck ladder, almost tumbling down it in his haste.

Mr Knight followed the direction of her gaze. 'Oh dear. I am sorry if I have added to your vexations. I hope they did not get the wrong idea.'

Elisabeth reached down and helped him up before he could say any more. 'Mr Knight – Walter – I have made a vow to Anne never to stand in the way of her happiness. You may ask for her hand if you wish, but I must warn you that I think it unlikely she will accept under the present circumstances. Your lives are on very different paths.'

'Perhaps I should rebuild her trust before making my case?'

'I think that would be wise.' She reached up and touched his cheek, hating to see this cheerful young man looking so sad. 'Shall we go and find Mr Strickland?'

They found him in his cabin, surrounded by scattered piles of papers on the desk, the chair, and even the floor. To Elisabeth's surprise, Mr Strickland listened with his full attention and admitted that he felt a degree of culpability for his actions.

'Gilbert was the best clerk I ever had. I'm finding the work to be impossible without him. Really, I cannot believe I knew so little of his circumstances. He should have spoken to me himself if he needed an increase in his salary.'

'Time has a habit of passing quickly when we are busy, Mr Strickland. And many employees are intimidated by their employers, whether or not it is warranted. Might you be willing to give Mr Gilbert a good reference so that his sentence for theft can be reduced to the minimum? I realise it is a lot to ask of you.'

'If you can be so forgiving, Mrs Godwin, then so can I. Can you have him brought to me?'

As Elisabeth rose to leave, she put a hand on Mr Knight's shoulder, pushing him back into his chair. 'Mr Knight also has something he wishes to discuss with you.'

It took her a while to get the key from Mr Thomas and permission from the captain, who came down himself to escort the prisoner and satisfy his curiosity. A miserable figure lay on the meagre mattress in the windowless cabin, which was no bigger than a linen cupboard. He looked startled to see them, but followed them meekly with sagging shoulders, resigned to meet whatever new fate awaited.

Mr Strickland asked to speak to Mr Gilbert alone for a few minutes and sent Mr Knight off to find the Reverend Robertshaw. When he called them all back in, Gilbert was sobbing into a large while handkerchief with 'ES' embroidered on the corner.

Mr Strickland directed his attention to the captain. 'New information has come to light, sir. I wish to withdraw the accusation of theft and take Mr Gilbert back into my employment.'

The captain rocked back on his heels and cast his eyes over the group. 'But he as good as admitted to the theft.'

'Extenuating circumstances and a genuine case of misunderstanding regarding the theft, Captain. I will take full responsibility for his behaviour until we disembark in New Zealand.'

'But the necklace?'

Elisabeth intervened. 'I have it back and I'm convinced that Mr Gilbert was not the thief.'

The captain got up and walked over to the door. 'Can't say I like it, but if you're all on his side, I am willing to agree. I must say I'm surprised by your attitude, Mrs Godwin, after how he treated you.'

Mr Gilbert turned his red eyes to her. 'I would like to offer Mrs Godwin my sincere and wholehearted apologies. I have acted abominably when she has done nothing but help other people and keep everyone's spirits buoyed by her charm.'

'Apology accepted. I wish you well, Mr Gilbert,' Elisabeth said, as the captain banged the door closed behind him.

Gilbert was not finished. 'Mr Strickland, your compassion is more than I deserve. I can only say that I will reward your trust with hard work, as God will surely reward you for your forgiveness. Mr Knight, I owe you a debt as well for believing in me. And you too, Reverend. I have agreed with Mr Strickland that I will offer my services to your mission as a volunteer, outside of work hours, to make amends.'

Mr Strickland clapped a hand to his shoulder. 'Well said, Gilbert. I thank you all for bringing this matter to my attention.' He smiled at them and strode over to open the door. 'Perhaps I might conclude our meeting, so we can make a start at bringing this mess of paperwork back to an orderly state.'

Outside the cabin, Mr Knight shook the reverend's hand and kissed Elisabeth's. 'Mr Strickland has kindly agreed that I might look into opportunities to take my surveying skills into uncharted territory, provided I put in a year's hard work for him, including training other men for the task of surveying streets.'

She kissed him on the cheek. 'That sounds like an excellent compromise. I wish you well and expect to hear great things of you in the future.'

He flashed deep dimples. 'I shall name the second highest mountain that I discover after you, for the highest is already promised to the admirable Mr Strickland.'

She smiled back. 'A pleasant valley or river named after me would do very nicely.'

After supper, Elisabeth took Anne outside to bring her up-to-date with the surprising developments of the day. They stood at the stern rail, looking up at a shimmering swath of stars overhead. Mr Enys had pointed out the Southern Cross and Pointers and explained how to work out the direction of south with their guidance.

Elisabeth also passed on the new information about Mr Amberley, in as casual a manner as she could muster. After all, he had never said outright that he and Templeton were old friends, and they had never pressed him for precise details of his past. Nothing had really changed. Except they no longer had the word of a man they trusted to vouch for Amberley.

Before Anne could say anything, Mr Amberley himself appeared on the poop deck, as if he had been conjured by her words. He strolled towards them with one hand on George Penrose's back, steering him their way. George and Elisabeth had exchanged no more than stiff nods of greeting since the discovery of the necklace and Mr Gilbert's mortifying words.

'Good evening, ladies. May we join you?'

'Of course you may, Mr Amberley.'

'How convenient that we found you. Anne, my dear, I have been meaning to talk to you about the Templeton's wedding. I gather you will stand with the bride?'

Mr Amberley moved to stand a little apart with Anne, talking to her quietly, leaving the doctor beside Elisabeth. They stood in an uncomfortable silence until Mr Amberley turned to them with an exasperated sigh.

'Oh, for heaven's sake, you two. Elisabeth, George wants to apologise for putting you in a position where your reputation could be slandered. Despite the obvious fact that not one person aboard this vessel, other than the one under arrest, thinks of you as anything other than the most respectable and delightful of ladies.'

Anne cut in. 'George, Elisabeth feels that she has put your position on board this ship at risk. Which she hasn't. In fact, the captain said only today, and I quote: "He's the best damned doctor I've ever had and a darned sight more of a gentleman than most of the titled folk I've met." Please, I beg you, talk to each other, or I shall have to bang your heads together.'

Anne slipped her arm through Mr Amberley's, with just a hint of a smirk, and they strolled off across the poop deck.

'I suppose they have a point. I would hate to lose your friendship, George, over a ridiculous, malicious remark.'

'That will never happen, Elisabeth.'

'Good, enough said.'

Still he would not meet her eye. 'Not quite. I must congratulate you on your engagement to Mr Knight.'

'There is no engagement between us and never will be. What you saw was an impulsive young man asking for my permission to propose to Anne. He was only kneeling because he dropped the ring.'

Finally, he looked up. 'Oh. And did you give your permission?'

'I wouldn't stand in her way if she loved him, but I don't think she does. I told him his offer was unlikely to be accepted without further efforts on his part to show his true character.'

'Anne is a fine woman. I've no doubt she will find a husband of wealth and distinction.'

'Neither of us cares much for such things. Far better to marry for love, than to accept a man who was deemed suitable only by an arbitrary standard of wealth or upbringing. To be able to work together to build a home, a family, a life, with laughter and companionship – these are the things that create true happiness. Don't you agree, George?'

'Yes, of course. But, even so, a princess does not marry a pauper – their ideas of what is needed to make a happy home would differ too much.'

'George, think of France. The princesses *are* the paupers now – those few who escaped the guillotine. Pomp and title are no more than a cloak wrapped around a person by chance, and all too easy to wrench away. But love goes deep under the skin and cannot be so easily discarded. My mother taught me that. She considered herself lucky to be an invisible nobody.'

He was staring at her now. 'I know very little of what happened in France, but I'd like to learn more. Your mother sounds like an extraordinary person.'

'She is. Our family story is a strange one, but then I hardly think you will be surprised at that after what we have been through on this voyage.'

'Well, it's fair to say being around you is never dull. I take it your mother was the same?'

'My mother's mother was a chambermaid for a wealthy French family, who kept my mother on as a companion to their own daughter when my grandmother died. She was treated as a daughter and received as fine an education as anyone could hope for.'

'She was lucky not to be cast out.'

'Until all of their luck ran out during the revolution. When the family was detained, my mother was eager to repay their kindness by helping them, so she hid their valuables. Nobody gave a second thought to a young girl of such little importance. After the family went into exile, my mother could marry my father and retreat to the farm, where happiness prevailed.' She paused as the memory of her forced departure from her family flooded back.

The reassuring warmth of his hand on her arm gave her the strength to finish the story. 'The existence of the pearl necklace became known to a relative of the family in 1830 and he was determined to possess it for himself. You know the rest – Cloutier was sent to get it back, my mother scarred his face, and I escaped with the necklace to England in a futile attempt to return the necklace to the rightful owner. And there I would still be, had it not been for a chance meeting between Cloutier and my brother-in-law.'

George was silent for a long time. She let the silence lie between them, knowing her story was a lot to take in. Finally, he said, 'What a life you have led, Elisabeth. Do you think you could ever settle into a quiet existence in faraway New Zealand?'

'More than anything, I crave a normal life. Family, happiness, security. The intrigues of the rich and powerful hold no delight whatsoever, I assure you.'

'I can certainly understand that.'

'Enough about my family. I want to hear all about Cornwall. I never had the chance to visit, but I hear the coastline is remarkably beautiful and rife with smugglers.'

He smiled. 'In Cornwall, we call smugglers "free-traders". My great-uncle owned an inn and wasn't above selling the odd drop of brandy that fell off the stern of a boat in the night. He didn't mind paying fair taxes, but the revenue services got far too greedy. Smugglers were local heroes. It was only the wreckers that ordinary folk despised.'

They stayed at the rails, sharing stories, separated only by a sliver of starlight, as the stars slowly circled the celestial pole.

Roaring Forties

12 October 1841

In the morning, the captain made his usual navigational observations and called for a turn to the east. After weeks of south-bound travel, the ship was finally heading into the rising sun. The voyage across the Southern Ocean would likely take another six to eight weeks, pushed along by the powerful 'roaring forties' winds.

There was no land at all between their current position off South America, in the South Atlantic, and New Zealand, in the mighty Pacific Ocean. The southern tip of Africa was to the north-east, with only the circling black-and-white Cape Pigeons to show that the Cape of Good Hope was over the horizon. Few ships would pass now, with the bulk of the trade heading north up to India.

The change of direction lent a sense of optimism to their meal-time conversation, only to be squashed by the cautionary tales of the captain.

'Storms fiercer than any other place on earth, raging winds, waterspouts and maybe even icebergs,' was the captain's grim warning.

The consensus was that New Zealand would be a welcome sight that couldn't come soon enough. Elisabeth sought the chief mate later in the day to get a second opinion on their fate.

Mr Enys attempted to add a positive slant but could not muster much of a smile. 'What the captain says is true, but it's not all bad. We'll have a tail wind all the way, so plenty of fast sailing. You'll see giant whales and albatrosses with a wingspan twice the height of a man.' He paused for a moment, his fingers still working on automatic to splice a rope. 'Am I to congratulate you? I saw Mr Knight–'

'Absolutely not. As I explained to Mr Penrose, he was not asking me to marry him, whatever it looked like.'

'The doc is a good man. I might be speaking out of turn, but it's fair killing the lad to abide by the strict rules about crew socialising with passengers. He'd lose his pay, which he can ill afford.'

'You're a good friend, Mr Enys. I'd hate to see that happen after he's worked so hard.'

Elisabeth wandered over to the stern rail, keeping an eye out for whales and icebergs. She saw neither, but did catch sight of one of the giant albatrosses. It truly was a monster of a bird, yet it floated in the wind without apparent effort.

Charlotte Strickland came over to watch it soar above the ship. 'Magnificent creature. What a voyage we've had.'

'I must admit, I'm relieved to be on the final leg of the journey, even if we have weeks of sailing still ahead of us.'

'I heard what you did for Mr Gilbert, Elisabeth. We are all very impressed that you stood up for him in the circumstances and had the brains to figure out the truth. Father is extremely relieved to have him back, keeping his papers in order.'

'Your father is an excellent man. Few employers would have been so willing to reconsider the evidence, especially on the advice of a woman.'

'He prides himself on being fair and objective. And just between us, he is used to taking advice from a woman.' Charlotte glanced over at her parents, strolling arm-in-arm on the deck with their heads together in quiet conversation.

'New Zealand will be lucky to have them both.'

'Elisabeth, I hope you don't mind, but he told me about the documents you gave him. His friend told us all about the railroad investment over dinner one evening, but Father could not recall much of what he said about the man behind it. As it happens, I know his friend's daughter, and she actually met the fellow who sold them the investment, when they passed him in the street one day. Her father introduced him and she talked of nothing else for two weeks at least. How handsome Mr Kingston was, what lovely eyes, how he smiled at her, his manners, his elegance … on and on. Until she saw him in the park, arm-in-arm with an elegant lady. That put an end to it.'

'Interesting. Kingston must be charming to inspire such devotion. There should be no problem identifying the man if there are so many enthusiastic witnesses, especially if he is still frequenting the Palace Club.'

'She can be a rather silly girl at times, especially when it comes to men, but he did make an impression. And not just on the girls. She said her father had been most impressed by the large nugget of gold he showed them from Canada. He wore a smaller, polished nugget on a gold chain, to show how common such things were and how rich they would all be when the railway was built.'

Anne's only comment, when Elisabeth recounted the conversation later, was about how typical it was for men's eyes to be turned by gold, regardless of facts. 'And,' she admitted, 'we woman only need a charming smile to turn our heads.' She was watching dark clouds gathering. 'I hope we're not in for one of those terrible storms the captain mentioned.'

13-16 October 1841

The barometer started dropping the day the *Lady Rosalind* turned east. At first it was merely cold and overcast, with waves surging above the level of the bulwarks. At one point, a giant waterspout appeared out of nowhere, causing frantic shouts and a rapid change of course. The captain had said that a waterspout can hold a vast mass of water, reputedly enough to sink an unlucky ship.

Mostly, the passengers stayed below decks, with occasional forays for fresh air, wrapped in layers of wool. As Elisabeth clung to the companionway rail, she noticed some idiotic young men were trying to catch an albatross with a baited hook. Despite the anger of the sailors, who feared that a dead albatross would bring bad luck, they finally caught and killed one. All so they could measure its wingspan and gather a few souvenirs.

That night, the storm hit with a ferocity beyond all imagination. Jagged lightning crashed all around the vessel, accompanied by booming thunder that echoed in their eardrums. Every member of the crew raced about their allotted tasks, knowing their life depended on it. Everything was lashed down, the hatches were closed, and the sails were furled, except for a few closely reefed sails so they could maintain their heading.

The vessel tossed around like a leaf in a raging torrent. Elisabeth and Anne tied themselves down in one of the beds, with blankets piled around them, and clung to each other to avoid being thrown about the cabin. They had packed away anything that could move in the first hours of the storm, after the contents of their writing desk had been scattered across the floor. Below their cabin, they could hear screams and furniture crashing about. They prayed the items in the hold had been tightly secured, or the vessel would be unbalanced and sunk for sure.

After a terrifying night, where every shuddering groan of timbers felt like it might be their last, morning finally came. The sky remained dark, so dense was the cover of towering black clouds. Three sailors were needed to man the helm, each roped for safety, as the waves had already swept one lad to his death. The three masts were skeletons draped with the barest covering of shredded rags.

But still the storm did not let up. The wind rose even further, into an unbelievable fury, screeching through the rigging like a million banshees wailing and driving them all close to madness.

Just when they felt they could take it no more, a mighty crack reverberated through the air, followed by an ominous crash, which shuddered through every inch of the vessel. Down in their cabin, Elisabeth and Anne could only hold each other close and pray that the ship would not be torn apart completely. They could feel the vessel was wounded by the change in her motion.

Up on deck, the ship's carpenter and a handful of desperate men were hacking at a tangle of wood, rope and sail from the broken yardarm. The debris was dragging alongside the ship and pulling the starboard bulwark under the waves. When the last rope was slashed by frantic axes, the ship righted herself. The crew rested their tired limbs for a few seconds before racing back to their stations.

By afternoon, the wind had dropped to a gale, but they were lashed with heavy rain. Waves almost as tall as the crow's nest surged past, occasionally crashing on to the deck with a thunderous boom. Freezing seawater and rain forced their way past latched portholes, battened hatches and caulked planks, leaving everything sodden. Teams of men and boys were tasked with pumping for their lives to clear the rising water in the bilges, which was dragging the ship further below the waves.
The storm held them in its grip for three more terrifying days.

17-21 October 1841

Elisabeth woke from a fitful sleep to the unaccustomed feel of the *Lady Rosalind* rocking gently back and forth over the swell. She felt as if she had gone deaf at the sudden absence of wind after the thunderous roar of the storm. The only sounds were the groaning of dismembered rigging and the cries of the injured, against the metronome of sloshing water.

Her whole body was limp with shock, exhaustion, and hunger.

Out on the deck, the ship looked like a battlefield. They were lucky not to have lost a mast, although lucky was a relative term given the chaos. All hands were needed to put the ship to rights – pumping the bilges, mending sails, repairing damaged spars, cleaning up the mess.

Everyone who was able was set to a task, right down to the smallest child. Anne and Elisabeth helped the doctor with the injured. Miraculously, only one man had a broken arm, another had snapped a collarbone, and a third had a dislocated shoulder. But there were dozens of sprains and cuts, and almost nobody had escaped without a patchwork of bruises. The most seriously injured were given the few hospital beds, while the rest were tended wherever they lay.

One of the first tasks was for the cooks to prepare a meal after four days of being restricted to ship's biscuits and water. They made a hearty mutton stew, seasoned with a generous dash of brandy, after it was discovered that one of the few remaining sheep had broken its neck in panic. Battered and hunched bodies draped in soaking clothes sat like piles of ragbags on the deck, eating their fill in grim silence.

The captain, chief mate and doctor formed a huddle at one end of the table in the cuddy, shovelling food and talking in low, urgent voices. Elisabeth edged closer to hear what they were saying.

'…broken water barrels could be a problem unless we get some decent rain. The food store is half-flooded with foul water and everything below decks smells of sewage. We'll need a thorough decontamination and a lot of luck to avoid disease and starvation. Thank goodness we took on those extra supplies…'

Elisabeth returned to her work in the hospital and tried not to think what it would be like to run out of food and fresh water in the middle of the Southern Ocean. Fish might keep them from starvation, but they wouldn't survive long without water. Not a thought to dwell on.

Repairs proceeded with sombre efficiency, thanks to a small army of experienced tradesmen and women. With two days of non-stop sawing and sewing, the remaining sails were reset, and they continued on their voyage. The full clean-up took several more days. Mr Penrose ordered that everything that could be moved be brought up to the deck and washed. Fortunately, the weather was fine, if far from warm, allowing mattresses and possessions to be more-or-less dried out.

Every surface of the compartments below deck was thoroughly scrubbed and decontaminated with chloride of lime.

Anne was assigned to do the floor of the cuddy, alongside Mr Amberley. She was in her oldest smock, wielding a mop, while he was on his knees scrubbing, wearing riding breeches and a loose shirt. As his muscular arms swept to and fro across the floorboards, she saw a flash of gold around his neck. When he leaned forward to the bucket, she glimpsed a gold nugget dangling on the end of a chain.

She looked away quickly, continuing to mop as if nothing had happened, though her heart was hammering so hard against her chest that she felt sure it must show. Handsome, charming Amberley, with his lovely eyes and smile, and his apparent devotion to her and Elisabeth. She resisted the urge to panic. He wasn't going anywhere, at least until this hideous voyage finally ended.

As in chess, it was always best to have a strategy before any move was made.

End Game

22-23 October 1841

The doctor's words proved prophetic. Despite all the hard work to decontaminate the ship, a dozen people had fallen sick with terrible stomach pains, diarrhoea, vomiting and a high fever that came on almost without warning. Dysentery, from the sewage-contaminated food, was striking more people down every hour, despite all the precautions.

He ordered extra measures to stop the spread of disease – thorough cooking of food and boiling of water, all hands to be washed before touching food, and toilet pails to be emptied and cleaned regularly. The sick were taken up on to the deck, despite the icy chill, and looked after by a rota of exhausted volunteers. It was heart-breaking to watch the afflicted writhing with stomach pains and constant diarrhoea.

Eleven more people, including seven children, were sick by the next day. To Elisabeth's horror, Anne was one of them. She didn't utter a word of complaint, but Elisabeth could see that she was in agony from her stomach pain and headache.

For two long weeks, they had fought to keep Anne alive. In that short time, she had turned into a skeleton of her former self. Her soft, white skin was sallow and wrinkled with dehydration and her jaundiced, unfocussed eyes were sunk deep into their sockets. Bright, wonderful Anne, who had rarely had a day of sickness in her life.

Right now, she was resting relatively easy, as George had used the last drops of laudanum to comfort her. Elisabeth dreaded to think how she would be tomorrow. All she could do was to cling to the faint hope that Anne would somehow pull through this terrible bout of dysentery. All the medicine was gone. Every knee was red and swollen from praying and scrubbing. The only small mercy was the rain that had given them fresh water to replace the foul.

George was gaunt from lack of sleep and the despair of losing two adults and five children to the scourge. Thankfully, many more had pulled through and no more people had fallen ill over the last few days. Matron and the band of volunteers were more than capable of looking after the recovery of the few remaining patients.

Elisabeth stretched out on her bed, fully clothed, grateful for a moment's rest. She closed her eyes and drifted off, while George and Charlotte tended to Anne.

George whispered near her ear. 'Elisabeth? Are you awake?'

'Half-awake, but I feel like I could sleep for a week. Anne?'

'Much the same. It's you I'm starting to worry about. You're exhausted.'

'I'm fine. Has Charlotte gone?'

'She's just left.' His hand went to her forehead. 'You don't look fine. You're very hot and dripping with sweat.'

'No wonder. I'm wearing my clothes and three blankets. If I expire before he comes, it'll defeat the point.' She pinched her cheeks and adjusted the hot cloth on her forehead, which had added to the red flush covering her face.

He gripped her hand. 'This is a crazy idea. I don't want you put at risk.'

Before Elisabeth could answer, she heard Charlotte and Amberley talking outside the door.

'How are they?'

'Not at all well, Mr Amberley, I'm sorry to say. Elisabeth is now extremely ill too – feverish and barely conscious. I would be very grateful if you would sit with them for a while, so I can sleep.'

'Of course, I will do anything to help.'

George gave Elisabeth's hand a last squeeze before he reluctantly got to his feet and opened the door. 'Thank you, Amberley. If I don't sleep soon, I'll collapse. Please try not to disturb them too much, as they are both in a critical condition. No point in talking anyway, as they won't even know you're here. Wake me up if they get worse, or in a couple of hours at the latest.'

Elisabeth heard Amberley quietly slipping into the room, closing the door gently so as not to disturb them. He pulled up a chair beside Anne, placing it side-on so he could see them both. Elisabeth appeared to be asleep and tossing fitfully with fever.

'Oh, my dear Anne, you look like you are not long for this world,' he murmured. 'And Elisabeth too, of whom I had such hopes.'

After what seemed like an hour, but was probably only five minutes, she felt him leaning over her. It took every ounce of nerve and courage not to flinch as he first touched her arm, then shook her gently and felt her feverish forehead. She let out a low moan and stirred slightly, but did not open her eyes.

He moved away. Then she heard the slight squeak as the lid of her mahogany trunk was raised. She didn't so much as blink in the silent seconds that followed. The rustle of fabric told her he was carefully unpacking the contents of her trunk. Dull tapping sounds and a faint 'ahh' told her he had found the false bottom.

Certain he would be fully occupied with his thievery, Elisabeth risked a glance at the door, which was now open a crack – hopefully enough for the listeners outside to hear what was going on inside and come to her rescue if need be.

She watched through the smallest possible slit in her eyelids as Amberley pulled out the bags of gold and money, followed by the jewellery box. Even with her limited view, she could read the triumph in his expression and posture. He might not be so happy when he opened the box and found the pearl necklace missing and no sign of the documents which would prove him guilty of fraud. All she had to do was get him to admit that his real name was Kingston.

'Damn.' The softly whispered curse was like a shot in the silent room.

'Something wrong, Amberley?' Elisabeth said. She was sitting upright and wide awake on the edge of her bed, the heat-inducing blankets cast aside with relief.

Amberley dropped the box and whirled around, his mouth open but speechless.

'Please be careful with my jewellery box. It is of great sentimental value to me, even if it no longer holds the pearl necklace you were after. Worth a king's ransom, Cloutier said, and he was right.'

Amberley stood up slowly, filling the small cabin with his powerful presence. He spoke softly, the habitual honey tones of his voice still aimed at lulling the unwary. 'Where is it, Elisabeth? Cloutier said it would be in your jewellery box.'

'I'm glad you're not trying to deny stealing from me, Amberley. That would be tedious, given the circumstances. I assume you took Anne's key and my sapphire necklace as well?'

Amberley's hand dropped towards his pocket for an instant before he pulled it away. 'I don't know what you are talking about. I was aware of the rumours that you were carrying valuable items, so I felt it my duty to check they were secure while you were both sick. Can't be too careful with thieves and ne'er-do-wells aboard.'

'Then you won't mind if I order a search of you and your cabin?'

'Of course I would mind. You can take my word as a gentleman that I am only trying to protect two ladies for whom I have the greatest of esteem. You are feverish, my dear Elisabeth, and not thinking straight. Let me help you back into bed.'

'Stay where you are.' Elisabeth continued to goad him, hoping for more admissions. 'You know, Anne saw you going into the Maynard's cabin the day the necklace went missing. She covered for you because she trusted you. She won't repeat that mistake.'

The honey slipped from his voice, replaced by a barely suppressed sneer. 'Look at her. She won't live long enough to testify against me. Anyway, I could have had any number of other reasons to be in Maynard's cabin.'

Elisabeth ignored this cruel jibe. 'But it wasn't just the jewellery that brought you sneaking into our cabin, was it? You were after the documents my husband left with me.'

He was silent for the time it took for her heart to thump through ten rapid beats, weighing his answer, moderating his tone. 'Look, I understand your desire for the truth. I know I should have asked you, rather than going through your belongings, but I didn't want to upset you. Your brother-in-law asked me to retrieve a document he said belonged to him. I never meant to get stuck on this ship, only to find you and ask for the document to be returned. If you hadn't switched cabins, I'd have been gone before the ship cast off.'

'Those documents are in safe hands, Mr Kingston.'

Amberley was obviously struggling to keep his temper in check at her persistent questioning. She could see his fists clenching and unclenching as he seethed, his eyes flicking back and forth as his brain worked through the best lie to tell next. He was so angry that it took a few seconds for his real name to register. 'What did you say?'

'I think it's about time we allowed the real Mr Amberley to have his name back, so he can rest in peace, don't you? His family will want to know who was responsible for getting him drunk, then pushing him down those steps to his death. You'll hang for that, Kingston.'

'How in God's name did you–' He snapped his mouth shut and stared at her with narrowed eyes and a rigid jaw.

'You say you never intended to get stuck on this ship, but Amberley's murder suggests you planned to use this as a chance to escape. I'm sure you cannot have been fool enough to think your fraudulent railway scheme would remain undiscovered for long, even without the documentary proof my husband found. What a perfect solution to your problems – safe passage far away from England, a new life, with a new name and papers certifying you as the owner of an estate in New Zealand. Easy enough to sell and move on when your crimes were discovered.'

He moved towards her swiftly, forcing her to step back against the wall of the cabin. 'Elisabeth, you are delirious. None of this is true. I am Edgar Amberley and all I was trying to do was help your brother-in-law with a small favour. I really must ask you to cease this slander or you will regret it.'

'Are you threatening me, Kingston?'

With a snarl and a quick dart of his hand, he grabbed her pillow and closed the gap. Before she had time to call for help, the pillow was over her mouth and nose. Her hand tightened on the small knife she held behind her back – a precaution she had been sure she would never use. But now, as the pillow pushed tighter, panic surged through her and she stabbed at his arm. Her hand was slippery with sweat, making the knife hard to grip. She felt it connect with his clothes and slide off. Before she could raise her hand again, he had knocked the knife to the floor.

The door of the cabin burst open. Templeton and Penrose rushed through the door, tripping each other up and landing in a heap of thrashing arms and legs.

Elisabeth stomped down Amberley's shin and lashed out with her knee, but he only pressed in harder. With the pillow blocking her breathing and his body pressing her hard into the wall, she was rapidly running out of both time and the capacity to act. She scrabbled around on the shelf to her side, desperate for a weapon, but only found a small bottle of perfume. She flipped the top off with her thumb and threw the perfume in the direction she hoped his eyes would be.

He let out a curse. The pillow loosened enough for Elisabeth to force her way out from behind it and gulp a breath. Amberley grabbed for her blindly, but Templeton launched himself off the floor and on to

Amberley's back, throttling him with one arm. Elisabeth scrambled for the knife, but George got in first, pushing her away with his left hand, while delivered a right hook powerful enough to topple both the other men backwards.

All three men tumbled to the floor, while Elisabeth jumped out of the way onto her bed. Mr Strickland stood frozen to the spot in the doorway as he watched the thrashing jumble of bodies, with Charlotte cowering behind him.

'Get help,' Elisabeth shrieked.

When the thrashing stopped, Amberley-Kingston was stretched out on the floor, with Templeton pinning his arms and George holding his legs. Elisabeth sank back in relief, her heart pounding with the shock of how quickly she had lost control of their plan to get him to confess.

An Unravelling

8 November 1841

Anne lay in a semi-conscious state for a further day, before her fever peaked and waned. When Elisabeth checked on her the next morning, Anne was awake. She was desperately thin but had a touch of colour in her cheeks and a hint of life in her eyes again, to Elisabeth's intense relief.

'Anne, thank goodness. How are you feeling?'

'Weak as a kitten.'

'I've brought you some broth, if you feel up to it.' Elisabeth sat beside her, absent-mindedly checking her pulse, as she had done so many times over the past weeks.

'I cannot believe I missed all the excitement. Did it work out as we planned?'

Elisabeth held the bowl and lifted the spoon to her sister-in-law's mouth. 'Yes, if the aim was to get enough proof of a crime to lock Amberley safely away. He could hardly deny trying to suffocate me with four witnesses.'

'He tried to kill you? Oh Elisabeth, how terrifying.'

'I knew I had help right outside the door, although I admit it was frightening for a second or two. I cannot come to terms with the treachery of the man. As Amberley, he was so sweet and amusing. As Kingston, he had the look of the devil himself.'

'I liked Amberley so much. It pains me to realise I was completely wrong about him. I suppose it will help to think of him as Kingston.'

'There's the rub. He did not admit outright to being Kingston, or to the other crimes. Having seen his reaction to my questions, I am absolutely sure that he was responsible for the burglary of our cabin and the death of the real Amberley, but he never admitted it outright so that our witnesses could hear. George did find our key in his pocket and he admitted to being in the Maynard's cabin after my necklace was stolen. But there is no evidence to prove that he killed the real Amberley, apart from the guilt I saw in his expression and the statement of a ten-year-old lad who didn't see his face.'

'Has Kingston been questioned?' Anne asked.

'He continues to say it is all a misunderstanding, and that he is simply an acquaintance of Frederick who was asked for a small favour. He denies knowing anything about the murder, fraud or theft.'

Anne waved away the soup spoon. 'With witnesses, surely he'll be in prison for a long time for assault, if not attempted murder.'

'I suppose so. But he is a slippery devil. He explained his attack on me as a momentary aberration due to his honour being questioned. I can easily imagine him persuading a judge that I was a malicious woman who goaded him beyond reason, provoking him to uncharacteristic violent behaviour.'

Anne sighed. 'I expect you're right. I would hate him to get away with his crimes, especially the callous killing of the real Amberley.'

Elisabeth looked towards the circle of blue sky ringed by the porthole. How she longed to be out in the fresh air on this fine day, instead of chafing at justice denied. Soon, her feet would touch dry land again for the first time in over three months, and all this would be over. She looked forward to that oddest of sensations – the feeling that the solid earth was swaying beneath her feet after becoming acclimatised to the roll of the ship.

She pulled herself back to the issue at hand. There would be years of fresh air ahead. For now, she knew she must do all she could to see justice done, for her husband and the Amberley family and all the victims of his fraud. 'There are people in London who can identify him as Kingston, if the New Zealand authorities agree to hold him while their witness accounts are sent. Or perhaps they will send him back to England.'

'Has his cabin has been searched?' Anne asked.

'The only thing even vaguely incriminating they found was a gold nugget, which he says was a gift. No items identifying him as Kingston, but plenty for Amberley. George has asked permission to make a more thorough search. In fact, that banging we can hear below is probably him ripping Amberley-Kingston's cabin apart.' Elisabeth noted Anne's pallor and decided she had had enough excitement for the moment. 'I'll leave you to rest for a while.'

Elisabeth was handing the soup bowl back to Thomas when George found her, a mallet and crowbar in one hand, a bundle wrapped in a sheet in the other, and the gleam of success in his grin. They rounded up Mr Strickland and William Templeton for a meeting in the cuddy.

When they were all present, George unwrapped the bundle. 'He had pulled up the slats at the bottom of his bunk and hidden these in the space between the bed and the top of the drawers.' He laid a large stack of papers on the table. 'Bearer bonds. I've done a quick tally and they must be worth thousands of pounds.'

'Good work, Mr Penrose,' Mr Strickland said. 'He'll find that hard to explain away. I'll get Gilbert to do a full count and make a list.'

'I expect he'll say they are funds provided by his family to set up in New Zealand,' Mr Templeton said. 'There seems no depth to the deceit of my so-called friend.'

'He'll have a harder job explaining this,' George said, pulling a ledger from the bundle with a flourish.

There was a collective intake of breath at the sight of the ledger, which had 'United British Canadian Railroad Company' inscribed in gilt on the cover. Elisabeth couldn't stifle a whoop of delight. Surely this would be enough to convict him of fraud, although he would no doubt come up with some excuse for having it in his possession.

'It's a list of dozens of investors and their investments, by the look of it,' George continued, 'including some staggering sums.'

Mr Strickland got up and peered over his shoulder. 'What do you make of this last column of letters and numbers?

'I haven't tried to make sense of it yet.'

'Perhaps Mr Gilbert could apply his bookkeeping skills to it?' Strickland flipped through the pages with a deepening frown. 'This appears to represent a truly massive fraud. I recognise many of the names. Noble families could be brought low by this scandal.'

'I hope they will be very grateful to Elisabeth and John Godwin for uncovering the fraud. And even more glad to get some of the money back from the bearer bonds.'

'Yes, very true, Mr Penrose,' Mr Strickland said.

'But does this prove that Amberley is this Kingston fellow who perpetrated the fraud?' Mr

Templeton asked. 'I can't see his name anywhere, although of course the fact that he has the ledger in his possession tells against him.'

'I would very much like to know the meaning of these extra columns in the ledger,' Mr Strickland said. 'Looks like initials and numbers, and thus possibly a code for the people involved. Perhaps we could work out to whom they refer?'

George looked at Elisabeth and pushed the ledger across to her. 'I do recall Mrs Godwin saying she was familiar with bookkeeping and Miss Godwin once told me her sister is a genius at number puzzles.'

Elisabeth blushed, but her innate curiosity had her itching to work out the answer. She opened the ledger. Frederick's name was listed near the top. From the amount listed, she could see why John had been horrified and worried that the Godwin family could lose everything.

She steeled herself and ran down the list of names, identifying several of their family friends and acquaintances. This was going to destroy the Godwin family's hard-earned reputation for honesty, not that it would matter with the business in tatters.

Elisabeth asked Mr Strickland, who was well-connected in London, to point out the names of investors who were members of the Palace Club or linked in other ways. Templeton added information on several other names.

'And what do you make of this last column in the ledger, Mrs Godwin?'

'I think you may be right that the letters refer to the person who sold the investment to each investor. The trick will be to work out to whom or what the codes refer to.'

'Perhaps it might be helpful if Mrs Godwin has some quiet time to work on it?' George said.

'Of course. I wish you luck. I'd dearly like to see these rogues pay from their crime.' Mr Strickland gathered up the stack of bearer bonds. 'Gilbert can tally these before I lock them in my safe. I will begin writing an account of the matter to the authorities in England.'

George shut the door behind them and came back to sit beside her.

'Do I detect a clever ploy to get a chance at solving the mystery yourself, George?'

'Am I that transparent? I do love a puzzle. Now, tell me what you've found, as I can see your eyes gleaming a mile away.'

Elisabeth had been running her finger down the last column and doing a few quick mental calculations. 'All the entries are sequences of two letters followed by numbers – some with a single set, others with more than one set of the two-letter/number combinations.' She angled the ledger so he could see it. 'There are only about a dozen unique sets of initials, each repeated multiple times, which suggests a small group of fraudsters. I think the number is their fee for each investment.'

'Show me.'

'You can see that if the last column only contains one set of initials, the number written after the initials is an exact percentage of the total investment. A seller's fee. Where more than one person is listed, the same fee is split, presumably between the seller and the man who recruited him. My guess is that the scheme was being operated as a hierarchy, with the instigators recruiting other people to do the selling to their own group of acquaintances, with each layer being paid a proportion of the investment as a fee.'

'With you so far. You really are brilliant at this. Any thoughts on how to crack the code?'

'Look at the last page of the ledger. I think it's a key to their identities.' Elisabeth flipped to the end of the ledger to show him the list of initials with the cryptic row of letters alongside them. 'The tricky bit will be in working out who they are from the code on the last page. The two-letter codes include unlikely combinations like "ZI", so I'm assuming it's not simply the person's own initials.'

'A Caesar cipher perhaps?'

She looked at him blankly.

'Julius Caesar sent secret messages to his commanders using a cipher. Sometimes it can be as simple as a substitution of letters. A becomes E, B becomes F and so on.'

'You have hidden talents, George. Not bad for a village quack,' she said, nudging him with an elbow.

'We make a good team.'

'How do you work out which letters are switched in the cipher?'

'Easily if you have the key. But in our case, we'll have to figure it out. It would help if we had a clue as to who any of them are, to give us some letters to start with.'

Elisabeth would have preferred to keep her brother-in-law's name out of it until she knew how deeply he was implicated in this scandal. Frederick Godwin was listed as an investor, but that only made him a dupe, like all the other investors. What she couldn't ignore was the many repetitions of 'ZI' in the last column, not long after the date of his own investment, racking up dozens of fees from members of the Palace Club and friends of the Godwin family. Clarissa's father was listed as one of the first investors of ZI, with an investment Elisabeth was sure he could not sensibly afford.

The only reasonable conclusion was that Frederick had not only invested but had profited from luring in other investors. She could only hope that he had done so thinking that it was a genuine railroad company with excellent prospects. He was certainly the sort of person who would believe in a such a grandiose scheme. And, surely, Frederick wouldn't have knowingly chosen to defraud his own father-in-law?

If she was right about the hierarchy of sellers, then Frederick had also recruited at least one other person, 'KB'. This man obviously had strong French connections, because all the investors he sold to had French names. Presumably émigrés who had escaped the horrors of the revolution, only to fall victim to these leeches. KB could only be Victor Cloutier, who had met Frederick at a diplomatic event, to their 'mutual benefit'. She felt sick to the stomach just thinking about him, let alone the appalling notion he had been in league with John's own brother.

'Elisabeth? Are you all right?'

Elisabeth felt a hand on her arm and warm breath by her ear as George whispered, dragging her from the grim depths of her thoughts. She lifted her head to find his worried grey eyes looking into hers at close range. A thought popped into her head, unbidden. What would it be like to wake up every day and see those kind, intelligent eyes? Wonderful, a small voice answered deep inside her, a voice she had been trying to shut out for some time.

He felt her forehead. 'Elisabeth? Are you feeling ill?'

She reached for his hand and put it back on the table, with hers on top. She felt in need of the contact for what she had to say – to feel as well as to see his reaction. 'Truly, I'm fine. I was only thinking. You need to know that my husband's interest in this scheme was because his brother stole from the family business to invest in it.' She pointed to Frederick's name, the large sum of money beside it clear evidence of the scale of his deceit. 'I suspect the initials ZI also refer to Frederick. And KB may be our old friend Victor Cloutier, recruited by Fredrick. If so, we have two names to help solve the puzzle. Presumably Kingston's name is there too.'

George didn't pull his hand away, or even flinch, as she thought he might. After all, she was related to a potential fraudster and had brought trouble to the ship and to him in the shape of Cloutier and Amberley-Kingston. Not exactly the kind of woman a normal man would want in his life.

Instead, he put an arm around her shoulders. His warmth flowed over her like a woollen scarf on a frosty night. 'This doesn't make any difference to who you are. In fact, it takes a brave person to act against wrong doing, when it's someone you love.'

'I can't honestly say there was ever much love between Frederick and me. But it will be a terrible burden to ruin the Godwin's fine reputation. Anne might never forgive me.'

'If your late husband was willing to act against his own brother, knowing that it would ruin both of them, then he must have felt very strongly. Anne will understand that. She told Mr Strickland as much.'

'That's not the worst of it. Cloutier told me he killed my husband for Frederick, to stop the truth from coming out. I…I believed him. Cloutier knew how John died.' Despite the warmth of his arm, Elisabeth could not stop shivering.

George pulled her into his chest and wrapped both arms around her, stroking her hair and rocking her gently. He knew the worst now, yet he was still being kind. Whether or not he wanted her, she would always be grateful to have had him in her life right when she needed him. The shivering died away, and she was ready to take the last step.

'That's quite enough of me wallowing in my woes. We've got the names. Let's get on with the puzzle.' She allowed her head to rest on his chest a moment longer before picking up a piece of paper and copying the codes from the ledger. She filled in 'F Godwin' over the letters next to ZI and 'V Cloutier' for KB.

Now that they had fourteen unique characters of the substitution code, the rest of the puzzle was relatively straightforward to work out. They ended up with a list of names, none of whom Elisabeth had heard of before. Kingston, Frederick and 'C Legrand' appeared to be the major players, to Elisabeth's dismay.

George went to get Mr Strickland, while Elisabeth took the ledger and went to check on her sister-in-law. She was still with Anne, who was looking much brighter, when the men came to find them.

Strickland looked through the list of names. 'I recognise several of these names. I would have staked my reputation on them being fine young gentlemen.'

'It's possible that many of these men truly believed in the railroad,' Elisabeth said. 'After all, there are genuine companies successfully developing rail businesses. I know my brother-in-law was a great believer in the wealth of resources ready to be tapped in Canada.'

'The original instigator must have known it was a fraud, though. The name Legrand rings a bell. I believe he might be the Canadian engineer Kingston was using to convince the investors of the potential. Highly believable, according to my friend, who was insistent he'd based his investment decision on qualified engineering advice.'

Anne's head jerked up at the name. 'I think you'll find that Legrand was no engineer, but rather a Canadian fur trader with an eye to making an easy fortune.'

Elisabeth saw the anguish in Anne's expression and felt sick at this latest blow. 'Mr Strickland, may we leave this in your capable hands? This ordeal has taken too much from us already.'

Mr Strickland agreed without hesitation and wished them a speedy recovery. George stayed long enough to ensure Anne wasn't about to relapse, promising her that he would be back later.

When they were alone, Elisabeth took Anne in her arms and gave her a summary of what they had found out. 'I'm so sorry, Anne. How could Frederick have done this to you? Or to John?'

'I hope you were right when you said Frederick really believed in the scheme and sold the investments in good faith. If so, he may have seen a marriage to Legrand's son as a good match for me.'

Elisabeth was seething and not willing to hide her feelings behind delicacy anymore. 'He was going to send you to Canada even after John proved this man was likely a criminal. I'll never forgive him for that.'

Anne had no response to this.

'Oh, Anne, let's take some consolation from the fact it's over now and we have helped to recover the investors' money, or part of it.' A small victory when set against the loss of her husband. She felt utterly drained of energy, but there was more to be said. 'This must have been a terrible shock to you, Anne. Amberley fooled us all with his charm.'

'I think we both detected a streak of self-interest in him, although I am shocked at how deep and dark that streak ran.'

'We all liked him. If anything, I thought him frivolous, but certainly not dangerous.'

'If there's one aspect of this that still troubles me, it is the coincidence of John's death and his investigation. It was as if John knew his life was at risk and made preparations for it. Changing his will, hiding the documents, leaving instructions with his attorney.'

Elisabeth felt the crush of Anne's logic. 'I don't know how to say this without causing you terrible pain, but you have a right to know. Cloutier told me he killed John on Frederick's instructions. I think it is possible he is telling the truth. Frederick might have panicked, knowing he would be exposed as a fraudster and would lose all of his investment. Perhaps Frederick thought he could on-sell the shares if he had more time. Perhaps Kingston pressured Frederick to stop John. We will never know.'

Anne sat with her head in her hands for a long while, curled up against Elisabeth. Eventually, she raised her head slowly, as if it weighed more than her neck could handle. 'Whatever we do, Frederick's involvement with the railroad will be exposed and he will be ruined, along with the Godwin reputation. But that is trivial compared to the other charge against him. Horrifying as the thought is to me, if Frederick had a hand in killing John, then he cannot go unpunished.'

'I suggest we write an account of what we know and send it to John's attorney. Mr Price was already looking into the circumstances of John's death, so he might have found more evidence or a witness by now. I don't see what more we can do. As it stands, without testimony from Cloutier, who was the only person who knows how John died, we can prove nothing. Besides, I still believe it is possible that Cloutier took it upon himself to kill John, because of his anger at me, and Frederick had nothing to do with it.'

'There is one more thing we can do. Ask Amberley. I mean Kingston.'

'Yes, I suppose we must face him. I'll leave you in peace for a while. The sooner I write down what we know for Mr Price, the sooner it will be done.'

About half an hour later, George came in to the cuddy, waving a letter. 'Gilbert found this tucked into the pile of bearer bonds. It's only a short note, and it may not be much help, as it's unsigned and doesn't mention Kingston by name. However, it does suggest he was planning his escape.' He paused. 'It appears Kingston might have had a lover, which is despicable in light of his behaviour on this ship.'

'May I see?' Elisabeth took the note. An icy hand gripped her heart as she read it.

'My love, arrangements for our departure are in hand for the end of the month. VC has dealt with the attorney, but I don't trust him with the other problem, which is better suited to your talents. Their address is enclosed. You must do whatever

it takes to get those documents back. I long for the day when we can be together, just us and our child, and be free of my idiot husband, who still does not know what he is involved in.'

'Elisabeth, you're trembling. What is it?'

'Please, George, don't show this to Anne.'

'Of course not. I'm sorry if I've upset you. I realise Amberley was a close friend.'

'He was close to Anne, not me, but that's not why I'm upset. I know what the note is about.'

George sat beside her and nodded for her to continue.

'We left London for several reasons, one of which was that my brother-in-law Frederick and Kingston were chasing me for the documents my husband compiled, proving that the United British Canadian Railroad was a fraud, although I did not know I had them at the time. We took refuge at a friend's house, at the address you see in this note. A second copy of the documents was held by our attorney, who was burgled the night before we left – by Victor Cloutier, I assume from the VC in the note.'

'Do you know who wrote it?' George asked.

'Yes. I think it is time to tackle Kingston again.'

Final Encounters

The interrogation of Amberley-Kingston took place in Mr Strickland's cabin. Only Mr Strickland and Elisabeth would be asking questions. Elisabeth felt a smaller number of inquisitors would be less intimidating and, therefore, more likely to put him off guard.

Amberley-Kingston was seated in front of Mr Strickland's desk, Mr Strickland behind it, and Elisabeth to one side. Mr Gilbert was in the far corner of the cabin, taking an official record of what was said. The captain stood at the back as a witness, while Mr Enys remained by the door as a guard.

As they had planned, Mr Strickland spent some time shuffling papers and ignoring Kingston, until their quarry could stand the tension no longer.

'What is the meaning of this? You have no right to harass me. I have done nothing wrong.'

Mr Strickland looked up from his papers. 'I have every right. I was appointed as a magistrate before I left England. You will be tried for the attempted murder of Mrs Elisabeth Godwin when we reach

Wellington. You are being given this opportunity to provide us with information, for which I may consider dropping the charge to assault.'

Amberley-Kingston sat back in his chair, rocking it on its rear legs, his expression hovering over the line between impassive and superior. 'I have no information to give.'

'Mr Kingston–'

Amberley-Kingston stopped rocking and slipped back across the line to impassive. 'How many times do I have to tell you? I am not Kingston. I have documents to prove my name is Amberley.'

Elisabeth could tell he was lying, as he was biting his bottom lip – ever so slightly – as he had done when he bluffed at cards.

Mr Strickland continued as if he hadn't spoken. 'Kingston is known to have been behind a massive fraud concerning the non-existent United British Canadian Railroad Company. You had hidden in your cabin a ledger containing the names of investors and the sums invested in that fake company. And thousands of pounds worth of bearer bonds.'

Amberley-Kingston tensed, clearly caught off guard by their discovery of the ledger and bonds, but his voice remained impressively calm. 'It is all a misunderstanding, as I have already told you. I was doing a small favour for an acquaintance, Frederick Godwin, and he asked me to hold on to the ledger for a few days while he dealt with another matter of which I have no knowledge. I am only vaguely aware of this railroad scheme, through casual conversations with Godwin, and had the impression that it was a well-considered scheme likely to be successful. It's Frederick Godwin you should talk to, not me.' His eyes remained on Mr Strickland, without so much as a glance at Elisabeth. 'The bonds represent funds from my family to establish my estate in New Zealand.'

'The railroad scheme is undoubtedly a fraud, Kingston. I have documents compiled by Mr John Godwin to prove that beyond doubt.'

Elisabeth watched as Kingston's eyes flicked to the door. He bit down on hard enough for his lip to turn white, and ran his hands through his hair, revealing a sheen of sweat on his forehead.

His voice now had a sharp edge to it. 'Nothing to do with me.'

It was her turn to rattle his confidence. 'We have a description of Kingston which fits you exactly, down to the gold nugget on a chain. Charlotte has a friend who knew you in London.'

'You'll be rotting in prison for attempted murder for the foreseeable future, unless they don't decide to hang you straight away,' Mr Strickland added. 'Plenty of time to get further eyewitness statements from London. And to get the inquest results for the real Mr Amberley. Roten luck for you that you were seen pushing him down the steps.'

Kingston broke. His shoulders slumped and his voice was pleading when he said, 'It was all Frederick's doing. The rest of us thought it was a genuine railroad company.'

Mr Strickland held up the ledger. 'Then how do you explain your name in this ledger, alongside Godwin and Legrand?'

Kingston stared in horror at the deciphered code. 'How in hell did you–?'

'And on the company documents as first-named director. You see, we know everything, Mr Kingston. Including your involvement in the murder of John Godwin.'

'No! I had nothing to do with that.' He was shaking now, on the verge of panic. 'It was all Frederick and C–'. He snapped his jaw closed before he could name the other person. 'Frederick and Charles Legrand.'

Elisabeth steeled herself to drive the final nails into his coffin on behalf of her murdered husband. 'You were about to say Clarissa. Did Frederick know that you and Clarissa had set him up as the dupe? Did he know you are the father of Clarissa's child? I can imagine he will have a lot to say when he finds out.'

Kingston looked at her as if she were a demon. 'How could you know that?'

'We found a letter in her handwriting, which I know well. We've always known Clarissa married Frederick for his money, but now we understand exactly what she did with the money, and how she exploited his contacts in England and Canada, while still keeping you as her lover. You and she were planning to vanish with all the money after John found out about it, and leave Frederick to take the blame.'

He tried one last time, his voice now high-pitched and trembling. 'It was Clarissa's idea. John Godwin was only supposed to be frightened, not killed, I swear to it.'

Elisabeth was out of her seat now, leaning across the corner of the desk, her hands knotted into fists. 'You really thought a man like Victor Cloutier would stop at giving John a telling-off? That my wonderful, honourable husband would give up on exposing your crime so easily?'

She could see him cringing under the blow of her words like a wounded animal. She hammered the last nail. All the countless hours of heartache she had endured poured out of her soul into the words she spat at him. 'You destroyed lives and yet you sit there smugly, thinking only of yourself. You killed my husband, Kingston, whether or not it was your hand that pushed him overboard. You killed Amberley in cold blood and tried to kill me as well. The devil has a special place in hell for vile scum like you.'

Kingston was a shattered shell of his former self when they dragged him away. Elisabeth was shaking too and Mr Strickland was mopping beads of sweat off his brow. She handed Clarissa's note to him to add to his pile of evidence.

He took it with a trembling hand. 'My dear Mrs Godwin, if I ever feel disposed to commit a crime, I will only have to imagine you on my trail and the temptation will vanish.'

14 November 1841

Elisabeth leaned against the stern rail, taking in the last rays of sun as it set directly behind the ship. She gazed out across the boundless ocean, longing to see green fields and trees again. Despite the sun, she couldn't stop shivering. She pulled the heavy cloak more tightly around her shoulders.

Her belly was now so round that she could not get into her corset. It was packed away in her trunk, the knife-rip mended and the blood washed out, but the memory still entrenched. The pearls could remain sewn up within it forever, as far as she was concerned. Only the three of them knew that the pearl necklace was still there. George had not added their names to the passenger manifest, so it would be difficult for her to be traced to New Zealand, and unlikely that anyone would think to try.

Two tiny feet fluttered against her belly like a pair of butterflies, making her smile.

George appeared beside her. 'You're smiling. It's nice to see.'

'The baby is tickling me with her feet.'

'Her?'

'The kicking is so strong, I'm sure it must be a girl. She is determined to remind me to look to the future. The captain says we may be in Wellington within a fortnight –'

'Look!'

George pointed off the starboard bow. It took Elisabeth a moment to spot the giant curved back amidst the heavy swell of waves. Within a few minutes, the massive creature was travelling alongside the *Lady Rosalind*, its length about the same as their vessel, their speeds matched. A smaller blue-grey shape rose up from the depths beside the first, its enormous eye seeming to take them in with benign interest. The pair kept pace with them for a mile or so, before arching their great backs and plunging under the waves.

George let out a low whistle. 'Blue whales, a mother and calf. The largest animal on earth.'

Elisabeth gazed into the depths, hoping to catch another glimpse. 'I have the oddest sensation that we have been blessed. Their eyes are as expressive as human eyes.'

'I'd like to think so too. We have a bright future to look forward to, Elisabeth. I promised Anne that I would look after you both.'

'Thank you, George, you are very kind. But you should not feel bound by such a promise.'

'I am expressing myself poorly. The fact is, I am in love with you, Elisabeth. I have been since we first met right here three months ago. The way you stood there so serenely, enjoying the sunrise, and then turned to me with the smile of an angel. I felt like I'd stepped out of a blizzard into a halo of warmth.' He reached out a tentative hand. 'I know you are still grieving for your husband, but, one day, when you are ready, I hope you might agree to marry me.'

Elisabeth locked his hand between her two. 'You would be willing to marry a widow carrying another man's child? After all that's happened?'

'She could be our child too. I would love her and any others we are blessed with, just like I love their mother. I haven't much else to share besides my heart, although I do have a little money put aside.'

'I don't need money, George, only you. I love you too, so much that it feels like my heart will burst every time I look at you. Nothing would make me happier than to marry you, as soon as you wish.'

He gathered her into his arms and kissed her, tenderly at first, then passionately, as she responded in kind. They clung together, three joyful hearts beating, each knowing they were exactly where they belonged.

Epilogue

Wellington, 1882

Elisabeth sat in a shady corner of the veranda, eyes closed, enjoying the scent of spring flowers in her garden. The unseasonable warmth was good for her bones after a chilly winter. George was on the lawn, helping their adult children to set up tables for her seventieth birthday luncheon. How had she become so old so quickly? She smiled at George, who was still as slim and almost as sprightly as ever, despite a mop of steel-grey hair and deep wrinkles. 'Laughter lines', as he called them.

They had had a wonderful life together. She gave thanks for her blessings every day. It hadn't been easy in those first years, when Wellington was little more than a swampy building site, but they had worked hard to create a strong foundation for their growing family. George had made a name for himself as a doctor, helped along by a loyal band of patients from the *Lady Rosalind*.

Aside from raising their children, overseeing the house and keeping the books for the surgery, Elisabeth had invested in a market garden and orchard venture in partnership with the extended Bell family from Kent. In her one act of sensible forethought before fleeing her childhood home, she had gathered up as many types of seeds as she could from her father's carefully preserved and labelled collection. These she put to good use. What pleasure it had given her to watch the plants grow and eventually to harvest juicy fruit and fresh vegetables, working alongside her own children. With even greater pleasure, she witnessed the marriage ceremony, underneath a canopy of apple trees, between one of her sons and a rosy-cheeked granddaughter of Harriet Bell.

Guests began to arrive, and a hubbub of greetings rose around her. George came to help her out of her chair and take her down the steps to her seat at the head of the table next to him.

She gazed with deep satisfaction at the joyful crowd around her. Her six children and their spouses were beside her at the long table, with eighteen grandchildren on picnic blankets or playing in the shrubbery. Elisabeth smiled at seeing her granddaughter, Grace Penrose, tending to a cousin's cut arm. Young Grace was determined to be a doctor, just like her father and grandfather.

Her darling Sophie, who had arranged the party, was beside her, looking very much like a younger version of herself. The other children had taken after George, making Sophie the odd one out with her blonde hair and pale skin. She adored all her children and was proud of their achievements, but Sophie had always had a special place in her heart. Perhaps because she had been born so tiny and weak, and yet had been a battler all her life. Lately, she had thrown herself into the women's suffrage cause, with Elisabeth's support. The vote had failed to pass in Parliament so far, but she held great hopes for the future.

Sophie was wearing the sapphire and diamond necklace, which Elisabeth had passed down to her when she turned eighteen, at the same time as they told her the full story of her biological father. Sophie's oldest daughter would turn eighteen soon and the necklace would pass to her. It made her happy to think that this token of John Godwin's love for her would link them all down the generations.

The one sadness in her life was in not knowing whether any of her family in France was still alive. She had had a strong bond with her nephew, François. She saw him in her dreams sometimes, still with his cheeky grin and rumpled hair, but now surrounded by his children, as she was by hers.

When the first course was cleared, George whispered 'I love you' in her ear, then rose from his chair. 'Nothing gives me greater pleasure than to see you all here today, gathered for my darling Elisabeth's seventieth birthday. Please join me in a toast to the extraordinary matriarch of the Penrose clan.'

Cheers broke out all around the table as everyone raised their glasses.

Sophie patted her mother's hand and passed her a handkerchief. 'Thank you, Father, for your fulsome speech, verbose as ever.' Laughter rippled around the long table.

'No need for wittering on when there is good food to be eaten and wine to be drunk. Your mother didn't marry me for my fancy words.'

'Whatever the reason she married you, we are very glad she did. No child could ask for better parents or grandparents, or a better life. And now, before the main course is served, we have arranged a little surprise. Could everyone please assemble in the front garden?'

Elisabeth raised an eyebrow at George, who shrugged his shoulders. He tucked her arm through his as they strolled down the path around the house. 'We've had a grand life together, my love.' He held her hand a little tighter and kissed her lightly on the cheek. 'I certainly never thought I'd find such love and happiness when I boarded the *Lady Rosalind* all those years ago.'

'Nor I, my darling.'

In the front garden, a photographer was assembling his equipment. A swell of excitement went through the crowd, many of whom had never had a photograph taken before. The photographer seated Elisabeth and George in the middle of the front row, surrounded by their children and grandchildren, with their friends at the side.

'Is there any room for one more old lady?'

'Anne!'

Elisabeth threw her arms around this most welcome of guests and hugged her tight. From the beaming smiles on the faces of her family, she was the only one taken by surprise. They saw each other so rarely now, although they wrote every week. Anne had lived with them at the start and worked as George's nurse for a couple of years, before being lured away to Dunedin by a visiting physician, Gordon Macmillan. He had promised both love and medical training, a winning combination. Elisabeth sat down again between Anne and George, her joy on this wonderful day complete.

The photographer appeared from under the black canopy shielding the back of the camera. 'Perfect, thank you, ladies and gentlemen. Hold that pose as still as you can, please.'

After the photograph was taken and the meal consumed, Elisabeth and Anne caught up with their old friends. Charlotte and William Templeton greeted Anne with delight. They had made a great success of their farming ventures and were pillars of the local community, thanks to their generous support of the Imperial Opera House and various musical societies.

Elisabeth hugged various members of the extended Bell family, then went to say hello to Mary and Charles Forrester. Their small shop and dressmaking business had grown into one of the largest stores in Wellington, 'Forrester & Jamieson'. Mary Forrester had continued to make dresses for Elisabeth long after her employees took over all her other clients.

There were many absent friends as well. The Reverend and Mrs Robertshaw had lived full and valued lives and died peacefully in their bed within hours of each other. Mr Knight had made a name for himself as an explorer and surveyor, before disappearing without trace on a journey deep into the wilds of Fiordland, chasing the fabled giant moa. Joseph Gilbert had lived a quiet life, working diligently and dying of a heart condition within a month of retiring from a senior position in the land deeds office. He had never remarried but had kept in touch with them a couple of times a year.

Mr and Mrs Strickland had passed on too, after serving the government with distinction. It was Mr Strickland who had arranged for the sale of the Amberley land. The Templetons bought it and used the profits from farming it to fund the Robertshaws' charitable work amongst the poor, and later to build a school.

Victoria Maynard had been one of their first teachers until she married one of the Robertshaws' many grandchildren and started contributing her own brood to the school population. Victoria smiled at Elisabeth from the far end of the table. She had been like a sister to Sophie and had lived with them for a while when the Maynards moved to Auckland, where Sir Julius had founded a gentleman's club. The name was something of a euphemism, given the club's reputation for drunkenness, gambling and women of ill repute. On his death from cirrhosis of the liver at the age of forty-three, Lady Maynard – to everyone's surprise – took over the club, ejected the seamier elements, and turned it into a highly successful and exclusive venture.

The man they knew as Edgar Amberley was sentenced to twenty years of hard labour for attempted murder and theft, while awaiting trial on further charges of murder, conspiracy to murder and fraud. He escaped from prison after two months, by charming the warden's wife, who was found abandoned and distraught in an alley two days later. Amberley was found in a flea-pit hotel three days after that, stabbed to death with a knife that was remarkably similar to the one the warden's wife used to dispatch chickens.

Mr Strickland had arranged the return of the documents and other evidence to England, along with the bearer bonds, which were used to reimburse the grateful investors in the United British Canadian Railroad Company. By the time the information reached England, Clarissa was long gone and

Frederick had voluntarily sold Godwin & Sons Shipping to pay his debts. When Mr Price confronted him with the evidence of John's murder, Frederick reportedly went deathly white and staggered back against the bookshelf, collapsing onto the floor under a cascade of heavy legal tomes. The seizure was fatal.

Elisabeth was exhausted by the time everyone left. She felt every one of her seventy years as she climbed the front steps of the wonderful house that they had built three years ago. It was a sturdy but beautiful two-storey building made of native timbers, with a sitting room and bedroom on the ground floor for her and George. The rest of the house was for Sophie and her family, and their many visitors. She knew she would be happy to see out her days there, playing with her grandchildren, pottering in the garden, reading, and helping Sophie with her pamphlets and speeches.

She had asked the carter's men if they would mind putting some items up in the attic for her when they had moved in. They had many things she could not bear to throw out, but for which they had no room in their new quarters. Among them was her old mahogany trunk. It had been a relief to see it sitting up there in the attic, out of mind's eye and covered in old rugs, surrounded by other treasures whose time had passed.

Elisabeth went inside and joined Anne and George in the sitting room for tea. The two people she loved best in the world, aside from her children. It was wonderful to be together again.

Thank you for reading this story.

If you enjoyed this book, I would be grateful if you could leave a rating or review to help other readers discover it.

Read on

The *French Legacy* story continues …
Book 3, *The Last Child At Versailles,* is a dual-timeline story, which reveals how the pearl necklace came into the possession of Elisabeth's family during the French Revolution, and the ramifications for the family two centuries later.

… and for the backstory
The story of how Elisabeth escapes from France and meets John Godwin is told in my free novella, *The Daughter's Promise.*

Coming next … a new mystery series
The *Penrose & Pyke Mysteries* are set during a remarkable period of social upheaval in 1890s New Zealand. Grace Penrose, the granddaughter of Elisabeth and George, is about to embark on her medical training, but has an unfortunate habit of getting mixed up in murder investigations. The series also features Anne Macmillan, née Godwin, as Grace's aging great-aunt (still as feisty as ever).

Find out more at https://RosePascoe.com

Historical Note

Every New Zealander has a family history featuring a long journey across an ocean, whether in a voyaging waka hundreds of years ago, a sailing ship from Britain, or a modern ship or plane from elsewhere. Gather a group of us together and you'll hear any number of truths stranger than fiction.

The idea for this novel was sparked by the journeys of my great-grandparents and great-great-grandparents. What courage they must have had to leave Victorian England and Scotland for far-off New Zealand. They travelled in steerage as assisted emigrants, enduring months of squalid conditions in pursuit of a better future. One of the English families originated in France, making me wonder just what it was that prompted a move between two countries that had so recently been at war with each other.

While the *Lady Rosalind* and her passengers are entirely fictional, I have tried to make her voyage true to the times, using diaries and letters written by various early immigrants on sailing ships, and the real events in Britain that sparked the wave of emigration. In particular, I would like to acknowledge the following sources:

Fell, Alfred (1973) *A Colonist's Voyage to New Zealand.* Caper Press, Christchurch, New Zealand.

Simpson, Tony (1997) *The Immigrants: the great migration from Britain to New Zealand, 1830-1890.* Godwit Publishing, Auckland, New Zealand.

Ells, Sarah (1992) *The adventures of pioneer women in New Zealand.* The Bush Press, Auckland, New Zealand.

Neil, Joyce (1975) *Plum duff and cake.* Pegasus Press, Christchurch, New Zealand.

Te Ara: the Encyclopedia of New Zealand (www.teara.govt.nz).

Acknowledgements

Many thanks to my friends and family for their support during my leap into the unknown, especially to those who read drafts.

I am very grateful to all the inspirational writers out there who share their thoughts and encourage other writers, through teaching, speaking and blogging. In particular, I would like to thank three fabulous New Zealand writers for their generosity: Mandy Hager (https://MandyHager.com) for her encouragement and helpful comments on an early draft, Diana Holmes (https://DianaKHolmes.com) for her knowledge of publishing, and Leeanna Morgan (https://leeannamorgan.com) for sharing her inspiring story at Books-at-the-Beach.

Thanks also to Jenny Waters (https://redheadediting.co.nz) for her copyediting skills.

About the Author

Rose Pascoe writes historical mysteries with a dash of romance, when she isn't plotting real-life adventures. She lives in beautiful New Zealand, land of beaches and mountains, where long walks provide the perfect conditions for dreaming up plots and fickle weather provides the incentive to sit down and write.

After a career in health, justice and social research, her passion is for stories set against a backdrop of social justice. Her heroines are ordinary women, who meet the challenges thrown at them with determination, ingenuity, courage, and humour.

Visit her at: https://RosePascoe.com

Other Books by Rose Pascoe

French Legacy series:
The Daughter's Promise
The Widow's Secret
The Last Child At Versailles

The Penrose & Pyke Mysteries
Murder in the Devil's Half Acre
Murder Most Melancholy
Murder By Vote
Murder in the Moonlight
Murder So Rash
Tinsel and Trickery
Murder Ignited
Murder Over Gold